The Sil

And then everything shifted.

Kissing Alfie was far, far more than any fantasy of kissing Alfie could have been. Once she had felt his lips – sort of firm and warm – against hers, along with his big hand on her shoulder and his other hand on the back of her head, she knew she was lost.

The fantasy version of kissing Alfie she had been able to resist – just. Now she knew what the reality was like, she was lost to him. Swept away forever.

The Silver Cage
Mathilde Madden

BLACK LACE

Black Lace books contain sexual fantasies.
In real life, always practise safe sex.

First published in 2008 by
Black Lace
Thames Wharf Studios
Rainville Rd
London W6 9HA

A catalogue record for this book is available from the British Library.

www.black-lace-books.com

http://lustbites.blogspot.com/

Typeset by SetSystems Ltd, Saffron Walden, Essex

Printed and bound in Great Britain by CPI Bookmarque,
Croydon, CR0 4TD

The paper used in this book is a natural, recyclable product made
from wood grown in sustainable forests. The manufacturing process
conforms to the regulations of the country of origin.

ISBN 978 0 352 34165 5

Distributed in the USA by Holtzbrinck Publishers, LLC, 175 Fifth Avenue,
New York, NY 10010, USA

1

Iris walked over a small bridge and found herself in the Botanical Gardens. She was looking for witches, the only people left who could help her. It was about time they took some damn responsibility for what she was going through.

Appearing as if out of the greenery, a woman dressed in a pencil skirt, seamed stockings and heels fell into step with her.

'Hey, Iris, right? The warrior wolf? Friend of Hecate?' the woman said with a sparkly long-toothed smile.

Iris rolled her shoulders. They still really hurt. In fact, her arms were aching all over. 'Hecate?'

'Yeah. Well, Cate. That's just kind of a joke we do. Hey, Cate! *Hecate.* My name's Lilith and I kind of get sick of being the only witchily named one.'

Iris nodded vaguely. 'Yeah, right.'

'Your wrists are bleeding, did you know?'

Iris looked at them. Her wrists were ringed with angry red bracelets flecked with blood. She rubbed the left one with her right hand. 'Oh,' she said, 'yes. That's from trying to ... Well you know.' Because of course Lilith would know. Being a witch, she would know everything.

Lilith smiled. 'Oh yeah. I know just who you are. You're the girl who was banging that ridiculously hot werewolf, aren't you? His girl Friday. Alfie, right? Hey, you know, tell me, did he ever do that modelling?'

'Modelling, no I don't think ... He probably wouldn't want to because of what happened back with the Beast. You know he was attacked by the Beast while he was doing some modelling for my brother.'

'And that's, what, given him a phobia of taking his top off for the camera?'

'No, I think he just ... Oh, I don't know. He hasn't done anything like that. Well, unless he's done it since I last saw him, anyway. That's kind of what I came to talk to you about –'

Lilith clapped her hands, cutting off Iris's words. 'Oh, the silly boy. Probably worried about being exploited. Tell him they're very tasteful. I mean, they'll be nude but back and white. All arty. And, hey, weren't you married to Blake Tabernacle as well?'

'Um, yeah, kind of. For a bit.'

'Wow. Hard to even see him as the marrying kind,' said Lilith. 'You do have an interesting *type*. Werewolf hunters, werewolves.' Lilith shrugged, laughing. 'What can it all mean? Are you trying for some kind of award? Weirdest back catalogue ever?'

Iris was confused by this, but ignored it. 'Please. Are you going to help me? Alfie's been taken by the Silver Crown and this, uh, this *woman*,' Iris said.

'She's not a woman. She's the Divine. The divine wolf. The she-wolf. The mother of them all. She's practically the werewolf god. Or goddess, whatever. I'm not so keen on gendered words myself.'

'Well, yes, her. She has Alfie. You have to help me get him back.'

Lilith stopped walking and turned to face Iris, her heels grinding in the gravel. 'I know. Thing is, doll, I think you're going to have to let her have him. I mean, he wants to be with her. I mean not *wants* wants. But she's got a power over him that can't be imagined. She's it.'

'She took his collar off.'

'Well, exactly.'

'But I love him. Is there really nothing I can do to get him back?'

Lilith wrinkled her long nose. 'Well, you know, that's

not really the question. The question is what will happen if you *don't* get him back?'

'What will happen?'

'The Silver Crown have been using the Divine's power for centuries. Now the circle is truly fucked and her power is barely contained. While they had her, everyone was safe. She gave them the power to keep werewolves hidden from the wider world and they kept her controlled. All of the supers agreed it was a reasonable arrangement. It's been going on forever. I know Sabrina was a little bit on the dark side, but it seemed fair enough to let her work with them. Make sure they had the eleven Beasts they needed to keep the Divine under control. Of course, we had the prophecies; we knew you'd be along to mess it all up sooner or later.'

Iris frowned, 'The supers?'

'What?'

'You said, "the supers agreed it was a reasonable arrangement". What are "the supers"?'

'Supernatural people, witches, vamps, lycs.'

'You call yourselves "the supers"?'

'Well, OK, no, actually, but I figured if I did it enough it might catch on. Now, to get on with the point – she-wolf – without the Silver Crown containing her she will probably unite all the werewolves in the world. Organise them. Bring them together. I expect she'll want them to wipe humanity off the face of the earth – that's normally the way things like this go.'

'She can do that?'

'She's the top of the werewolf food chain. The number-one sire. Every wolf answers to her.'

Iris straightened up. 'Is she an Ancient Beast?'

'I don't know. Perhaps technically. She's certainly both ancient and bestial. She is literally a wolf. It's only magic that makes her look and sound human.'

'So I could kill her. I kill Ancient Beasts.'

'Hmm,' said Lilith, letting her weight sway from foot to foot. 'You could. But that might kill every werewolf on earth.'

Iris swallowed. '*Every* werewolf?'

'Well, I think so. She's the top of their power chain. She holds it all together. Thrall. The bonds of power between werewolves that keep them all in line. Without her, without those controls, they'd just all start killing each other. You've seen how they operate. Savage creatures. They'd all die. But you could try it. I mean, it's understandable, if the alternative is watching the Divine wipe humanity off the face of the earth.'

'But Alfie. Would it kill Alfie?'

'Oh no.' Lilith smiled.

Iris's heart leapt. 'Alfie'd be OK?'

'Alfie'd indeed be OK, because you're not going to do it. You're not going to do anything. You're still trapped in the tunnels under Oxford, chained up, dying.'

'Oh.' Suddenly Iris's grip on where she really was felt very wobbly. 'Is this ... ?'

'A hallucination? Yes, sorry, didn't you know? You're really not well at all down there.'

'Well, actually, now I come to think of it, I have no memory of how I got here.'

'Yeah. Quite. So that's the thing. I don't see how you're even going to get out of those tunnels, let alone save the world.'

'I don't suppose you could do some magic and help me out.'

'Ah, well, that's the other thing. Stuff like this, we really don't like to meddle.'

'But the wiping humanity off the face of the earth thing.'

'Yes, but, well, if we witches intervened every time *that* was threatened ...'

'Seriously? No chance?'

'Sorry.'

'But I'm the warrior wolf. It's my destiny. I'm the one who kills them all.'

'Well, yes, you are, but you said it. Prophecies are never clear until the events they talk about are over. When this is played through, I'm sure we'll see how to apply what is written. I'm writing this paper about that actually. Prophetic hindsight . . .'

Lilith's voice trailed off and the two women walked a little further down the gravel path together. Now she knew she was still in the tunnels, the constant dull pain in Iris's arms seemed to increase until it was almost unbearable.

Lilith said, 'God, this is feeling kind of awkward.'

'I know. Shouldn't I have woken up screaming in the chains by now?'

'Yeah. Actually I could fix that for you. Then we could call it quits.'

'Quits?'

'Yeah. So no whining that witches never help you out.' Lilith made a gesture like she was wiping a crumb away from her bottom lip, then snapped her fingers.

2

Wednesday, 30 January 2008

Blake Tabernacle, werewolf hunter and Director of the Institute of Paraphysiology, fiddled with his coms set. But he knew it was no use.

Before Iris left on her suicide mission to rescue Alfie, she had been locked with him in the cellar of a werewolf pack house in Oxford. While she was there, in typical Iris hardass style, she'd cut her own arm open with a scalpel and stuck a tiny transmitter from her coms set into it. Blake had been trying to trace her signal for four days, but it just led him to a busy shopping street in the middle of Oxford – with Iris nowhere to be found – no matter how he fiddled with the calibrations.

Alfie had a chip in him too. He hadn't been quite as brutal as Iris about acquiring it. Blake had sliced him while he looked away. Alfie was the best doctor of the three of them, having done half a medical degree before he was bitten. A doctor *and* a werewolf – but he still said he'd rather Blake did the butchery for him.

Blake scoffed, mocking him for not being as tough as his girlfriend, but then Iris said, 'It's because he needs it really deep, Blake. Mine's just popped under the skin; you need to sink his right into the muscle so the wolf doesn't rip it out when he changes.'

Blake looked at her. 'Why don't you do it for him then? He's your boyfriend.'

Iris bit her lip. 'Because you're the sadistic bastard around here.'

Blake sunk the scalpel as deep as he could into Alfie's

bicep, feeling Alfie tense and then shudder as he fought the pain. Alfie's face was turned away, but even at this angle Blake could see the tautness in his jaw. Blake understood the reactions he was looking at quite intimately. He had hurt people deliberately before.

Alfie was looking at Iris as he suffered. She reached out and stroked the back of his hand.

Blake picked up the chip with tweezers from his med kit and rammed it hard into Alfie's wound. Alfie bellowed in pain.

'Blake!' Iris shouted.

Blake sniffed, ignoring her. 'That's puppy dog chipped,' he said as he turned away from them, shutting out the inevitable tableau of Iris comforting Alfie, before she took the suture needle to sew up his poor wound. He concentrated instead on popping a third chip under his own skin.

And that had been the whole idea. Iris's idea. They were trapped in the cellar, the werewolf authorities, the Silver Crown, were coming for them – they needed a way to find each other again when the Crown inevitably split them up. And so, when Iris and Blake managed to escape – Blake's doing, his heroic moment – Iris used the trace from Alfie's chip to go back for him. When she hadn't returned, Blake tried to find her with the signal. But Iris's chip wasn't doing its job.

Several hours after Iris left, she had definitely met up with him; Blake had replotted the whole thing with the cached data on the coms system. Then Alfie had left. But the signal from Iris's chip hadn't moved. Alfie had gone east and then Iris's signal had flickered. Then faded completely.

Blake stared at the signals, tracing the co-ordinates on maps, trying to work out what had happened to Iris. Was she dead? Had she died trying to save Alfie just like Blake had said she would? Or was Iris with Alfie and had she removed the chip so Blake couldn't follow?

If he could at least find the chip itself – according to his data, it was still in the centre of Oxford, pulsing away.

If he just had a bit more time.

He sighed and turned off his computer for the last time. All around him his precious lab was cleared or packed into boxes.

He walked back into his office through the adjoining door. The imposing figure of Erin Cobalt was standing there, watching casually as his library of books – a collection that was his life's work – was loaded into crates by several identical lackies. She turned, immaculate as always with her neatly swept-up grey/blonde hair, perfect dark-green suit and tiny-heeled pointed-toed black shoes. She was tall and didn't need a heel lift to tower over Blake.

She was holding a clipboard, Blake's own aluminium clipboard. She set it down on the edge of his otherwise empty desk. The computer that usually sat there was boxed. He knew the drawers were empty. His heart was heavy and the inside of his mouth tasted sour. It was all gone. It was over.

'Ah, Mr Tabernacle,' said Erin. 'Ready to go?' She picked up the handcuffs sitting on the desk next to the clipboard.

Blake nodded and crossed the room, dragging his feet a little on the forever-worn carpet. He looked down, just watching his progress; his combat boots, his dark-red fatigues, the edges of his white lab coat just edging into his vision as he watched himself walking away from everything he knew.

When he got to where Erin was standing, he turned his back and offered his wrists to her for the cuffs.

3

Alfie Friday – 21 years a man, 11 years a werewolf – had never really stuck at anything in either of his lives. Right from the start. Even his schooling had been erratic. His parents – both doctors – were in the military, and he'd been bundled about the country and the world; saying goodbye had been a way of life.

He'd often felt like an afterthought. Another job that needed to be done before his parents could get on with something else – something that usually amounted to the greater good.

He'd got into Oxford to study medicine mainly down to luck and charisma rather than academic prowess. When he dropped out after three years – although the circumstances were way beyond his control – it still felt like part of a pattern.

Alfie the werewolf hadn't been raised by a single pack, with a single set of werewolf beliefs. He'd been all over the world. He knew how werewolves worked from an outsider's point of view. That was not the same as being brought up in a pack. For a start, he knew that what individual packs believed was often different.

Like anything, like anywhere, werewolves believed a lot of different stuff with varying degrees of faith. Alfie had seen packs where the rules of alpha worked differently, where the line was seen as an archaic nonsense, where the ritual of a cub summoning his sire by going to the place where he was bitten and shedding more blood was completely taboo.

Alfie was a scientist before he was a wolf. He knew that, whatever lay at the heart of what he was, he wouldn't uncover it by picking and choosing what to believe from a bunch of contradictory myths.

For example, some werewolves believed in life mates, a lot didn't. Alfie didn't. Some werewolves believed it as their ultimate totem of truth – that if a lycan found his mate then he would never rest, would never be happy unless he took her. And took her by any means necessary. A lot of terrible behaviour was tolerated, even encouraged, under the excuse of taking a so-called life mate.

Alfie knew packs had hunted women down on the word of one of their number who had seen her and just *known*. Some packs complained that women were stalked and kidnapped by lascivious werewolves who thought destiny and lust were interchangeable. Others claimed that it just *looked* that way, that, once the chosen life mates understood their calling, they were happier than they had ever been once they were living in the pack, either taking the bite or remaining human and keeping the honorary status of wolf's woman. (It was common enough for women to remain human and it made a lot of sense. The life of a werewolf was notoriously brutish and short – they were, in reality, often no more than warring animals even in their smooth human skins. Women often chose to stay human, stay with the pack for their wolf mate's lifetime and then return to the world they knew.) A wolf's woman was practically a werewolf. Everyone knew that. Iris, as Alfie's girlfriend, had apparently achieved enough status through being a 'wolf's woman' that she could fulfil her prophesied role as warrior wolf.

And, despite Alfie's scepticism on the matter, those who believed in life mates would look at Alfie, bitten when he was in love with Iris, never able to make any kind of bond with another woman, pining, then reunited with her after eleven years, and say that surely there was evidence of life mating.

Alfie knew this – too well. But he had decided that he had felt the same way about Iris *before* he was a werewolf. And Alfie had betrayed her before. He was not a faithful man. And werewolves – for all their touting of life mates – were not faithful creatures.

Alfie had been unfaithful to Iris when he was human, but only in body, never in mind. When Alfie had kissed his ex-girlfriend Lara at that student party it had been a moment of the body. A body that was full of alcohol. He didn't make excuses for it and never asked Iris for forgiveness. It had happened. And after Iris stormed out he had taken Lara to bed, but he had never stopped loving Iris, even when he had his big hard dick buried deep inside another woman. Even as she rolled and reached for his hair, tugging him down to kiss her. Even as she gasped and begged for it harder. Screamed about how big and hard he was. Moaned as he rolled the root of his dick to tug at her clit somehow. Even as she pressed her tits together and urgently whispered to him to withdraw, to come over her there and on her face, to mark her body like the animal he wasn't. Yet.

He did as she asked, pulled his hot heaving cock from the slickest place between her legs, supported himself on the wall behind her with one big arm and looked down at her and roared as he came. Covering her. Looking into her eyes. Knowing she wasn't Iris – a fact that turned him on with its wrongness and broke his heart too.

Even then, he still loved Iris like his heart would burst from it.

And after he and Iris split up, when he prowled the planet a lonely wolf, every women he took couldn't help him. He thrust his dick into a thousand more woman, feeling it burn, feeling like he could fuck his memories of her away. But he never could. Iris's face, Iris's body, Iris's cunt and dark eyes and orgasmic cries were the only thing he could think of when he came.

Even when his body became unstable, and he had to

lock himself in a cage or chain himself down to protect his lovers and those around him from the wolf that was taking control of his body, he still thought only of her.

Yes. Iris – life mate or not – had been the only thing in his life that Alfie had ever stuck with.

Until the Divine.

When she came to him, just after his body had been battered into submission by the torture methods of the Silver Crown, just after Iris had appeared, come to save him, Alfie had been unable to resist. Every part of him had been entirely hers the moment he saw her.

When Alfie followed the Divine, when he felt her power, when he turned away from Iris, left her, he knew what he was doing. He was giving his body, his mind, his soul to someone else for the very first time.

He didn't really have any choice, but, at the same time, it felt good.

Where had it led him? Following someone else? Leaving Iris?

Right now he was in a cellar, dark and gloomy, lit by two bare swinging bulbs. And he was in a cage. The cage was against one wall of the dank black room, furthest from the wooden door.

He had no real idea how he'd got here.

His cub Leon was here too. Alfie had brought him, unconscious, as the Divine had ordered. Leon was nestled in one corner, his big body curled up in the dirty straw on the floor. Alfie was naked; Leon in just his jeans. The top two buttons of Leon's fly were broken now and, the way he slept, Alfie could see the top of his pubic hair as it shaded into the contours of his hard bite-scarred belly. The belly was where Alfie had sunk his fangs into Leon and ripped out his intestines into the steaming night, four years ago.

The cage they were both housed in was big. Not like the one he used to lock down in, which barely held his crouching body. But it was smaller than the ones they had in the Vix basement. Alfie could stand up in it and walk around, but not more than a couple of paces. The bars were made of silver. (But just coated with it, Leon had said. Leon was good with metal.) But it was spelled like the collar and the crown had been so that when he leant against them they didn't burn him – just hummed and tingled against his bare skin.

He wasn't wearing the Silver Collar any more. His precious collar had been taken off him by the Divine and cast on the floor of the cavern, right in front of Iris. A demonstration of the Divine's power over Alfie. Only the person Alfie loved most in the world could take his collar on and off. He couldn't even control it himself.

He didn't have the Silver Crown he had been wearing either.

The collar and the crown had been all he was wearing when he'd first seen her. And, without them now, he was totally naked. Naked before her.

Naked felt right. More real. More true to the animal in his soul. The animal that she brought him closer to.

Without the collar on, Alfie was dangerous. He was a wolf who was close to the skin. He didn't just change at full moon – he changed in response to other stimulation too. Fear, anger, anything that overwhelmed his senses seemed to let the wolf take charge. And orgasm – or even just strong arousal – was the biggest trigger after the full-moon light itself.

So, when the Divine had first slung Leon into the cage after him, he baulked. Thralled as he was with his mind full of little but his need to please her, he found a corner of himself that had to protect his cub. 'No,' he said weakly. 'It's not safe for him in here with me.'

Leon puffed himself up at that. 'I'm fine, sire,' he muttered, clear fear leaking into his voice and betraying him.

The Divine closed up the door of the cage and drew

the bolts. 'This is just by means of a demonstration of your new environment,' she said. Her voice was like music throbbing through Alfie's soul. He gazed at her, almost tearful with joy and awe.

'Fuck him,' the Divine said with a bare nod at Leon.

'No,' Alfie said quickly, feeling the thrall inside him stretch painfully as he defied her. 'Sorry,' he said almost straight away. 'Sorry.' But he didn't move.

'Do it, wolf,' the Divine said coldly. 'Cub. Tell him to take off his jeans.'

Alfie swallowed. *God, no.* But that one word of defiance had been all the fight he had. He turned to Leon.

Leon was standing gazing at him, his weight on one hip, his eyebrows high on his forehead. His expression said, 'Are you really as weak as I thought you were?'

Alfie heard his own voice, strange and real and throbbing with the low burr of his alpha voice. His sire voice that Leon couldn't disobey. 'Take your jeans off, Leon.'

Leon cocked his head and began to unbutton his fly – all defiant swagger. 'Sure, sire.'

He let them slide down and kicked his feet free. Now naked in front of Alfie, Leon grinned again. 'Come on then, what are you waiting for?' he said, spreading his arms wide.

Alfie shook his head. The inside of his mouth tasted like bile. 'I – I'll kill you. I'll change when I come and . . .'

Leon shrugged. 'You've bitten me twice. I'm still here.'

Leon was right. As well as the night he had turned him, there was another time Alfie had bitten Leon. He had flipped in Brazil and Leon had used himself as a decoy, saved the day by making Alfie's wolf chase him, taking a bite to his arm as reward.

Alfie shook his head. 'I can't.'

'Yes you can,' said the Divine. 'Do it now.'

Alfie couldn't disobey. He crossed the cage to Leon in two strides and grabbed him by the shoulders. He forced him up against the barred wall at his back with a loud clang and then slammed his mouth into Leon's.

Leon returned the kiss like he was starving for it.

Outside the cage, the Divine shouted and applauded. 'Oh yes. Oh yes. My animal boys. Be savages for me.'

Leon found Alfie's ear. 'Just fuck me,' he said. 'Who cares about that perverted bitch. Let's ignore her and make this good. I want your dick, sire. I want you to fuck me.'

'But I'll change,' said Alfie. 'I'll change and kill you.'

'Yeah, well, it isn't like being alive is working out so great for me right now.'

Leon's cock was hard against Alfie's thigh. Hot, hard and wet. Alfie fisted it roughly and made Leon moan with sudden neediness.

'I don't really have a choice,' Alfie muttered.

'Then stop angsting about it and do it. Fuck me.'

It wasn't the first time for Leon and Alfie. As he turned Leon around and pushed him to the ground, Alfie remembered the first – and last – time they had done this. In a bedroom that was part of the Silver Crown's lair in the tunnels under Oxford. Leon had been so clearly in love with him and he had been certain Iris was dead. It turned out she wasn't – not then. Of course, she was dead now – he'd killed her himself.

It had been just like this time then too, with Leon slicked with nothing but sweat and spit and precome. He tried to be gentle, but Leon roared and snapped his hips back, forcing himself fast on to Alfie, working at his sire's cock.

Alfie lowered his head to lick and bite Leon's neck. Leon turned so they could kiss sloppily and messily with their bodies connected. Alfie found Leon's cock and worked it fast and firm.

He was rising fast, remembering suddenly that the last time he had come had been inside Leon too. But that had been different. He had been collared. Safe. Neutered. Leon had never liked him wearing that collar. Was this why?

He looked out of the cage at the Divine. She was so beautiful. She said gently, 'Come for me, wolf cub.'

And he did, screaming. Without the Silver Collar the pleasure was so much more intense. He felt the wolf. All around him. Rising . . . Rising . . .

But he didn't change.

He looked around, blinking his confusion. 'I . . .' He looked at the Divine. 'Did you cure me?'

The Divine laughed. 'No. Oh no. Cure you of your most precious gift? It's just the Silver Cage. It holds your form like the Silver Collar. It's another of the Sacred Silvers.'

'Another of the what?' said Alfie.

Beneath him, Leon was laughing.

They had fucked a lot in the days that had followed since that first time. Him and Leon. Fucked and sucked and wanked each other.

There was nothing much else to do.

4

Outside the Institute on Cowley Road, a black Mercedes with tinted windows was purring by the kerb. Handcuffed, Blake walked in front of Erin Cobalt, watching his step on the blasted pavement.

The driver held the door open for him and he slipped inside. The car smelt new, like leather and rubber. As well as the blacked-out windows there was an opaque screen between where he sat and a driver's and passenger seat in front. The back seat was its own little private world.

Erin Cobalt slid into the back seat next to him and he shucked along the seat a little to make room for her, but not so far that she didn't look at him a little oddly when she realised how close together they were sitting.

Blake sighed. Erin Cobalt. Everything about her was intimidating. He knew what she was doing. Her immaculate hair, her soft, refined make up, her clothes – tight and proud. It made Blake think the filthiest things about her.

And now he was her prisoner. A pointless stupid mess of a situation that could have been avoided so easily if Blake had been smarter, had been thinking smarter. But she caught him at one of his dumber moments.

Four days ago when Erin had first turned up from the funders, to conduct an audit of the Institute of Paraphysiology, he had been psyched up and mixed up. Iris had just left him, gone to her doom. He'd been up all night in a dirty cellar of death in that bloody pack house, he'd saved the day – in his own way. He'd shot Aurelia. That was meant to make Iris understand but it had made her hate him. Really, it had closed the door between them forever, just when he thought he'd started to get it open a little.

So Blake had shown Erin around the Institute acting hyper and bouncy. In emotional turmoil. His mind on nothing more than whether or not he might be able to fuck her. She was taller than him by several inches; he liked that – it made him hard. Tall women had always done that to him. Blake was a small man, tight and compact. He was strong and he knew it. But he liked the illusion of power that height gave a woman. He wanted her to slap his face and then suck his dick. He wanted her to tell him that Iris still loved him.

But she was – quite unsurprisingly – concerned with different things.

'Are you Dr Malcolm Tobias?' she said.

'Uh, no. I'm Blake Tabernacle. Doc's dead. He turned out to be a lyc.'

Erin's eyebrow's flashed. 'A lyc? A lycan. You mean a werewolf?'

'Yep.' They were in the basement where Blake was showing her the cages and cells. He leant against the rough wooden door of one of the cells and stuck out his crotch, displaying himself, half conscious of it. 'Killed him myself.' That was a lie. Iris had killed Dr Tobias. But she wasn't here right now. Maybe she was coming back alive, maybe she wasn't – either way, Blake decided, it was time to stop caring about Iris. She'd shown she didn't care about him.

He didn't know who he was trying to fool.

'Because he was a werewolf?' said Erin coolly.

'Yep.'

'You are aware that under Cobalt and Home Office regulations werewolves are still classified as mythical creatures.'

'Well, yeah, but I mean, that's just a formality, surely. You're Cobalt. You know the score. You hunt vampires.'

'We *regulate* vampires, Mr Tabernacle.'

'Sure, sure.'

Blake knew all about Erin and her husband's semi-private, semi-government, unaccountable vampire *regulation* organisation. He didn't trust them one bit. The one thing he hadn't known until today was that they were the mysterious funders his late boss Dr Tobias had secured for the Institute.

Erin flipped open the lid of a palmtop computer she had fished out of the inside pocket of her jacket. 'So, you're Blake Tabernacle ... and you're the new director.' She jabbed the keys as if inputting these new details. 'Iris Instasi-Fox? Is she here?'

'Iris is on an important mission right now, recovering an extremely dangerous lycan. Actually, you know, now I come to think of it, she actually killed the Beast not me.'

Erin looked at Blake and said nothing.

'So, er, yes, they should be back at any moment. He, er, Alfie, that is, Alfie Friday, the unstable lyc, he had some trouble with a werewolf governance organisation.'

Erin sniffed. 'The Silver Crown, by any chance?'

'You know of them?'

'Tch, lycan rabble.'

'*Mythical* lycan rabble.'

'Well, quite.' Erin drew her bottom lip into her mouth. 'So when will she be back?'

'Oh, I don't know. Tricky business. She's after Alfie, a very unusual specimen. A wolf who is close to his skin. He changes outside the full moon.'

Erin's face betrayed a different expression for just a moment. She jabbed at the keys of her palmtop again. 'I see, I see. Well, perhaps the rest of the tour, Mr Tabernacle.'

Blake nodded and led the way back up the stairs.

The building the Institute was housed in was an old bingo hall. The auditorium was a strange space, sweeping and baroque and full of fixed-down plastic tables and chairs. Blake offered to show the space to Erin as they were on their way upstairs, and then, suddenly, somehow, Blake was pressed up against an old fruit machine that, even though it had never worked properly, was still plugged in. As he leant against it, pressing into the large flat buttons, flashing coloured lights lit Erin's face. As Erin moved a little closer, towering over him, Blake thought, just for a second, how much energy they wasted maintaining a building like this.

Erin kissed him, forcing him uncomfortably backwards. Her lips were cool and dry. She whispered, 'I could tell you wanted me from the way you were looking at me on the doorstep. Did you know your reputation precedes you?'

'My what?'

She laughed, brief and sinister. 'You know the main reason a person becomes a werewolf hunter, Mr Tabernacle? The reason they start – about ninety per cent of the time?'

Blake nodded, his face still in her grip. 'Friend or relative killed.'

'That's right. But that's not the case with you, is it?'

'No,' Blake said plainly.

'So why else would someone become a werewolf hunter? What drives that other ten per cent? You know what they say – bunch of fucking sniffers. Turns them on. Why else would they do it? No money in it. No reward but the creatures themselves.' She kissed him again, a long kiss that made him want her and hate her for it. 'Is that why you do it? You a sniffer? Or do you just like the power kick?'

'The power kick?' Blake said a little weakly, as Erin stroked his face.

'Oh yes, Mr Tabernacle. The power. Or the lack of guilt. That's the thing about lycans, isn't it? They're not human, but they look like humans most of the time. Their status gives you licence to indulge all sorts of delinquencies. For a certain kind of person, that can be a very attractive proposition.' She was holding Blake's face tight.

'Are you saying I'm some kind of pervert?'

'Why are you here? If not to indulge appetites you can't sate any other way?'

Blake looked up at her and inhaled hard and slowly through his nose. Then he reached up into the inside pocket of his dirty lab coat and pulled out a packet of tobacco and a little packet of cigarette papers. In the tiny gap between their bodies he slowly began to roll a small thin cigarette. As he worked he said, 'So, you're a widow now?'

'What? What has that to do with anything?'

'Vampires, wasn't it? Darius Cole. Seduced your daughter and killed your husband. Terrible business. The talk of last summer amongst the paranormals. They say Cole was after revenge, that you tortured him and killed his true love in front of him. Unconventional stuff. Got some nasty appetites yourself there, Dr Cobalt.' Blake took a match from behind his ear, struck it on the fruit machine behind him and lit the cigarette.

'Why do you ask? You want to try me?' Erin's face was still set, firm and hard, but Blake saw something else – something right in her eyes.

'Me? I'll try anything.'

He took one slow drag before Erin back-handed the cigarette out of his mouth. It skittered away and lay smouldering on the floor. Blake wasn't worried. There was no way the hard industrial carpet tiles in the auditorium would ignite.

Erin looked at him. 'You run this place now, do you, Mr Tabernacle?'

'Uh, yeah. Actually Tobias left it all to me. This place is mine.'

'Not quite, Mr Tabernacle. He bought it with our money. Cobalt funded this project. A little experiment of ours.' Her eyes narrowed. 'But we're thinking of calling in our loan. Which means that you – as his successor – owe us. Seven million pounds.'

'I . . . Seven mill – Oh.'

'So are you going to pay back what you owe us? Or do we need to take possession of your assets?' She waved her arms around her. 'We can take everything, Mr Tabernacle. If we want to.'

Blake opened his mouth, but Erin silenced him with one long finger.

Blake spoke around her finger. 'You know I can't afford . . . Well, what then? What do you want?'

'You, the Fox girl, the unstable lyc. Your whole operation under our control. I don't know what you were thinking, taking over as director, but you had no right. Our deal was with Malcolm Tobias. We'll be watching you, don't run. Get me that unstable lyc. And get ready for a change of location, or when we come back we'll be closing this place down and you'll be under arrest for killing your employer.' She leant in and kissed him one more time.

As Erin stroked Blake's narrow thigh in the back of the Merc, he couldn't help thinking that he really could have handled this situation better. Not telling her about Alfie being unstable – that would have been good move number one.

They hadn't fucked when she had kissed him before. She had just bent him backwards over the fruit machine and forced his mouth open with one gloved-hand tight on his chin. He'd liked it, got hard. He liked a woman who could make him frightened – not much frightened him any more. But Erin dangled seven million pounds' worth of debt, his livelihood and a potential murder charge. Now that was a powerful woman. *That* got him harder than anything had for a long time.

She'd kissed him hard and pulled away, leaving him gasping and wanting, and said, 'One way or another, this can wait until I come back.'

So, in the back of the Merc, Blake knew that she was going to screw him – one way or another. And, as he was still handcuffed, he knew he wasn't going to get any say in the matter. She unfastened his flies and climbed on top of him. Pushing him back into the deeply upholstered seats as she mounted herself on his cock. Before she could kiss him, her phone rang.

Erin moved slowly on Blake's dick, rocking herself idly, but in ways that made it very hard for him to follow the conversation she was having. Until he heard her say, 'Yes, Miss Pepper, yes, I see what you're saying.'

'Pepper?' Blake said.

'Excuse me,' Erin said into the phone then put her neat manicured hand flat over the mouth piece. 'I'm sorry, Tabernacle, is there a problem?' She wasn't moving on his dick any more. She was frozen and cool.

Blake said, 'Pepper? Are you talking to Pepper? *My* Pepper? One of our werewolf hunters? I thought she was in hospital?'

'Oh she was. We went to see her. Transferred her to the medical facilities at Cobalt. Much more conducive. She's a bright girl, very well trained. But she wants a desk job. She going to work with us.'

'That little fucking turncoat,' Blake muttered.

Erin took her hand off the phone mouthpiece and reached out. She put her hand around the bottom part of Blake's face again and squeezed. She covered his mouth and then let her hand slide a little higher so she could pinch his nose closed with her thumb and forefinger.

Blake couldn't breathe. He fought Erin and the cuffs. He was still inside her as he squirmed. Fuck, she was strong. He was easily as frightened as he was turned on.

Erin whispered, 'Turncoat? But aren't you and I on the same side, Tabernacle?' She moved her hand and freed his nose but not his mouth.

Blake inhaled, hard and jerky. 'What?'

Erin Cobalt spoke into her phone again, 'Have you located Miss Fox yet, Miss Pepper. I believe her contribution to future operations could be vital.'

Blake strained hard and could just about hear Pepper's tiny tinny voice. 'Not yet, ma'am. Sources and seers seem to agree that she has taken out the Silver Crown, which would explain the detectable changes in lycan activity too. But there's no sign of her. Sources say the Silver Crown had a preference for underground hideouts. Caverns, tunnels, caves, when they were away from their London base, but over and above that . . .'

'OK, Miss Pepper. We might need to bring in a witch on that one. Put me through to the director of finance. That'll cost us a little.'

Blake looked out of the tinted window of the Merc. They were heading out of Oxford towards the M40, whizzing towards London. Tunnels. There were loads of tunnels under Oxford. Blake thought of the signal from Iris's chip that had led him to a shopping street in the middle of Oxford. She was still there. Right there. Underground. Fuck.

Erin was still on the phone, looking distracted. His cock was still inside her, just about. He wasn't hard now that she wasn't massaging him to distraction. If he was going to get out of this car – going to jump – he had to do it as they slowed for the last roundabout on the ring road, anything else would be fatal.

Blake tilted his head back a little into the sumptuous leather upholstery behind him. He braced himself a little, then headbutted Erin right in the face.

5

In perfect Gothic dungeon style, the heavy wooden door creaked and scraped on the floor as it opened. When she walked through it a second later, Alfie felt his breath catch, just as it did every time. She was so beautiful. Not human beauty. In human terms she was very ordinary. Her hair was short and greyish-brownish – so like the colour of his pelt when he changed. Her features were neutral. Her body was average and simply put together.

But when Alfie looked at her he didn't see the human. He saw the animal. He saw a beautiful wolf. A female. A mother. The wolf sire that rejected him. The human parents that were too busy setting the world to rights. All better now she was here. He felt like he had come home at last.

The Divine smiled at him as she crossed the room and unlocked the cage door. Alfie felt the hairs on his skin stand on end. She was coming into the cage. She was going to touch him. She had been telling him for days that she might. That soon she would. And now, now . . .

Yes, yes.

She walked towards him. He didn't dare move. When she was near enough, she took a handful of his hair and pulled him to her. He lurched from a sitting position on to his hands and knees and crawled the short distance to kneel before her. He wrapped his big arms around her legs.

She wore a long grey dress, a shroud of cobwebs. Unearthly. He'd barely noticed it before. Her clothes were nothing to him – part of her irrelevant humanity. He noticed it only now as the dusty fabric got in his face. He started pushing her skirt up, scrambling for her skin.

The Divine cooed as Alfie pushed her skirts right up out of the way and nuzzled his face between her legs. Instantly addicted to the scent of her. A craving that hit him and floored him like a punch in the guts. Blind need. He pushed his tongue into her and looked up, craving the response, the pleasure of her pleasure. He saw her head tip back and her lips part as she exhaled. She threw out one arm and grabbed hold of the bars of the cage on one side. 'Alfred,' she said. Her voice was musical, magical. 'Alfie.'

Alfie held both her thighs – one in each big hand. He felt like his heart would explode with love and longing. The feel of her, the taste of her, the Divine. It was also melancholic, the feeling of being this close to her, like it could never be enough. He could climb up inside her body and he still wouldn't feel close enough to her.

And, as he disappeared into his work, he heard her say 'Leon,' but he didn't look up. He drew his tongue back and forth along the seam of her.

He was slightly aware of Leon, who had been awake since the door to the cellar opened, getting to his feet. Alfie barely registered him – just a vague image of his long blond hair falling on his bare shoulders – until he felt Leon's hands cover his own on the Divine's hard narrow thighs as he used his tongue on her too, echoing Alfie's movements.

Alfie could feel the reverb from what Leon was doing to her – long strokes, rimming her and twisting deeper – in his own mouth as he worked. Alfie took it easy and slow, wanting this to be forever. He wanted to stay in this place for the rest of his life. He was already overwhelmed and despairing at the thought of her orgasm.

After a few more long strokes, up, down, Alfie met

Leon, right under the Divine. The scent of the Divine on Leon's face was too much. Alfie pressed between the Divine's legs and kissed Leon hard. His tongue swooping and diving into Leon's open wanting mouth. The taste of his sire, of *the* sire on his cub's lips was overwhelming. He moaned out loud.

The Divine growled and reached down, pulling Alfie away from Leon by the hair. She forced him back, still on his knees, his back arching over. She bent at the waist, leaving Leon kneeling behind her, slightly dumbstruck, his reddish lips moist and kiss-swollen.

'You attend only to me, Alfred. Your cub is nothing to you in the presence of the Divine.'

'Yes, yes . . .' Alfie was stammering, his heart beating so hard it seemed painful. 'I'm sorry. I don't know why I –'

'It really is simple, Alfred,' the Divine said slowly, 'you must let the power flow the correct way. You attend to me, your cub attends to you. Let me make it clearer.' The Divine turned to Leon, kneeling on the floor of the cage. 'You, wolf, pleasure your sire.'

Leon met the Divine's eyes with one silent moment of sullen resentment. He looked at Alfie.

The Divine smiled. 'You tell him,' she whispered. 'My power over him is still through you until the next full moon.'

Alfie looked up at her.

She exhaled hard and then slapped Alfie's face. 'Tell him.'

Alfie looked at Leon. 'Pleasure me,' he said dryly, the phrase making him cringe.

And then Leon – with no choice in the matter – shuffled forwards on his knees, as the Divine stepped out from between their bodies so he could press his face right into Alfie's crotch.

As Leon drew Alfie's cock hard and tight into his

mouth, the Divine walked around his arched body. She positioned herself behind Alfie's head, making him tip it right back to look at her.

'In a moment, wolf, I'm going to show you exactly the way the dynamic flows. But first –' she reached up and grabbed a generous handful of Alfie's hair, twisting it in her fist until he gasped, bucking into Leon's mouth '– I'm going to explain why you're getting confused. The power between you and me should be utterly pure. You're a Beast cub. You're the longest-living Beast cub alive. The Silver Crown, the circle of Ancient Beasts, has been destroyed. You have ascended. You are an Ancient Beast now. The Ancient Beast. You are cub and sire. Wolf and man. And you are mine. There is nothing in the line between you and me. And yet, you still find some shred of resistance. Why?' The Divine jerked Alfie's head so he hissed with pain as her fingers ripped in his hair.

He didn't answer.

'Why?' the Divine said with a harder jerk.

'Iris,' Alfie muttered as Leon let his tongue slide the entire length of Alfie's rock-hard cock and the wrench of pain in his scalp made him see stars.

'Iris,' said the Divine. 'Yes. It's disgusting. A wolf lying with a human woman is one thing – but letting her have power over you, letting her interfere with the lines of your thrall. I can smell the taint of it all over you, sapping your true power. She's linked to you still, were-wolf, making you weak.' The Divine backhanded Alfie casually across the face. 'Dirty and weak, not lying with a human woman, not mating with a human woman, *loving* a human woman. You couldn't be a proper wolf, just like you couldn't be a proper man. Look at you, werewolf, blessed as you are with the body of a god, the face of a cherub, a powerful master of a wolf inside you and yet you wasted all that power seducing human women to your bed, trying to fuck that bitch out of your mind. Once you became unstable, you spent your last years searching the world for chains and collars just so you could fuck, drag more human women into your filthy pit of desire, driven by your basest needs. Never a thought for a higher purpose.

'My higher purpose.

'No wolf should live this long, Alfie. You're special. You're meant for great things. Or you should be. As soon as I saw you I knew you were the one.' She straddled his face and put one hand behind her and around his throat. 'Now, wolf. Beast cub,' she said, her voice sounding muffled to Alfie as her thighs closed around his head, 'feel the power flowing as it should.'

Alfie let his mouth open underneath the Divine as Leon continued to tease his cock. It felt good. It felt perfect. The Divine was right; he could feel the power flowing between them. He twisted his tongue against the Divine's clit and felt her thighs tighten. Her feathery grey skirt had half fallen down over his face. There was no world except her slick cunt in his mouth, on his face, her hands still woven in his hair, holding it painfully taut, and the grey curtain of her skirts around him.

He used his tongue. Just his tongue.

With other women, he would have used his hands too, his nose, his stubbled skin. Iris always dissolved when he pushed the tip of his prickled chin into her pussy.

With other women, he'd have worked to hold them on their rising edge for as long as he could. Made them sob, beg him to let them come as his will o' the wisp tongue danced around their orgasm.

But not with the Divine. She was different entirely. He worked his tongue perfectly for her, brought her right to the point and then circled her clit closely in the perfect motion to tip her over.

When she came, the Divine moaned, but softly, leaning back against the barred wall behind her and tugging on his hair.

A second later she stepped away, regaining her composure instantly as her skirts slipped down her legs to brush the dirty straw-strewn floor of the cage.

Leon's mouth was still around Alfie's cock and, with nothing else to distract him, Alfie suddenly felt the sensations overwhelm him. He thrust hard down Leon's throat. The Divine walked around behind Leon and put one bare foot up on his back, bending down, watching, almost like she was inspecting.

Alfie moaned. He was still in the same position. Kneeling, leaning back, his arms supporting him. Arms that should have been wobbling by now, ready to give. But they weren't. Alfie kept thrusting. Leon's mouth felt so good. Tight, warm, wet. Alfie was two thrusts away from orgasm. Then one. Then . . .

Nothing. His hips bucked into empty air. His cock was cold where Leon had taken his wet mouth away. He moaned out in frustration. Opening his eyes, he saw that the Divine had lifted Leon bodily away by his long blond hair.

Alfie looked at her. He was panting, his nipples tight and hard. His cock was desperate for the one final caress that would drive him over the edge.

She looked back at him and smiled. 'No, werewolf. The first thing you need to learn about your power is to stop wasting it.'

From the pocket of her dress she pulled a pair of silver manacles – connected by a short chain. Alfie, dumb with thrall, barely moved as she cuffed his hands behind him, feeding the chain between the cage bars.

His hips jerked a little.

The Divine reached over and stoked his cock, running the flat of her palm over his twitching aching length. 'I know that these chains aren't really strictly necessary. I don't think you'd be able to disobey me, even when you're needy like this, but, as my power isn't as pure as I'd like it to be yet, it's better to be certain.'

'Please,' Alfie mouthed, as she pulled her hand away from his cock, but she was already stalking out of the cage, dragging Leon with her.

6

It was best to be kept waiting. Cate knew this. Waiting for Lilith was infinitely preferable to keeping Lilith waiting – if you liked all your limbs and your skin in the usual places. Lilith was not only one of the most powerful witches in the world, but also one of the most eccentric.

Cate was drinking a strawberry milkshake. Lilith had wanted to meet in the Dairy Maid on Aldgate, which was hopelessly overcrowded and stuffy and had essentially no privacy, but it did do honey and lavender ice cream, for which Lilith claimed to have a craving. In the twenty years that Cate had known Lilith, she had discovered that Lilith's seemingly random ice-cream-flavour cravings were as sensible a thing to base a decision on as anything reasoned and rational.

Cate drained her glass. Lilith was twenty minutes late. Cate shifted. The place was so full that the lanky student patrons in their ripped jeans were standing up to drink their shakes and lick their ices. They crowded around her table.

No one really looked twice at Cate. With her long red hair, pale skin and flowing-to-the-floor ethnic-print dress, she fitted in nicely. Unlike Lilith, who had just made a sweeping entrance through the heavy swing door. Lilith was wearing her usual this-witch-means-business look, a look she had pretty much made her own. Today it consisted of a fancy little pinstripe peplum jacket with a nipped-in waist, and a matching ridiculously tight pencil skirt. Cate frowned when she noticed that today Lilith's stockings were both seamed *and* fishnet and her heels were five, possibly five and a half inches high.

It was such a giveaway really. Not that witches worried too much about 'passing' in the same way as other paranormals did – being so powerful, they didn't tend to worry about much. Every witch had a mind wipe at her fingertips. But Cate knew, as she looked at Lilith, that any ordinary human with the vaguest grasp of paranormal behaviour would be able to spot what Lilith was.

Cate might have more of a traditional floral, floaty hippy-witchy look, but plenty of young women in Oxford dressed the same way. Lilith dressed like a business-woman, but the way she moved in those crucifying shoes, that hobbling skirt, the way the cut of that jacket always, always sat just right, her stocking seams like laser beams – well, that wasn't natural.

Lilith slid through the throng and plonked herself in a chair at Cate's table – there hadn't been a chair there before.

'Sorry, Hecate, doll,' Lilith said as she picked up her spoon. There was a huge and sudden dish of lavender and honey ice cream in front of her and another straw-berry milkshake in front of Cate.

Cate didn't comment. This was usual in the world of witches. 'Everything OK?'

'Yeah, maybe. I don't know really. No more Silver Crown. The Divine on the loose. That Iris chick got a psychic connection through to me somehow. It's all look-ing messy.'

Cate took a long slug of her shake. The icy-sugariness made her feel suddenly tense behind her eyes. She looked up at Lilith. In the streaky sunlight coming through the greasy windows of the Dairy Maid, Lilith's smooth brown hair looked unnaturally sleek and shiny.

Lilith was broadly handsome but not pretty. Cate was almost certain that Lilith's face didn't bear a single magical enhancement. The direct opposite of Sabrina – the rogue witch Lilith had had to lock away a few days ago. Sabrina was so beautiful it was practically all artifice.

But there was something else to Lilith. Quiet strength. The kind of confidence that came from being unimaginably powerful. Even for Cate, who, as a witch, lived in a world of power most humans couldn't imagine, Lilith was something else. Lilith was barely a step down from being a god.

And she had ice cream on her pointed chin.

'Things are going to get messy?' Cate said. 'How messy?' She realised too late that Lilith might think she was referring to her eating habits.

'The Divine's the problem. Big bad wolf on the loose. Queen Bitch. She's a bloody nuisance anyway. What a pain in the arse. Some god wants to fuck a wolf so he makes her into a human then when it all goes wrong he sprints off back to god land and leaves her here like some unexploded bomb.'

'You think she's going to go off?'

'I have no idea. God knows what her plans are, but she'll have them. And they involve Alfie. She's got him thralled to her. Tight enough that he turned away from his woman. He's an Ancient Beast now as well as being unstable.'

'Damn. An unstable Beast! Well, at least there's only one of him.'

'And wolf's woman is in real trouble. I'm not even sure if she's going to survive unless things start moving for her quick.' Lilith shook her head and took a large spoonful of ice cream. With her mouth full she said, 'I think we should do something.'

'What? Intervene?' Cate clapped her hand to her mouth.

'Kind of.'

* * *

Leon was slumped against the wall of the cellar. It was rough stone, old and uncomfortable. There was only one window and, if he tipped his head back, he could see it, high on the wall he was leaning against.

Alfie was looking at him from inside the cage with his wrist chained behind his back. Leon knew Alfie had fought the chains violently as soon as the Divine had left the cellar and closed the door. She hadn't told him he couldn't after all.

Alfie had been desperate to get free because he wanted to come. She'd teased him so well. It must have been torture when she'd forced Leon to pull his mouth away. It was actually no fun for Leon either. He'd been hungry for the taste of his sire in his mouth. Not that he hadn't tasted that several times while they'd been locked together – but it was still harsh to be denied something so magical.

His cock swelled a little at the memory. Fucking Alfie.

'Oh look at you, sire,' he said, noting the way Alfie's naked hips were still thrusting a little into the air, the way his cock was still hard, even though Leon's saliva had long dried away. 'So desperate. Are you really that much of a slut? Anyone'd think you hadn't come for a month.'

'Like you'd know about that,' Alfie growled, still squirming.

It was the first time Alfie had spoken to him. Something about that dark voice he had – he was only a shade from his alpha tones – made Leon's cock swell further. Not thinking, he flipped open his jeans and found his cock. 'I can't believe you made me kiss that bitch's arse,' he muttered, wrapping his fist around his dick.

'I didn't make you do that. You obeyed her. You wanted it. The taste of the Divine Wolf? I thought you were all about our heritage, who we really are. And in any case,' said Alfie, leaning closer, 'don't pretend it wasn't your idea of fun when I kissed you. I know how you feel, Leon.'

'That so, sire? You know how I *feel*, do you? How your dick feels in my mouth or in my arse.' Leon was stroking himself blatantly now. 'You want to think about that. Wish you were doing that right now, do you, huh?'

Alfie gasped. Then moaned a little with need.

'Or maybe you just wish you could do this.' Leon slowed his pace a little. 'God, man, my hand feels so good on my cock right now. Tell you what, everything I've done, all the fucks I've had, there are times when nothing feels as good as your own damn hand. Right, sire?'

Alfie's voice was thick. 'I know what you're doing, Leon.'

'Really, recognise it, do you? 'Cause, you know, I think you ought to get a good long look. I don't know about you but, from the way that bitch chained you up, the look in her eyes, I reckon this could be the new shape of things to come. I reckon she's not going to let you get your hands on your cock for a good long time. I reckon she's decided it might be fun to see what happens when the sex-beast doesn't get to come for a while. Huh? What do you think?' Leon's hand was frantic now. The idea of Alfie watching him, frustrated, was turning him on so much, so fast. 'I bet you wish my hand was on your dick right now? Right, sire?'

Alfie gulped visibly. His cock was harder than it had been before, tight against his taut belly. 'Yes,' he said weakly. 'Yes.'

'Oh, God!' That was all it took. Leon arched off the floor, into his hand, and came.

7

Once Upon A Time

Myrtle grinned. Iris knew that grin. 'You got some last night! You bloody got some.'

'Guess who off though, you'll never believe it.' Myrtle raised her eyebrows – all tease.

'Who?'

'That fucking incredible-looking guy who you work with in animal behaviour.'

'Alfie?' Iris felt her heart wince. *No, please.* But they'd just sat down in the student union bar. There was no polite way to escape. She'd have to suffer this.

'Yeah. Him. I met him in the library and, oh, God, I don't know how you can concentrate on your work partnered with him.'

'Well, I just have to, I guess.'

'Seriously, Iris, sleep with him. He is hot as fuck.'

'I have to work with him. It would be stupid. Anyway, who says he wants to sleep with *me*?'

Myrtle just laughed. 'Have you seen yourself? That dark tousled hair thing you're working is really doing you a great service.'

Iris rolled her eyes. Dark and tousled? More like messy and uncontrollable. Much like the rest of her life. 'Look, I know what you're saying, he's gorgeous and I've heard what a great lay he is, really. But he's so good looking and he knows it. He's the college slut. A recipe for heartbreak – and other clichés.'

Behind Iris, a low voice said, 'The college slut? Now that's not nice.'

Iris turned around. *Fuck.*

'Hi,' Alfie said, sitting down at Iris and Myrtle's table. Iris didn't dare ask herself how long he'd been listening to their conversation. 'And Myrtle too,' he continued, rolling the R in her name and flashing teeth that looked almost too white against his caramel-coloured skin.

'Hi, Alfie,' said Myrtle, seeming about as tongue-tied as Iris felt.

God, she thought, I am so shallow. How can I be in the throes of a full-blown unrequited crush on a man who is so damn good looking, and witty and charming and bright?

Alfie took a sip of his pint of Guinness and smiled right at her as he set it down again.

How could I not be?

'I've been looking for you, Iris,' Alfie said, turning to her.

'Yeah? I thought we were meeting at the lab at four?'

'Oh we are, we are. It's just, there's this guy I think you should meet.'

'This guy?'

'Yeah, you know I've been taking that extra maths class? There's this guy I work with, Pete, fucking bright. Maybe even as bright as you, babe. And he, I don't know, he's not so good at talking to women. But he's cute and funny and everything I know you girls like. I just thought you ought to meet him.'

Iris almost spluttered out her mouthful of lemonade. 'You're setting me up on a blind date?'

Alfie grinned and broke Iris's heart for the thousandth time. 'Yeah. Guess I am.'

That was the closest Iris came to sleeping with Alfie the first year they knew each other. He set her up with one of his friends, Pete.

But, by the second year, Iris and Pete were ancient history. Over before it began. The fact Iris was in love with the guy who had set them up really wasn't good for the relationship. And then, just after the Easter break, Iris's twin brother came to visit.

It was the first properly sunny day of the year. Iris would never have introduced them, but Matthew had pointed Alfie out, asking Iris whether she knew 'that tall really good-looking guy over there'. When Iris admitted that she worked with him sometimes for biology practicals, Matthew demanded an introduction. Seconds later, Matthew was waving his camera around and asking Alfie to pose for him, as Iris backed away across the manicured grass of Green College.

'Oh my God, Iris, that *has* to be your brother.'

Iris turned to see Myrtle standing behind her. 'Yeah,' she said, 'twin brother actually.'

'Oh my God,' said Myrtle again. 'He's photographing Alfie Friday. Damn, if they do any naked shots, be sure and let me know.'

'I don't think that's all that likely.' Iris looked over at Alfie. He was sitting on the grass, leaning back with one big knee up, flashing Matt a killer smile. She looked back at Myrtle.

'Did I tell you I slept with him once, back in the first year?'

Iris sniffed. She'd never been able to forget. 'Alfie slept with the entire college in the first year. More or less.'

'Yeah,' Myrtle mused, mostly to herself. 'I met him in the library and, seriously, Iris, you really should sleep with him. He is hot as fuck. Have you seen him naked?'

'He has a girlfriend now.'

'Oh yes. I think I've seen them together. Lucky cow. God . . .' Myrtle tipped her head back rapturously. 'Just the sight of his back, all muscled and everything. Well, and then there's his cock. And his arse. Fuck.'

'Yeah. He's hot. I get it, but he has a girlfriend.'

Myrtle chuckled. 'You should have moved faster, girl.'

Iris rounded on her. She knew Myrtle had touched a

raw nerve and she knew she ought to control it but ...
'Well, I didn't! It never seemed like a good idea. I had to work with him. It would have been stupid to screw him. Anyway, he never showed any sign he wanted to sleep with *me*. He set me up with his friend!'

Myrtle just laughed. 'Yes, well, that was clearly some stupid male thing. Ug, I'm in love with this girl who is all cold with me. Ug, I'll set her up with a friend of mine to stop myself thinking about her. Ug, nice work, now me go back to cave.'

'What?'

'He fancied you. He told me.'

Iris felt herself stiffen. This she did not want to hear. 'Yeah, well, so I missed out on bedding the college slut. Poor me,' she said, speaking too quickly.

Behind Iris, a soft dark voice said, 'The college slut? Now that's *still* not nice.'

Iris inhaled hard.

'But, as it's you, Iris, I won't punish you too mercilessly. And Myrtle too,' Alfie continued, rolling the R in her name in that way that he always did. It made Iris quiver – God knows what sensation it would invoke if Alfie was doing that silver-tongued thing to her own name.

'Hi, Alfie,' said Myrtle.

Alfie nodded at her, but turned back to Iris almost rudely. 'Anyway, Matthew's going to buy me a drink because I've been so accommodating. You coming, Iris?'

'Sure,' Iris said, flashing a warning glance at Myrtle, who had her mouth half open.

In the pub round the corner from the college, while Matthew was still at the bar, Alfie said, 'I heard what you said to Myrtle. Your information's out of date. I split with Lara.'

'Oh.'

'Just this morning, actually.'

Matthew arrived with the drinks before Iris could say anything else. He plonked them down on the table, splashing lager around, just as Alfie launched into a sudden tirade about Lara. Lara, the woman Iris had spent the best part of the year listening to Alfie talk about in the lab. ('She's so great, Iris. I know you're going to like her. Stunning, like a model and really smart. Not like as smart as you, smart, but smart enough to talk to all evening, easily. And her dad is in the government. Lord somebody ... And she's just lovely. So sweet.')

Lara. Lovely Lara. She was the poshest girl Iris had ever met. Iris tried not to hate her. But in the end she didn't have to worry about that. In the end everyone got to hate Lara.

'She did what?' Iris said.

'She slept with her tutor to get a better mark,' Alfie said. His voice had a heavy sad quality to it, deep and dark. 'Well, that's what she said when she told me. She didn't seem to think it was anything to do with me even. I think she only told me because she was so pissed off that it seems he didn't even give her a good mark.'

Matthew and Iris made sympathetic noises. They didn't really say anything. What was there to say? Matthew decided that this situation needed salt and headed back to the bar for crips. Iris put her hand on one of Alfie's big bare forearms. 'Never mind. I'm sure you two will work something out.'

Alfie talked to the rim of his pint glass. 'We won't. I don't want to work things out with her. She was all wrong for me. Stupid rebound thing anyway. I don't think I ever really loved her. I just – oh, God, I was really looking forward to having sex this afternoon.'

'What?'

'Oh, you know, we've all been busy with exam revision. I was just looking forward to taking a study break and having sex with her later. And now I'm not going to.' He shrugged like this statement was really normal.

Iris looked at him. 'God, Alfie. Have you seen you? Just pick someone up. That's what you used to do all the time before you were with Lara.'

Alfie said. 'Oh, yeah, like you said, college slut. Well, actually, that's what I'm trying to do.'

Iris looked around the pub, trying to figure out who Alfie had his eye on, but she couldn't see anyone who fitted the bill. She looked back at Alfie and the way he was looking at her made her mouth go kind of dry. 'Oh no,' she said softly, shaking her head. 'Not now. Not while my brother's visiting, and I have a ton of revision and you are so totally on the rebound.'

'*She* was the rebound, Iris.'

'Don't give me a line, really.' But Iris knew her protest came far, far too late. Alfie Friday. Resistance was futile.

Iris tried not to seem too excited, tried to remain cool. But here she was standing in her kitchen and she was about to kiss Alfie. With no guilt. With no fear of rejection. Matthew had been dispatched on a trip to try to hunt down some more black and white film and they were alone. It was going to be as pure and clear and real as she had always dreamed kissing Alfie would be. She thought that right up until the moment when their lips met.

And then everything shifted.

Kissing Alfie was far, far more than any fantasy of kissing Alfie could have been. Once she had felt his lips – sort of firm and warm – against hers, along with his big hand on her shoulder and his other hand on the back of her head, she knew she was lost.

The fantasy version of kissing Alfie she had been able to resist – just. Now she knew what the reality was like, she was lost to him. Swept away forever.

They tumbled into bed. As she stared at Alfie's long-imagined naked body, big and firm and strangely comforting, her stomach flipped and her limbs dissolved.

When she touched her tongue to one of his tight brown nipples, electricity seemed to shoot through her. His mouth tasted like home, and later his cock tasted like heaven.

The first time she let her lips slide over it, Alfie groaned, rolling his head back against the pillows. The second time, he reached down, grabbed her with a firm hand under each arm and pulled her back up on to the pillows.

'Don't you like that?' Iris said as he tumbled her on to her back and climbed to straddle her naked body.

'God, I do. But too much. I don't want to come yet, Iris. I want this to last forever.'

Iris sighed.

'Our first time. Never have this again. Never want it to end.' He dropped pecks of kisses over her face, down her jaw.

'Oh, God,' moaned Iris. 'There. Do it again right there.'

Alfie had just kissed her right on the corner of her jawline. He did it again. She moaned even more loudly.

'You like that.'

Iris gasped. 'Apparently.'

Alfie chuckled, dark and deep, and then opened his mouth and gently bit the sensitive spot.

Iris levitated.

'Fuck,' said Alfie, taking his mouth from Iris's skin and looking up at her. 'That's hot. Doing that to you is so fucking hot. I used to ... I've always, uh, thought about you.'

'Thought about me how?' Iris said, although she had a pretty good idea.

'You know, in that way?'

'In a dirty way?' Iris grinned at the way Alfie was blushing. 'In a dirty *rhythmic* sort of way?'

'Yeah. If you like. Yeah.'

'Wow.'

'And when I did, you know, I always kind of got off

on the idea of controlling you. There's something wild about you, Iris. Something savage. I want to fight you.'

Iris laughed, pulling herself up on her elbows so she could look at his bulky body. 'Fight me? I'd totally lose.'

'Maybe. It's kind of hot, though. Hot to think about.'

Iris leant forwards and drew one finger down Alfie's hot smooth chest. God, but he was beautiful. 'Maybe. But right now I'd rather you just fucked me.'

'Yes. I knew you were smart, Iris. That's a great idea.'

Alfie lined himself up as Iris lay back down. He slid inside so easily. She was wet, but, even so, his cock was big enough to make her catch her breath. Alfie moved inside her. 'Oh, God, Iris. I've always wanted ... Never knew ... I'm in fucking love with you, Iris. It's the wrong time to say it, I know. Too soon, while fucking. Double wrong. But, oh, God, it's true. I just want this to be it. I just want forever. Uh. Oh, God. Never want this to end.'

Iris clenched her muscles, hugging his cock. The waves of how he moved inside her were ripples of pleasure.

Alfie moaned as she moved. 'Oh, God. That feels amazing.' He thrust a little harder then, making her moan in turn as he found spots inside her that made her see stars.

'That's like ... explosions,' Iris moaned, not caring whether or not she made real sense.

In return, she gripped Alfie's cock and twisted on it, overwhelming him with sensation, taking charge of him, of every part of him. He moaned, mouth open, head shaking as he began to come.

Iris whispered, 'You're not the only one who has fantasies about control.'

8

'Alfie?'

But Alfie wasn't there. Iris was dreaming, but awake – delirious and confused. She was still dangling in the manacles in the underground cavern, every muscle in her arms screaming, feeling like they were being wrenched out of their sockets. At first it seemed like everything was the same. Almost the same. The table and chairs, Alfie's collar lying abandoned on the floor, the six dead werewolves, but there was something else. Something flitted across the doorway.

Iris craned forwards in the chains. Her mouth felt bone dry and she was nauseous and dizzy. She wouldn't be in the any state to fight. And if she was going to have to fight for her life then the chains were going to be a problem.

When he stepped out of the shadows and grinned at her, she felt her heart flip over. White coat, red fatigues, hair like a flock of crows were circling his head.

Blake took a couple of steps forwards. 'So, Iris,' he said, grinning, 'you dying of dehydration, chained up in an underground cavern – or are you just pleased to see me?'

9

Wednesday, 20 February 2008

Iris had no idea where she was or how long she'd been there.

Often she thought she was still in the cavern. Her shoulders still screamed. But then, each time she opened her eyes, she was in a clean quiet room, diffused sunlight coming through the big grease-streaked windows, distant traffic noise, a cool clean fresh smell in the air. A warm soft bed. There was a building site near by, or something like it. She could hear the shouts of workmen, machines and the crash-smash of those workmen and machines not quite in perfect harmony. Sometimes, she half opened her eyes and through the window she could see sky and a dark-blue crane moving lazily, back lit by spring sunshine.

Matthew – her twin brother's ghost – appeared sometimes, sitting on her bed, but he was smiling, unspeaking and he usually vanished again in moments.

Iris felt strangely content. More than once she thought she might be in heaven.

She drifted. She didn't really want to come back to reality.

But then there was a time when she opened her eyes and a tall tightly put together woman with neat grey hair was staring down at her.

'Hello, Iris,' the woman said, her voice low and pleasant.

Iris didn't sit up – didn't feel like it – but she kept her eyes open. 'Am I in hospital?'

'Sort of. I'm Erin Cobalt. This is Cobalt. Have you heard of us?'

Iris shifted her head on the pillows in a sort of nod. 'Um, yeah. Yes, of course. Blake told me, I think ... You're part of the government. The Home Office. You hunt vampires. You're like us. Like the Institute, but with vampires.'

'Well,' said Erin, 'you're almost right. First of all we *regulate* vampires, rather than hunt them. We simply ensure that they abide by the various co-operation treaties. The other difference – the very big difference between us and you – is that we're official. We have a permanent status. Vampires are classified as non-mythical. Werewolves aren't.'

'Yeah, right. Werewolves are mythical,' said Iris dryly. 'You are talking to someone who has killed over a hundred werewolves.'

'Oh.' Erin picked up a glass of water and took a sharp sip. 'Don't get me wrong, Miss Fox, I am fully aware that werewolves exist. I am simply saying they have mythical classification. That's why when we set up the Institute we had to –'

'What?' said Iris, a little of her mistiness dispersing. 'When you what? *You* didn't set up the Institute ... What are you talking about? Dr Tobias. Malcolm Tobias, he ...'

Erin shook her head and smiled. 'Well, yes, I know that Tobias had some kind of small set-up going. Working out of his basement, weren't you? Mixing your own magical covers? Tobias came to us for funding and, after he convinced us that what you were doing was valuable, we decided to fund you so you could actually do something. We'd been talking for years about expanding into lycans. The deal was we'd fund the operation for a year before officially bringing it under the Cobalt umbrella.'

'Right, I – I think. The Cobalt umbrella?' Iris looked

away from Erin and up at the distant ceiling. Her head spun. 'Where's Blake?'

Erin made a sad, almost pitying face. 'I was getting to that. Mr Tabernacle did a rather wonderful job rescuing you. He quite definitely saved your life –'

'I've saved his life plenty of times,' Iris snapped. They didn't count debts like that. That was a rule.

But Erin talked right over her. 'He did, however, use some rather unorthodox methods. I am not sure if his plan was to spirit you away somewhere … In fact, it may be that he didn't have a plan at all. But, clearly, when he found you, you were in a bad condition. So, he made what I can see to be the only really sensible choice: he brought you to us.'

'What? He left me here! Where is he now?' Iris started trying to sit up. Erin took a step towards her and placed two strong firm hands on her shoulders, pinning Iris down on the bed.

'Don't,' Erin said, 'don't sit up.'

'Where is he? I want to see him right now.' It was then that Iris felt them, the firm, yet mostly unobtrusive medical restraints on her wrists, holding her down to the bed. 'Listen, Mrs Cobalt …'

'*Dr* Cobalt.'

'Dr Cobalt, you can't do this. What's going on? I'm confused. I need to see Blake.'

'I know you are, Iris. You nearly died down there.'

'How long was I … ?'

'Four days. Then Blake finally figured it out. And you've been here ever since.'

'What? How long have I been here? How long since Blake rescued me?'

'Just over three weeks.'

Iris gasped out loud. 'Then he's been gone for …' She wasn't sure, as her voice trailed off, if she was talking about Blake or Alfie.

Iris squinted. Her brain felt all soft and mushy, so treacly it might start running out of her ears. 'Did he trace the chip?' She looked over at her right bicep where she had gracelessly forced the chip from her coms set into her arm. There was a neat row of stitches there. They'd taken it out.

Erin saw her looking. 'Not a bad idea that. Shame Mr Tabernacle didn't tell us about it or we could have found you sooner. Of course, when we looked at that wound – it was horribly infected – we realised what you had done. You were about twenty-four hours away from death, we think.'

'He probably thought I was safe with Alfie,' she said softly, weakly.

'Who's Alfie?'

Iris was about to say something, but she paused, suddenly wondering if she should tell this government-sanctioned paranormal regulation agency that she had a werewolf for a boyfriend.

And, as her sentence died on her lips, Erin said, 'You don't mean Alfred Friday?'

Iris frowned, but nodded her head very gently.

'We've been going through the paperwork. Mr Tabernacle and Dr Tobias both had extensive files on Mr Friday. I haven't found very much paperwork written by you at all, actually.'

'Oh, I, uh, well, I was always mostly field work.'

Erin nodded blankly, flipping a little wisp of hair out of her eyes. 'Yes, I see. We understand that Alfred Friday was an unstable werewolf. Close to the skin. We have been examining the possibility of capturing such a creature for a while.'

'But Cobalt deal with vampires.'

'Minor scuffles aside, the vampire threat is mostly contained. Oh there's still Darius Cole making a few angry noises now and then, but he got married recently and that has kept him quiet. But we're going to push for a change in the status of lycans, an upgrade from mythical to non-mythical.'

'Lycans are going to be made non-mythical? When is this going to happen.'

'Well, strictly speaking it's not fully processed yet. We used to think that, whatever the lycans were using to cover up their presence, it was clearly so good that we didn't need to intervene. No one believed in them, and that meant it was wasteful to spend money protecting humans from them. But we knew that things might change, that's why we took so much interest in your Oxford project. What Dr Tobias was doing was of enough interest for us to fund it.'

'You do know that Dr Tobias turned out to be a lycan himself?'

'Oh, yes, it's all in Tabernacle's files. That kind of thing is more common than you might think. We receive most of our funding, in fact, from the Vampire Clan Council themselves. Most paranormals like a quiet life. They often fund humans to keep control of their fringier elements without having to get their own spooky hands dirty. Tabernacle did tell us he'd killed Tobias. But we've seen the reports now. Clearly, that was just showboating. It was you, I believe, the warrior wolf. And our unstable Mr Friday is your ex-boyfriend.'

'Er, yes, my ex.' Somehow it seemed very clear to Iris that not telling Erin any more than she already knew about Alfie was for the best.

'So where is he?'

'I don't know.'

'We know he has some kind of tracking device embedded in him too. Tabernacle was kind enough to have written up a report on the whole thing. But that signal seems to be being jammed or damped somehow. We need you on this. Your experience. We need to find Alfie Friday. Can you imagine how powerful he must be? He ascended to the level of Ancient Beast, didn't he? You killed the rest of the Silver Crown. He's the only one. And he's thralled to the Divine Wolf...'

Iris shuddered. 'But you still haven't told me what happened to Blake. Uh, Mr Tabernacle. You said he'd brought me here. Where's Blake now?'

10

Blake was sitting on a bench in the Botanical Gardens. He'd been on the run from Cobalt for weeks. This was the first time he'd dared come back to Oxford.

Finding witches was never an easy task, but he figured that this might be his best bet. The Silver Crown had been destroyed, and witches were bound to be interested in how that panned out, even if they weren't planning to do anything to actually help.

He waited. He wasn't exactly sure how much time Lilith spent here, but one of her covens did meet here. And the Oxford Botanical Gardens had a reputation for being a place where the normal and the paranormal intersected. He didn't know if it was true. But he'd been sitting here for an hour and there was no sign of Lilith, and he shouldn't stay. He was on the run – not good to stay still for too long.

That was when he saw someone else. A tall elegant redhead emerged out of nowhere – or, rather more succinctly, emerged from what was clearly a cloaking spell. Blake jumped up and chased Cate down the crunching gravel.

Lilith and Blake might have had a little history. But Cate was the witch Blake knew the best. Cate had worked for the Institute of Paraphysiology as magical interfacing officer since ... well, technically she still *did*.

He caught her shoulder and she turned and smiled. 'Oh, there you are, Blake.'

Blake frowned. As if a witch would ever have trouble finding someone they were looking for. Witches were always doing stuff like this, pretending they weren't unimaginably powerful – and then getting it weirdly kind of wrong, slightly off. 'You were looking for me?' he asked, not sure whether he wanted to play witch games or not.

'Yes. Well. I was just wondering what was going on. The Institute is locked up.'

'Yes. It's been empty and locked up for almost a month. Iris and Pepper are at Cobalt. And, Cate, *I* can get into that place without a key so I seriously doubt that you would have any trouble if you really wanted to get inside.'

Cate stopped Blake with a look that told him he was way off the point. 'Are they OK?'

'Iris and Pepper? I don't know. But things are serious. Cobalt want ... They want Alfie. Unstable werewolf. Oh, God, this could go wrong so many ways. Um, I'm not sure if Pepper and Iris are prisoners, exactly.'

'OK. Right,' said Cate vaguely.

'Yeah. Sure. OK. Shady government organisation want to get their hands on powerful supernatural creature. Not news. However, the real question is where is Alfie Friday? Iris was pretty delirious when I found her, but, if what she was muttering in the back of the truck is right, the Divine Wolf took him. The mother of them all. And she had him thralled tight enough that he left his beloved Iris to die down there. And, if that's the case, well, I'm more than happy for Cobalt to find him. I'd rather they had him than she did.'

'Yes,' said Cate in that cool-mouthed way that witches sometimes spoke when they were trying to speed things along by subtly conveying that they already knew simply *everything*, without making the person they were talking to feel the fabric of reality wobble. It never worked. Blake swallowed. *Eurgh, gross, witches.* 'I want to see Lilith,' he said. 'I need ... We all need her help. She has to intervene. Help Iris find Alfie.'

Cate's pale face lost a little more colour. 'Inter – Uh ...

Are you sure? You're going to ask...? You know that Lilith is, well, rather powerful, and, you're a ... OK, I'd never call Lilith a man *hater*, but she isn't the best man tolerater around. She tries, but –'

Blake made a sharp laughing noise, sarcastic and resigned. 'Oh don't worry,' he said, 'Lilith and I have a little understanding.'

11

Alfie had been chained up in the cage for weeks now. Divine came in twice a day to feed him and help him wash himself. Often he thought being kept like this was worth it for her touch and ministrations. Other times not.

Thrall was a funny thing. It stretched and twisted. He could see the patterns it made in the way he felt about Divine and the way Leon felt about him.

He hadn't come in all that time. His cock was so sensitive breezes seemed to rouse it. His balls ached all the time. Often, after Divine had given him his first meal of the day, she took time washing him. It was almost a ritual, a sacred thing. She whispered to him about how he would be her consort. She would tease his cock to the edge of orgasm over and over. It was torment, pure torture. And yet, somehow, just the touch of her hand was better than nothing. Better than the time when he had been chained in the cage with no way of touching himself, permanently hard, permanently needy.

The days she didn't touch him were the blackest of days in this black, black month of misery.

Alfie was certain of this, even when she pulled her hand away at the very last moment, leaving him bellowing, bucking into space, with Leon in his usual spot in a corner of the cellar outside the cage, laughing, obviously hard in his jeans from watching Alfie's arousal.

Alfie had said to Leon so many times in quiet moments that he should run when the Divine was distracted. That she always left the door standing open.

But Leon never ran.

And Alfie never forced him to.

12

Blake didn't know where they were or how they'd got there. All he knew was one minute he'd been talking to Cate in the Botanical Gardens and the next he was walking across the drawbridge of a castle, a perfectly authentic medieval castle that seemed to exist somewhere out of time and space. It made Blake shudder, kind of seasick again. *Witches! Gross!*

As they walked into a big flagstoned entrance hall – that was anachronistically comfortable and warm – Lilith was walking down a majestic staircase, resplendent in all her usual pin-striped, high-heeled glory. 'Mr Tabernacle, my favourite humanoid creature,' she said, as usual her low musical voice making Blake's spine tingle. She danced over the flagstones, her heels click-clacking, and almost threw herself into his arms like a Victorian lady in a fainting fit. 'It's been too long, darling,' she cooed, reaching up to touch his cheek. 'You know how I miss you and your little ways.' She grabbed two handfuls of his hair and pulled him down into a kiss.

Blake let her kiss him, once, on the mouth and kind of smooshily. *God, this was weird. Why was she being like this?*

'You can go now,' Lilith said over Blake's shoulder to Cate, as she let him up.

Cate locked eyes with Blake. 'Oh, uh, OK. Um, are you all right here, Blake?'

Blake turned in Lilith's arms. Cate's face was full of concern. He smiled at her. 'Oh yeah. I reckon so.'

* * *

When Cate had gone, Lilith bustled Blake into a plush little nook of a lounge and forced a cup of very good coffee into his hands. The room was somewhere between flouncy and austere, the walls rough stone and wooden panelling, the furniture all boudoir. It was like being in the waiting room of a medieval brothel.

She sat down next to him on the sofa. Far too close.

Blake shifted. 'Lilith . . .'

Lilith smiled as his voice trailed away. 'Go on,' she said, 'ask me.'

'Ask you what?'

'Ask me to help Iris. I know why you're here, Tabernacle. I'm a witch. Help her get Alfie back. Isn't that right? So noble.'

'It's not like that,' Blake said hurriedly. 'I just don't want that creature, wolf bitch queen, to do whatever she's going to do with a thralled unstable werewolf.'

'He's not just an unstable werewolf now . . .'

'I know. You think I'm not aware of what he is? Of what his power could be harnessed to do? Why do you think I'm here? Talking to a witch who likes me to do things to her that witches kill men for doing? I'm here because I need you, Lilith. You need to help. Even if I knew where he was, he's thralled to her and killing her, well, that's not straightforward.'

'Fine, fine,' Lilith cooed. 'It doesn't matter. Although, actually finding them might be your biggest problem. But, OK, you're asking a favour of me, right? Get him back. Which means that in return I can ask you to take my witch's binding.'

Blake tried to draw away from Lilith, but the arm of the sofa was right behind him and he didn't have anywhere to go. 'What? You have to ask three favours of a witch before she can ask a binding.'

'You have asked three favours of me, Tabernacle.'

'I have not!' Blake shouted suddenly. 'God, can't you count? Whoever heard of a dumb witch?' Blake held up his palms as Lilith's face stiffened. 'Sorry, fuck. Please don't kill me! But, really! Three? How do you work that out?'

'That first time we met. You tied me up and I sucked your cock.'

'What! That was all your idea. You seduced me, tricked me, made me think you were powerless so I'd tie you up and dominate you a bit. I shoved my dick in your mouth, sure. But that was all your idea. I've shoved my dick in more than a few mouths and, actually, they've always been very willing. And, sweetheart, *you* are a witch! If you hadn't wanted that, I am pretty sure I wouldn't have a dick right now. Or I would have it growing out of my face, or some other kind of witchy attempt at humorous maiming.'

Lilith's face changed to one of almost girlish excitement. 'Ha, you know, actually there was this one woman, Petranella Snow. This was about twenty years ago. But this guy stuck his dick down her throat when she didn't want him to and she fixed it so his dick grew out of the back of his tongue. Right down his throat. One of those witchy ironic punishment things.'

'Really?' Blake felt cold inside.

Lilith, clearly, thought this was funny. 'Yeah. He died though, choked or something.'

'OK, well, look, that's just great and it just proves my point. I'm still alive. And my dick is where it should be. The sheer fact you didn't smite me means when you sucked my cock you weren't doing it as a favour.'

'What? Didn't you enjoy it?'

'That's not the point. I wasn't asking a favour of a witch.'

'Oh no? Well, let me remind you of the moment where you had me tied down in the bed underneath you, you were hammering into me with a cock like a fucking iron bar ...' Lilith's voice faded away for a second. She blinked. 'Hmm, how do you do that, you're what? Forty?'

'Forty-one,' said Blake. 'What can I say? I'm a voodoo sex god.'

'Ha! Good one!' Lilith said with her familiar bark of a laugh. 'Hmm, yes, well, you were fucking me like that, and then you slipped your hand between my legs, twirled your fingers on my clit and you said, "Come on, witch, come for me." I believe I did exactly what you asked.'

Blake shifted. *Oh, fuck.* 'Damnit, Lilith, that really wasn't ...'

Lilith was smiling. 'Yes it was, Tabernacle. It really was. You asked a favour of a witch.' Lilith held up one finger. 'And then you came back and asked me to fix your arm. Favour number two.' She held up a second finger.

'I took out those vamps for you in return for that.'

'Well, I know, but it still counts. And now, here you are again. Asking me for another favour.' Lilith moved closer and held up a third finger.

The soft scent of her was a little like Iris – grassy, cottony, lemony something. It was a trick, a witch trick, making him think she was like Iris. Damnit, though, it was hard to resist. Too easy for Blake to just close his eyes and believe her witch lies. 'Yes. Another favour,' said Blake tightly, pulling back a little. 'Yes I am.'

'You want me to help her? Iris? Your poor wife. Help her find her long-lost werewolf true love. Her life mate. Her bonded one. Help the warrior wolf become the wolf's woman again. It's so tragically romantic, Blake. Who'd've though it of you?'

'That's not what I –'

Lilith ignored him. 'So you know how this works. You're asking a third favour of a witch. So I'm offering you my bond. Take my bond and you can ask what you wish of me for your third favour.'

'So this is it, then? A proposal?'

'If you like, yeah?'

'You're not going to go down on one knee or anything?'

Lilith twisted her mouth a second. 'Oh, darling,' she said softly, 'I thought you'd never ask.'

Lilith slipped off the sofa on to the floor. Blake felt his heartbeat faster. Sex with Lilith was never an easy proposition. Lilith liked him, he knew, because once upon a time she had persuaded him to treat her very mean indeed. But she had tricked him. There would have been no way he would have done what he'd done to a witch if she hadn't promised him she had removed all her powers and so there was no danger she would smite him in anger if he pulled her hair too hard or slapped her face at the wrong moment. That had been the deal. But she hadn't done anything to her powers. She had still been possibly the most powerful woman in the world when Blake had tied her up with his tie and stuck his dick in her mouth. It gave Blake the sweats just to think about it.

And the worst thing of all was Lilith had made it pretty clear in their subsequent meetings that she wanted a replay. But that hadn't happened. Until now.

The way Lilith scared Blake was different from the way Erin Cobalt scared him, or even the way Iris sometimes scared him. If she wanted to, Lilith really could reach inside him, take hold of his soul and squeeze.

His only protection was the fact that, for one reason or another, Lilith seemed to like him.

Her long fingers reached for his fly. 'You know what I want, Blake,' she said softly. 'And I know what you want. So how about you show a girl a good time, huh?'

Blake looked at her, inhaled as hard as he could and reminded himself he was a brave man. He was the bravest man he knew. He leant forwards and put his hands over Lilith's on his fly. 'No,' he said.

'No?' Lilith drew back. Her eyes looked a little black.

'Blake,' she said, and her voice was black too. Dark and hard and firm.

Blake leant forwards and put one finger across her lips to silence her and, with the other hand, he reached into the top inside pocket of his white coat and pulled out a pair of handcuffs. 'No. Don't do that with your hands.'

He leant forwards and reached around her and fumbled the cuffs on to her wrists behind her back. Her head was on his shoulder and he heard her sigh as the cuffs went tight. Something inside Blake couldn't help admiring her ability to compartmentalise. There was no way in the world a pair of handcuffs could make a witch helpless – and yet, the way she was acting, he almost believed it himself.

His dick certainly believed it, stirring at his groin as he pulled away and she lifted her head. Their faces were very close together. Her eyes weren't at all black now, just pure liquid blue. Her pupils dilated with lust. 'Now,' he said, 'no magic. Understand?'

Lilith nodded. Soft.

'Good. Well, let's see if you can get my dick out with your mouth, witch.'

Blake leant back, already half-hard as Lilith moved. He grew harder as she squirmed in his crotch. She grunted in frustration as she tried to get a hold on his zipper. After a couple of failed attempts, she got it open and then, using her lips and tongue, she lifted Blake's hard, hard dick out of his underwear.

Blake leant forwards a little and took hold of a clump of her hair in each hand – copying her earlier move in the hallway when she had forced her way into his mouth. 'No magic, remember,' he said as he forced her head down, sheathing his erection in her skull. 'Take it like a woman, not a witch.'

Lilith felt good. So tight and hot. Her mouth seemed

endless. A slick hot well of joy. He thrust up harder and held her head down.

The idea that she could kill him with a single thought suddenly became an amazing rush.

Blake fucked Lilith's face harder and harder as if at any moment he expected to suddenly find himself whisked out of her mouth and nailed naked to the stone frontage of her magically created castle.

He ached and screamed. He felt his orgasm rising fast, too late to hold back. He jerked Lilith's head up and back – off his dick – as he came in rhythmic thrusts, his semen smattering over her face. Lilith's eyes were closed. She moaned a little as the droplets hit her. Blake's hips jerked again and again and then finally stopped.

He lifted Lilith, still handcuffed, into his lap and turned her around so she was cradled in his arms like a baby. Lilith was a shade taller than he was. Maybe three-quarters of an inch. But with her nestled like this he felt like the strong man. He felt like Alfie Friday.

He slipped one hand between Lilith's legs, working his fingers into her silk-sheer underwear. Then he slowly rubbed her hot tight clit as he dipped his head and licked her face clean, pushing as much of his come as he could into her eager mouth. Kissing her finally, twirling his fingers around her clit as he spun her on the edge of her orgasm for a few moments before letting her come, feeling her buck and twist in his arms.

Blake watched Lilith's face as her eyes fluttered open.

'Thanks,' she said softly, bringing her hands from behind her back and holding out the handcuffs he hadn't unlocked.

He took them, feeling his knowledge of how powerful she really was return like a sickening wave.

'I've got you a present,' Lilith said, standing up.

'You have?' said Blake. 'That's, er, nice of you.'

Lilith was standing over him. Her suit was creased and rumpled. She was listing to one side because she only had one of her stilettos on. Her shoeless leg's stocking had also popped off its suspenders while Blake was working her clit and was pooled around her ankle. Her hair was almost as wild and untamed looking as Blake's own. One hand was behind her back. 'Do you want to try and guess what it is?'

'Is it a broomstick? Actually I've always wondered if a man could learn to –'

'Ha! Oh, God, no. A man on a broomstick? That'd never work. How would you stay on?'

'What?'

'Well how would you mount yourself on the knout? Are you going to stick it up your arse?'

Blake blinked. 'What? Are you trying to say that you . . . ?' Blake shook his head in disbelief. 'You're winding me up.'

'You think? Anyway,' said Lilith, casually oblivious, 'it's not a broomstick. It's a sword. A magic sword.'

Blake tried to look around her body, as she still hadn't revealed what she was holding. 'You mean a sword, as in, a *real* sword. This isn't an ironic witch thing? It is actually a sword?'

Lilith smiled and brought the sword she was holding from behind her back. A long delicate small-sword. Its slender flexible blade glittered, the complex pattern of its hilt fitting snugly over Lilith's bony knuckles. Blake gasped out loud, certain his dick would have twitched at the sight of it if he wasn't feeling so spent. 'Oh! I, er, I've actually always wanted a sword,' he said, his voice sounding rather breathy.

Lilith smiled, and turned it around, taking the blade carefully and holding the hilt out to him. He stood up and took it from her.

'What's magic about it?' he said, taking half a step back to balance himself and then cutting at the air almost reverently.

'Oh,' said Lilith, 'well. Swords are lovely and everything, but they can be rather cumbersome. That one, Tabernacle, fits right in your pocket.'

'Wow,' Blake said, childish and awed.

'Swords have meaning, Tabernacle. You know that.'

'Destiny,' said Blake. He knew the score. 'If a witch gives you a sword, it's not for nothing.'

Lilith nodded. 'I'm sure you'll be fine. A man like you. I know you know what to do with a sword.'

'And Iris? Alfie? The intervention?'

Lilith smiled. 'Leave it all to me.'

13

'Who are you?' Iris said, sitting up. A dark-skinned Asian man dressed all in black – a soft thin expensive-looking polo-neck and jeans – had just unfastened her restraints.

He held out a hand and Iris shook it. 'I'm Vikram,' he said, 'Vikram Rose. Dr Cobalt wants me to work with you.'

'Work with me?'

'On the new werewolf project. Assessing the threat. Formulating a strategy. Just basics. I'm Cobalt trained as far as vampires go. I just need you to fill in the gaps. We need to sweep.'

'To sweep?'

'That's what you call it, right? I've read the files. You sweep for stray lycans at full moon.'

Iris looked up at the drip still attached to her. 'I don't think I'm really ready to . . .'

Vikram grinned. 'Oh I can take care of that for you.' He moved closer and bent over Iris's arm, efficiently removing the drip and covering the needle set into her arm with a sticking plaster.

'Er . . .' said Iris, suddenly aware, as Vikram bent over her, so close, that she was only wearing a backless hospital gown. 'Well, I need to get dressed.'

'I have some clothes for you.' Vikram pointed to the long low cupboard that ran under the dark window. A small stack of familiar dark red sat there.

Iris twisted and slipped out of bed. She made her wobbly way over to the window. Her old uniform, dark-red army fatigues. They'd been washed and pressed – they would've needed it after the state she was in when

Blake found her; in fact, she was surprised they hadn't been incinerated. But, despite the laundry processing, something about the smell of them still made Iris ache with nostalgia. Her uniform, practically a part of her. She sighed, removing her hospital gown as Vikram turned away.

Iris wasn't ashamed of nudity, certainly not in practical matters like these. She looked at the back of Vikram's head. He had shaggily straight dark hair that grazed the collar of his black sweater at the back. He had almost as much hair as Blake, although his was far sleeker. Blake was a man who could exert control over almost anything, except, for some reason, his own hair. Vikram was tall, almost Alfie-tall, but unlike Alfie he was waif thin, supermodel thin. His sweater and black jeans hung off his skeleton. There was almost nothing to him.

'I'm done,' Iris said, fastening the last buttons of her shirt.

Vikram turned. His face was nice, well balanced, regal. All about his nose and cheekbones. He couldn't have been much older than 25.

'So,' he said, 'it's already dark. Moon's up. We should go.'

Iris frowned. 'Moon? Oh, I didn't know it was ... Do you have a route planned? This is central London. I have no idea what the lyc situation is.'

'Well, yeah,' said Vikram, 'that's kind of the situation, isn't it? We need to find out what the situation is.' He smiled and passed her the familiar crossbow that was sitting on the table by her bed.

Cobalt was really nothing like the Institute. The Institute of Paraphysiology had been housed in an abandoned bingo hall in a rundown and tired part of Oxford, with not a single thought given to repairing the damp proofing or redecorating. The foyer still had the old posters advertising various long-past special deals and promotions. Cobalt – if the bare fact that they had their own medical ward wasn't enough – was bright and shiny through and through, like a pharmaceutical company crossed with an advertising agency. As Iris followed Vikram through understatedly plush corridors, past big glossy windows open to the darkening London skyline and into a shiny lift, she wondered if maybe she had landed on her feet.

Cobalt she knew was slap bang in the middle of Westminster, just off Whitehall. Officially/unofficially it was part of the Home Office, jointly and generously funded by both the British government and the Vampire Clan Council itself.

As they exited the lift, Iris couldn't help comparing the dusty old yard behind the Institute with this brightly strip-lit underground space. And, where transport at the Institute had been a rickety old army truck with a canvas roof, here at Cobalt, Vikram ushered her into a luxuriously upholstered black SUV, with tinted windows and every premium added extra. And, in fact, Iris noticed, there wasn't just one. The underground garage boasted a whole fleet of these luxury streamliners.

Vikram drove. Iris listened to the gentle purr the engine made compared with the Institute truck's hacking splutter. The SUV glided up the ramp out of the garage and into dusky London.

'So,' said Vikram a little while later, as they slid along Park Lane, 'where should we head?'

'Um, hard to say. Have you looked into any reports of animal attacks at full moon? I don't know what the situation is in London at all.'

'I did look briefly. I didn't find anything.'

'Maybe there aren't any lycs loose in London. I just don't know. They don't like it too urban. And you can't get much more urban than this.'

'I guess,' said Vikram. 'I mean, if there were lycans in London, we'd know. Someone would have spotted them.'

'Maybe. But the Silver Crown covered a lot of things up. We can't be sure.'

'The Silver Crown? I saw that in the files. The reason lycs have managed to stay so secret is that they had some kind of governance organisation keeping attacks hushed up.'

'I guess, yeah. The Silver Crown. They had a lot of power because of the Divine – the mother wolf. She was part of their circle of twelve. They used her power. Somehow.'

'God, yeah, maybe they siphoned it off somehow and sold it to witches. Witches love a source of ancient power like that.'

Iris nodded. 'Yeah. Maybe. I think there was some witch involvement. I'm not really sure how it all worked. Blake was the expert in that side of it. I just used to kill stuff, mostly.'

'I'd imagine it would be easier for lycs to keep things covered up. They're human most of the time. Completely undetectable and full human reasoning. It's pretty clear they'd be able to police themselves. Vamps are different. They need us. It's the vulnerability to sunlight that's the kicker for them. But it means that a band of humans can control vamps pretty easily with light boxes – even with all the damn power they've got. That's why vamps keep themselves to themselves and don't cause much trouble any more. They know we can take them.'

'So what does Cobalt do?'

'Mostly we work for the Clan Council. Sort out any problems. We work like the vamp police force. And we help keep their existence secret. I guess we're their Silver Crown.'

'Yeah, well, the Silver Crown are over. I killed them.' Iris said quietly, feeling almost ashamed of it. She had a woozy confused memory of Blake helping her down on to the floor of the cavern where he'd found her; manipulating her into the recovery position; covering her in a blanket and then standing back and saying, 'Fuck. You killed six Ancient Beasts in here, Iris.' She remembered him collecting their sparkling crowns and putting them in his bag. He ignored Matthew, who was still slumped and silent in one corner. He took the Silver Collar that lay on the floor too.

As she lay there, sucking gently on a damp cloth Blake had slipped into her mouth, he took his time photographing all the bodies before disposing of them with the magical powder he used. Typical Blake. Work first, medical emergencies second.

'Yeah, well,' said Vikram, bringing her back to the SUV stopped at a red light, 'that's good, right? It means now we'll be able to take the motherfuckers out.'

'I guess.'

'But what will really get us into Dr Cobalt's good books is if we find this unstable Ancient Beast guy. They seem to think he's in London.'

'Yeah. Blake traced him to . . .' *God, where was Blake?* All Erin told Iris in the end was that Blake left after he rescued Iris. 'Um, London. Yes.' Iris twisted her mouth. 'He's, uh, he's my ex-boyfriend, actually.'

'Blake?'

'Alfie. But Blake's my ex too. My ex-husband. Well, we're kind of still married. Estranged, I guess.'

'Really? That must be weird.'

'Yeah, well, that's why I do this. There was an attack. My twin brother Matt was killed. Alfie was turned. Um, well, and here I am.'

'Makes sense,' said Vikram. 'Most lycan-hunter types have some kind of reason to be in the game.'

'What about vamp-hunter types? Do you have some kind of reason to be in the game?'

Vikram shook his head. 'Nah. We're just recruited in the normal way.'

Iris didn't ask what 'the normal way' might be. Something covert, no doubt. It wasn't like Cobalt advertised for trainee operatives in the paper. Instead, she said, 'So, what's the plan?'

'Well, I thought we'd park up here,' said Vikram, pulling into a small side street, 'and keep an ear on the radio. London's full of green spaces we could hit. We're only a block from Hyde Park here. Maybe we'll get lucky.'

14

They sat in the car and waited. Iris still felt a little woozy. Four days in the cavern, and before that she'd been trapped in the cellar. Then – what? – nearly a month recovering at Cobalt. And now here she was, back at work. The car heater was warm around her legs. Her eyelids felt a little droopy. It was so unlike Iris to lose her edge like this, to give in to sleep. And yet . . .

She drifted. She was back in that underground cavern. The six Ancient Beasts she had killed were dead on the floor. Alfie was standing in front of her naked, his body covered in scars from the crown's torture, and she was telling him how she had killed four more beasts in the tunnels to get to him.

But then, instead of the Divine appearing behind her and whisking Alfie away into thrall, Alfie strode over to her and took her in his arms. He kissed her deep and long, the way she craved like she was starving.

'Oh, God,' he whispered against her cheek. 'You came for me, Iris. I knew you would.'

Iris squirmed, slightly aware of where she was, in the Cobalt SUV. She knew she was dreaming and yet she couldn't bear to lift herself back to reality.

Alfie was licking at her jaw. She felt something. Something real. There really was someone licking her jaw. But Alfie, she wanted Alfie.

Iris. Iris half opened one eye. She looked out of the passenger window. Matthew's ghostly figure stood out on the pavement.

Iris, wake up. Don't let this happen. But Iris shook her head. In her lucid dream she was on the floor of the cavern. Alfie was on top of her and she could feel the weight of his body, half crushing her. So real. *So real.* He wrenched at her combat trousers, ripping a chunk of the fabric away. Enough to fuck her. Thrusting into her, fast and greedy, he whispered, 'You came to find me, Iris. You came for me.' His fingers were on her clit. She screamed at the sensation. 'You came for me, Iris. Come for me. Come for me.'

Iris. Matthew was yelling, his voice enough to rip her eyes open again.

'Matt, I . . .'

Alfie was receding. She couldn't feel his cock inside her any more, or his thick fingers on her clit. But she still felt the weight of his body on top of her. Except . . . no. Not *his* body. Not Alfie.

The next thing she felt was a strange damp tickle at her mouth. She spluttered and tried to pull her head back, but the deeply padded headrest was firm behind her and Vikram's hands – because, of course, it was Vikram – were unnaturally strong on each side of her face. He was sitting on her lap, straddling her, his groin tight against hers.

'Vikram,' Iris said, muffled into his mouth.

Vikram pulled back a little, but still held Iris's head. 'Iris? Is something wrong?'

'Is something wrong?' she whispered. 'You're kissing me.'

'I know.'

'Well, er, why?'

'Why? You fell asleep. Don't you bond like this at the Institute of Paraphysiology? At Cobalt we think it's good to have a sexual bond in a team. It helps if you are working together. I thought . . . You said that you and Blake . . .'

Iris squinted. 'What? No! Blake and I were just . . . We fell for each other. We were married. You're telling me Cobalt are some kind of sex cult? 'Cause I'm sure if that were the case Blake would have known about it. And Blake would have said. In fact, Blake would have never shut up about it.'

'Really?' Vikram said, his voice a soft burr. He was still holding Iris's face. He seemed so much stronger than he ought to be.

Iris looked into his big dark eyes. God, they were amazing eyes – melting chocolate pools, huge long camel lashes. Why did she want him to stop kissing her again? 'Vikram,' Iris murmured. She knew it was an open invitation.

'Vik. Call me Vik.'

As he leant back into the kiss, something inside Iris thought that maybe this was something magical. That she shouldn't want this, not like this. Alfie had told her about lure, a power male werewolves had when the full moon was close to convince women to come to their beds. Was this lure? But Vikram wasn't a lyc.

Iris could see the moon hanging in the sky, fat and creamy white. Except, no, that wasn't a full moon . . . Not quite.

'It isn't a full moon,' Iris said dreamily. 'It's a day off, going to be full tomorrow. That isn't quite full.'

'No. I know. I never said it was a full moon. This is just an exercise.' He kissed her again.

'An exercise?'

Vikram's lips were soft and oddly cool on Iris's. He tasted faintly of coffee.

'I mean,' Vikram said as he pulled away a little, 'unless you still want that wolf?'

'What?'

'They say werewolf hunters are mostly sniffers.' He shrugged.

Iris's mouth opened to say something but he went on.

'Nothing to be ashamed of. It'd give you an edge. I can see that. Do you still love him? Your ex? Even now he's what he is?'

Iris shook her head. 'No. God, no. I'm not a sniffer. I don't love him. Can't. He's a lycan. Lycs killed my brother. I just want revenge. My brother . . .'

'Hmm.' Tight close and heavy on Iris's lap, Vikram drew back a little and slipped his hand up her red shirt. He cupped it over her left breast, stroking her nipple with his thumb. 'Well, that's good. It's not really the same with vampire hunters. We don't tend to become bloodfuckers in the same way. Well, except for interrogators. You know, it's almost impossible to really interrogate a vampire 'cause of their psychic powers. When they had Darius Cole that time, God, they tried everything. But vamps love human sex. They're drawn to it. It's their biggest weakness. You know, another reason we sometimes have sex with each other at Cobalt is that it can be a good lure for vamps. They love it. They can't have sex. Well, they can, but they don't have orgasms unless they do this creepy blood-rites thing. They're attracted to human sex. It's the hottest thing to them, mysterious and freaky. Taboo.'

'Really,' Iris said, a little breathless as Vikram kept teasing her nipple as he spoke. Something about the way he was talking turned her on. She'd never thought about vampires before, only heard Blake and Dr Tobias dismiss them as corpses. All the times Blake had called her a sniffer, he'd never once suggested she might be a bloodfucker, turned on by vampires. The erotic power of vampires was a story, nothing like the reality. But, God, the way Vik was talking made them sound so, well, so sexy.

'Lycs aren't like that,' Iris muttered as his mouth hovered above hers. 'They love sex, though. They're really highly sexed. And sometimes they take human women, claim them, call them life mates. Sometimes at the Institute we talked about looking into that – but we never did.' She closed her eyes, drifting. 'Alfie, just after he was bitten, before we knew . . . I was in a bad place, confused and full of grief. And all he wanted to do was fuck. That was the first thing that changed. He was incredibly sexual before, but that first month, sometimes, it was like there was nothing else to him. And the way he fucked me then. The way we were together. United in grief, in horrors we couldn't talk about. No one believed us. We described the monster and no one listened. Of course, now I know the Silver Crown had probably been there, covering things up. But then it felt like there were just the two of us and then the rest of the world. I was between worlds, I guess. Moving from the human world I knew into a world of the paranormal.'

'Hmm.' Vikram ducked his head down and kissed her again. For the first time – and with her head full of Alfie – Iris kissed him back.

Vikram kissed her lips, her cheek, her chin. He slid down and around and pressed his lips to her neck. Iris moaned, almost in frustration as he missed her secret spot – that sensitive place on her jawline.

'The way he fucked me then,' Iris half sobbed. Thinking of Alfie. Nothing but Alfie. Partly her dream, partly her memories. Alfie's body over hers like a canopy, like a shield, blotting out the world. The world defined by her dead brother, ripped open in the night only to be replaced by his screaming ghost. His body. Alfie. Safety and protection. A harbour. Out of the storm. Except, except it wasn't safe under Alfie. She'd been in his bed the afternoon before his first full moon. Only luck had sent her home before his first change.

His eyes were gold in her memory. Had they been gold that afternoon? She wasn't sure. Golden eyes, that subtle werewolf tell that somehow only ever seemed obvious in retrospect.

And the way he'd fucked her. That afternoon. That month before he changed. Even before he was bitten. Even later when they found each other again. Vicious, almost cruel. Driven, powered by his lust, his need. Alfie had always been a slave to his own body.

Vikram kissed Iris's neck over and over. And then Iris realised she really didn't feel well at all.

Everything swam into darkness.

15

'Really, Iris, what were you thinking?'

It was Erin Cobalt talking; Iris was lying in her bed at Cobalt. It was dark outside, still night. 'Have you any idea how unwell you are? I could tell from the files that you were dedicated to your job but this is quite ridiculous. You were dehydrated, seriously infected, both your shoulders were dislocated. You were hours from death when Tabernacle found you. *Hours*. I don't care how being this close to a full moon might affect you after all this time. You are in no state to be out of bed yet, let alone attempting to plan a werewolf hunt. We'll sedate you, if we have to. You need to rest.'

As she listened to Erin's voice, Iris wondered how Erin knew she was listening to her. Iris still hadn't opened her eyes more than an undetectable crack.

Erin continued, 'Now, I must say, we don't really agree with solving medical problems with witchcraft. Of course, we all know what happens when fatal injuries are reversed by witchcraft. Nasty business. But, as you are so very important to our future plans, I am willing to give you a small dose of –'

Iris's eyes snapped open. 'No. Sedate me.'

'Iris, it's really fine.' That wasn't Erin speaking. It was someone else, someone standing behind Erin, someone heart-soaringly familiar.

'Cate?'

Cate was standing right behind Erin, looking strangely messy and shabby-dusty in the sparkling spot-lit hi-tech of Cobalt. As she moved forwards, Iris blinked; Cate seemed to be actually trailing dirt and dust in her wake.

Even though it was night-time – the clock on the wall said half-past eleven – the building site next door seemed to be still hard at work. Iris could just make out the floodlights bouncing off the cranes and the low hum of machinery.

As Cate leant over the bed, Iris found herself coughing. Cate put a hand on Iris's forehead. Her skin felt sticky and warm. Iris squirmed. Cate looked over her shoulder and said to Erin, 'She could do with a little dose. Just something to aid her recovery.'

Erin nodded.

'Cate. No. No magic,' Iris said weakly.

'I'll have her back within the hour,' Cate said and suddenly her hand on Iris's forehead felt very heavy and tight.

Iris felt panic rising inside her. She couldn't move or speak, and she couldn't keep her eyes open . . .

16

In another moment Iris was lying on something hard, something stone. Her eyes, which had felt like they were glued shut a moment ago, opened naturally. Iris looked up. Above her was a huge vaulted ceiling, the light that fell on her face was dirty, dappling candlelight. She tipped her head back. Behind her was a huge stained-glass window, its colours muted to various shades of black-with-a-hint-of by the night sky outside. She was in the belly of a building, something magnificent and sacred. She was lying on the floor of a church.

Cate was crouched over her, her palm still flat against Iris's forehead. She smiled. 'Sorry, Iris,' she said. 'It just seemed like the cleanest way to get you out of there for a while.'

Iris sat up, realising the building she was in was more a cathedral than a church, huge and ancient. 'Where am I?'

'Don't you recognise it? Maybe from that angle it looks different to when it's on TV. This is Westminster Abbey. I didn't want to pull you too far. And the coven who use it are very amenable.'

Iris looked around, the silvery-grey architecture suddenly snapping into familiarity. 'Westminster Abbey! A coven meet in Westminster Abbey?'

'Yes,' said Cate, 'nice, isn't it? Are you OK here for a moment? I need to join the ritual.'

'Mmm.' Iris looked around again at the silver-dust-shot surroundings. There were a few other people in the Abbey, all witches, all moving in a precise regimented way and chanting in low breaths, making magic. There must have been some kind of elaborate cloaking or even a dimensional shift in place for this trick to work. She knew the only way to really cope with being enmeshed in witchcraft was to try to ignore it.

And then she saw who was sitting on the far end of the front pew. A shock of dark hair and a white coat.

And her insides just flipped over. *Oh! Oh!*

She got up jerkily and, even though her legs felt kind of watery, she ran.

As she got close to Blake, she went to hug him and he held out both his arms straight in front of himself, blocking her and keeping her from making contact with him. She took a step back, oddly humiliated, just managing to half recover herself and say, 'Hey.' She sat down shiftily on the pew next to him.

'Hey,' he said, still looking out towards the altar.

Iris felt a weird sort of homesickness, a nostalgia. Normally, Blake was quite blatantly pleased to see her, often to the point of it being an irritation. But suddenly he was blank and cold. Iris was surprised how much that upset her. 'Um, look, you saved my life. Thanks. You never stayed to let me tell you.'

'That's OK, Iris. We save each other's life. You know that's what we do.'

'Yeah. Also, you left me there. At Cobalt. Why didn't you stay with me?'

Blake turned his head but just looked at her blankly. 'Complicated.'

'Well, yeah. Sure. God, it's so good to see you. Are you OK?'

Blake still seemed to be acting oddly, twitchily. 'I'm on the run, Iris. Cobalt want me.'

Iris narrowed her eyes. 'Are you trying to say . . . ? You mean they want to kill you? Why would Cobalt want to kill you? We're on the same side.'

Blake raised his eyebrows. 'Sure, Iris, sure. Well, perhaps I'm wrong, perhaps I misinterpreted a few things, but it's either that or Erin Cobalt wants to keep me as her permanent fuck-slave. I don't know which is worse.'

'What?' Iris said, her voice suddenly whooping and swooping off the vaulted ceiling. Several witches stopped their marching and chanting and looked round. Iris flushed slightly and dropped her voice. 'What about me?'

'I don't think Cobalt wants *you* as her fuck-slave, Iris. I don't think her tastes are that irregular.'

'Yes, but, do they want me dead?'

'No. Or you'd be dead already. They want you 'cause they want to start working on lycs. And you're the Institute's killer-bitch, the doc's protégé, the warrior wolf. You've got to remember though, Iris, Cobalt aren't a charity. They aren't about keeping people safe, or about reuniting you with your boyfriend. They're about what's best for Cobalt. Financially. Nothing more. They want Alfie.'

Iris nodded. 'I know. They already said that that was my priority.'

'Yeah, well, ask yourself why. It's not 'cause you're missing his spectacular wolf dick.'

Iris was about to ask Blake what he meant when Cate and Lilith came up. Lilith twirled around girlishly in front of them and sat right on Blake's lap.

Iris frowned. She wondered for a second if this was something magical. There was a couple of seconds where she half expected Cate to sit on *her* lap.

But then Blake smiled sheepishly in a way that made Iris decide not to say anything. Lilith was a hugely powerful witch, after all. She was probably used to sitting on any lap she felt like.

'Hi, again,' said Lilith, turning her body slightly towards Iris, blocking Blake almost completely from view. 'Nice to see you. You OK?'

'Fine thanks,' said Iris a little stiffly.

Cate, still standing in front of Iris and looking slightly awkward, said, 'Iris, we brought you here because we need to find Alfie. Well, what we really need to do is find the Divine . . .'

Iris frowned. 'Well, can't you? You're witches.'

'We need you to do it, Iris. We can't interfere directly. We can assist you, but there are limits to be observed. Balances to maintain.'

Iris frowned. Witch logic hurt her brain. 'What?' She looked at Lilith. 'But you said the Divine would end the world?'

Lilith just shrugged.

'Oh, God, whatever. OK. So I need to find him. That's my job anyway. So how?'

'He has a tracking chip inside him, right?' said Cate.

'The signal's dead though,' said Blake, looking a bit shifty as Lilith twisted sideways on his lap and leant close to his chest to twiddle his hair. 'Either the chip's out of order or . . .'

'It's cloaked,' said Lilith. 'The Divine'll have the whole place locked up tight. She knows we'll be trying to find her before moon rise tomorrow night. Well, tonight, actually. It's gone midnight.'

'Why? What happens at moon rise?' said Iris.

'Boom-shack-a-la,' said Lilith, clapping her hands together and grinning. She clapped quite close to Blake's ear. He flinched. Lilith laughed and cooed, 'Sorry, baby.'

Iris frowned at them. 'What? Could you say that in Eng –'

Lilith looked confused.

'Oh, forget it.'

'OK, so here's the plan,' said Cate. 'We take the cloaking off the chip and then you can trace him. There's just one tiny matter. The spell I want to use is tricky. I need to spot clean the magic off the chip without destroying it.'

'I thought witches could do anything.'

'We can, by human standards, but this is interfering with magic already in place. That can be awkward. This spell is kind of strong. It can be a little volatile. But I can use it because Alfie is a magical creature. If the chip is inside him, his magical body will absorb any fall-out from the spell.'

'It's inside him,' said Blake. 'I put it there myself.'

'We need to be sure. The Divine could have removed it somehow. Alfie knew about it. He might have told her. Thrall might have made him.'

'Well, don't you *know*?' said Blake. 'You're witches.'

'It's complicated. The cloaking is very dense. The Divine has a lot of power. She was made by a god.'

Iris was shaking her head. 'Well, we can't know it's inside him, can we? I mean, we can't know for sure.'

'No, but we have another plan. A back-up in case the decloaking of the chip doesn't work. You can ask him where he is.'

'I can?' Iris frowned hard. 'Well, forgive me but if I can ask him then maybe we don't need to go through this charade to find him because, if I can go and ask him, then surely . . .'

Cate laughed. 'Your mind is so logical, Iris. It's funny. You can ask him because you're connected to him. You just have to open your mind to it.'

'Oh, come on,' said Iris, taking a step back. 'What, so I have psychic powers now? Am I a vamp or something?'

'It's very simple,' said Lilith, sounding irritable. 'You are connected to Alfie. We can smooth that connection. Open it up so you can communicate with him. Either we decloak the chip and trace it, or you get Alfie to tell you where he is. Two chances to find him. Then we all live happily ever after.'

Blake said, 'Yeah, now, when you say, "we all live happily ever after", what does that mean exactly? We find the Divine, then what? You said you were going to stop her. Does that mean destroy her? How can you?'

Lilith sniffed. 'It might not come to that. It depends what she's actually planning. Destroying the Divine is tricky but not impossible. And it is actually foretold. I thought destroying the Divine would destroy all were-wolves. Eradicating a species is a difficult trick to pull off without Armageddon-like repercussions. But there is this prophecy – it's not so well known – but I think it might be relevant to us. It's quite clear about the fact she will be destroyed. Hang on . . .'

Lilith twisted on Blake's lap and pulled some papers out of a neat shoulder bag. Iris craned to see but the text was indecipherable.

Lilith wrinkled her nose as she read aloud. 'So, it says, basically, "The lines of the wolves will stay true so long as the true heir of the first Beast pays the Divine." '

'Great,' said Blake, 'er, what does that actually mean?'

Cate said, 'It means that, when the Divine dies, if we have to kill her, the werewolf lines won't dissolve like we thought. But it does mean that whoever does kill her needs to be this "heir of the first Beast".'

'And,' said Lilith, 'they'll die. Whoever is the heir needs to kill her. And ensure they absorb her power somehow, which will probably be what kills them. That'll be the price. You can bet on it. Prophecies don't muck about with terms like that.'

'Great plan, then. Someone, this "heir", kills the Divine and they take her power, but the power will kill them,' said Blake.

Iris tutted. She was more interested in something else. 'So who is this true heir? Is it me? The last prophecies were about me.'

'Well,' said Lilith, ' "the first beast" probably means your Beast, Dr Tobias, who you killed. And he did con-sider you his heir in some ways. His werewolf-killing protégé. But it could also easily mean Alfie, as his oldest living cub. So I expect one of you will kill the Divine. And pay the price.'

'But how do we know which one of us it is?' said Iris.

'I'm sure all will become clear. My money's on you,

Iris, you have "chosen one" written all over you. You pretty much don't stand a chance, but that's the good thing about a nice doomsday scenario – the stakes are so high you can try anything. It's really quite liberating.'

'Why is this a doomsday scenario?' said Iris. 'We don't know what the Divine's doing yet.'

'Yeah, course. It might not come to that.' Lilith did that nose wrinkle again.

'But if she doesn't die . . . If I don't kill her, she'll keep Alfie, won't she? He's thralled to her.'

Lilith shook her head. 'We're racing ahead here. Stage one is to find them. Then we'll see what has to be done.'

A few minutes later, the witches were assembled ready to carry out the plan. Iris still wasn't sure why this was the plan. Witch logic was so cracked. Cate had told her once that the basic premise was to help humans to help themselves. Iris had no idea what that really meant.

Iris was on the altar, lying on her back. It felt kind of weird. She looked up at the high dark ceiling, the swooping shapes. It was like being inside an animal, in the belly of a whale, or a dinosaur. She thought about the Oxford Natural History Museum. She missed Oxford.

Tipping back her head, she could see Blake standing in the pulpit, smoking a roll-up cigarette. He flicked the ash into the air. Everything was hazy, dreamlike. There was a huge stained-glass window behind him. Candle-light was bouncing off it and twinkling back on to him, throwing choppy darkened colours on to his white coat and into the reflected highlights in his hair. Iris felt slightly deranged, lost. It was probably the magic, heavy in the air like thick sickly incense.

The witches were circling her, moving and chanting. She tried to dissociate from it. Then Lilith stepped forwards and placed her hands on Iris's forehead.

Iris's eyes snapped open. She hadn't realised they were closed. She saw Alfie in front of her.

'Oh.'

Alfie smiled. It was her Alfie. The Alfie who loved her. Clean and neat. His white teeth sparkling and his eyes flashing joy. The last time she had seen Alfie in reality he had been naked. His body bruised and scarred from where the Silver Crown had been torturing him. He'd been thralled to the Divine. But now his body was unmarked and he looked at her with love.

'Alfie,' Iris said. 'I didn't think it would be this easy. Did the witches bring you to me?'

Alfie smiled and leant closer. His mouth was a breath away from hers. She felt her lips tingling with the wanting of him. And Alfie, so close that she felt the words rather than heard them, said, *I still love you, Iris*.

And then Iris heard a scream. Alfie was gone. Lilith was standing over her. She tipped back her head, opened her mouth and gasped out loud. Then there was an explosive bang, Lilith's touch was gone and she was borne across the cathedral. There was a crash as she hit the ground and Iris heard Cate shouting, 'Shit! Shit! Oh, God. Oh, God, no.'

17

Somewhere and nowhere, there was a place that wasn't really a place at all, a small golden cage dangled in a well of darkness. Inside that cage sat a witch.

Sabrina was a different kind of witch from Lilith and Cate. She knew those Glindas frowned on her. Every witch used a little magical enhancement to improve her looks. Even when the crone look was really in, most of that was done using magic. Hairy warts don't just sprout by themselves.

Everyone knew all witches dabbled a little. It was hard to look in the mirror with the kind of power witches had and not think that it might be nice to smooth out the odd wrinkle, or straighten the odd line. Every witch did it. Well, maybe every witch except bloody Lilith.

Sabrina, on the other hand, was almost entirely constructed of artifice – only another witch would really see it, of course. Sabrina didn't see what was wrong with looking the best you could look. A few little spells to make her dark hair glitter like it was shot with stars, to make her face a balance of delights, to make her body the shape men dreamt of, well, it just saved her spelling herself a smooth path through the rest of the world.

Pretty people got away with more, got an easier ride. That was how it had always been and how it always would be.

Sabrina had been in the golden cage for no time and for forever. There were other cages here, swinging in the dark – Sabrina wasn't sure who or what they contained, but she was aware of them sometimes. A soft cry. A shadow in her periphery. Someone new had arrived recently, insofar as time meant anything in the endless dark. Someone who had cried out more than usual, someone human.

But Sabrina had other things to worry about than who else was here. Sabrina knew that Lilith simply didn't know what to do with her. But one thing was for sure, she couldn't keep her locked up like this.

Every supremely powerful witch needed an evil nemesis. You can't rewrite rules like that.

So, when the golden cage suddenly shattered/melted/dissolved around Sabrina, she wasn't at all surprised. And, as she tumbled through the veils between her prison world and the one she knew, she only thought for a single moment about what might have happened to Lilith to make her magic fall apart this way.

18

Iris was back in her bed at Cobalt. She wasn't sure how she had got back here, but she was almost used to it. This was the third time she'd woken up confused in this room, and it was starting to feel familiar. According to the clock on the wall, it was only half-past midnight. Even so, that meant less than 24 hours until the full moon.

Cate was standing over her. 'Sorry,' she said, 'I thought it might be best to get you here as quickly as I could. We need Cobalt to trust you.'

Iris nodded against the pillows. 'What happened to Lilith?'

'Um, well, she seems to be in a sort of coma. Some of her body's usual functions seem to have shut down to power the spell opening the connection between you and Alfie. It's not unheard of. She'll be fine. I think.'

'It's OK?'

'We don't know for sure. A witch like Lilith going down is rather rare and the outcome is unpredictable.' Iris went to say something and Cate held up her hands. 'Yes, even for witches.'

'And, um, am I connected to Alfie. Right now?'

'Yes, but the connection will be strongest on your morphial plane.' Cate paused. Iris made a face. 'Just accept it, Iris. It'll be easier. The morphial thing means that you will probably dream about him and be able to communicate with him in your dreams, but that might not be the most useful thing. Dreams can be slippery. Try to speak to him as you are falling asleep. In that state. That's probably best. Meanwhile, I'll work on the decloaking spell'

'OK.' Iris shivered, thinking of the last time she had seen Alfie; he had been totally thralled to the Divine, chaining her up in the cavern under her directions. She swallowed. 'He might not want to talk to me.'

'He might not. But his feelings for you are still there, even if the thrall has control of him. He still loves you or this connection wouldn't work. Use your power. Use your love for him. The more you open your heart to him the stronger your connection will be.'

Iris felt suddenly frightened. The reality of having to communicate with *that* Alfie, not her Alfie. The Alfie that could cheerfully leave her to die. 'But I can't. He hurt me. I can't let him hurt me again.'

Cate smiled, nodded seriously and walked away. At the door she turned and said, 'You don't have a choice, Iris.'

19

Sabrina stepped through the alcove into the little underground room. The Divine was startled. 'Sabrina! I thought the witches had taken you.'

'Well, yes, they did,' said Sabrina, clopping into the small dark low-ceilinged space in her wedge-heeled sandals. She was only wearing a thin white dress. She never seemed to feel cold.

The only light in the room was from a mismatched collection of candles and the fire. The room had little in it except a rocking chair, a low table and another hard-backed chair drawn up close to the fire. The floor, ceiling and walls were bare rough stone. At the back of the room was the heavily bolted wooden door that led to the prison where Alfie and Leon were being kept. Sabrina was brushing her hands together and she marched through the room to sit smartly on the empty chair. She lifted one leg to take off her shoe. 'Oh, stop looking like that. I'm not going to put you back in your cage.'

The Divine settled back into the rocking chair. 'Well, good.' Her expression was bristling. The Divine wasn't scared of much, but Sabrina terrified her.

'Oh, stop.' Sabrina smiled casually and the Divine shuddered. 'Look, it's you and me now, Divinia. We're not rivals anymore. If we even ever were. No more Silver Crown. The warrior wolf came for them like it was written that she would. It's a new era. Wolf and witch. We can do what we like. And I hope you have a plan to screw over as many humans as possible.'

Divinia felt her heart lift. Sabrina back and on her side. That was too, too perfect. She grinned a dirty grin.

'Well, you know. I kind of do. But why don't I tell you about that later. 'Cause I have some really fun non-humans to screw over right through that door there.'

Leon was looking at Alfie. He did that a lot. He didn't know how long he'd been locked down here or what was going to happen to him. But looking at his sire helped. It made him feel safe.

Alfie was lying naked on his side. His cuffed wrists pulled up and twisted a little behind his back where the chain was twined around the bars of his cage.

In a rare lucid moment Alfie had wondered aloud about this set up. Why he was still in the cage and Leon outside it in the cellar room. Leon knew why. Firstly and most simply, the cage was magical, working like the collar to hold Alfie's form. The reason they weren't *both* in the cage any more was obvious – Alfie would thrall Leon into making him orgasm. Leon could see how tormented Alfie was by the constant frustration and teasing. The Divine clearly wanted to drive Alfie mad by not letting him climax. There was no way she'd let him and Leon go back to their earlier ways of comfort through rutting. But it was safe to keep Leon outside the cage because, while Alfie was locked up, no matter how many times Alfie told him to run, there was no way Leon was going anywhere.

He didn't hear the door opening, but when a musical lilt of a voice said, 'Well, ain't love grand!' Leon knew he would have recognised her anywhere.

'Sabrina,' he said, rolling over.

She was standing in the doorway. She looked just the same as she had the last time he had seen her. Bare delicate feet, long brown legs, a stretchy tight white dress that seemed to make her look more naked. She smiled. Leon's broken heart went heavy and tight in his chest.

The magic Sabrina had used once to temporarily break

his thrall to Alfie and make him loyal to her was still there, somewhere inside him, pushing its way to the fore again now he was in a room with her. Looking at her seemed to activate it.

'How are you, Leon?' Sabrina said, crossing the room. She threw a single wary glance at the sleeping Alfie. Leon didn't get up; he let her approach him and drop into a crouch. She covered his body with hers and kissed him.

All Leon could think about was how Sabrina was so beautiful.

She ran her fingers through his long blond hair, melting away the tangles that had matted their way into it while he had been locked up. Every morning, while the Divine bathed and tormented Alfie, she gave Leon a bowl of water to wash with, but it was barely adequate. However, Sabrina, as she touched him, seemed to cleanse him. The grime and sweat of weeks of captivity seemed to melt away.

Leon let his gaze wander to Alfie. Sabrina's hands had come to rest on the fastening of his jeans. She reached down and turned his chin, making him face her again. 'There's something different about you, Leon,' she whispered. 'You used to be blind to anyone but me when we were together. Let me remind you.'

Sabrina bent back over his crotch and popped open his fly, his erection sprang out, but Leon didn't know whether he was hard from Sabrina's petting or in that way he often got from idly gazing at Alfie, naked and frustrated in the cage.

Sabrina leant closer still and took Leon's cock into her mouth. Down and down into her throat.

'Oh, God,' Leon moaned, almost shocked at the raw ridiculous pleasure of it.

Sabrina laughed and those vibrations flowed into his cock and seemed to spiral out through his whole body. The pleasure was intense. Too much. Every hair on his body stood on end. His nipples were pinched taut. Sabrina let her mouth work his cock a few more times then pulled free. She worked it a few times with a tight fist. Then she whispered, 'Stand up, werewolf. See me.'

Leon obeyed her. He got shakily to his feet, his body still buzzing, overcome with almost debilitating arousal.

'Touch it,' Sabrina whispered. 'Touch yourself.'

Leon took his cock in his hand and brought himself to the rising edge of his orgasm, fast and sudden. He stroked again. Nothing. The sensation suddenly gone.

He looked at Sabrina. She smiled.

'Witch,' said Leon, frantically working his cock and suddenly feeling nothing. 'What did you do?'

'Very little, actually. You've been wondering, haven't you? How it feels for him, for your sire. Your heart is breaking for his suffering.'

'No,' said Leon sharply.

'He has your pleasure, Leon.'

'What?' Leon turned his head and looked at Alfie. His eyes were closed or almost closed. He looked peaceful and pleasured.

'Touch it,' Sabrina whispered.

Leon stroked his cock. He felt nothing, but in the cage Alfie moaned and bucked, thrusting his groin into the empty air.

'Just as you wished. I know you've been taunting him, making him watch you. And I also know that, deep down, your only wish was that you could give that pleasure to him.'

'No.' Leon shook his head. 'That's rubbish.'

Sabrina smiled. 'This spell doesn't work like that, Leon. I made magic to give you the sexual experience you most desired. And it would seem, what you most desire is for your sire to have your pleasure.'

'No, no.' Leon shook his head hard.

'So you don't want him to feel you come?' Sabrina said, getting to her feet.

'I – I . . .' Leon was shaking his head.

Sabrina moved closer. Leon was backed up against the stone wall. Sabrina's long cool fingers closed around his cock. 'Well?' she whispered. 'The Divine won't know. It won't affect her potion. He won't actually come. Just feel it when you do.' Her fist was tight, moving on Leon's cock.

Leon bucked and gasped, squirming, his back against the wall – but he felt no pleasure from what she was doing. He looked at Alfie. He knew that look on his sire's face – the pleasure was clearly all his.

'If you wanted to enjoy it yourself, you would,' Sabrina whispered, and her voice was harsh and bitter.

Leon moaned and felt himself ejaculate. He looked at Alfie, writhing as Leon came.

After a second, Sabrina brought her semen-smeared fingers up to Leon's lips and shoved them into his mouth. As he cleaned her up, she muttered, 'Wow, werewolf, who's *your* daddy?'

20

Iris lay on her bed. Cate was gone and it was dark outside. She couldn't see the clock without putting the light on. She guessed it was maybe one thirty now. Iris lay down and closed her eyes. She couldn't wait to see if the connection worked.

She lay still, wondering what was going to happen. She felt exactly the same. 'Alfie,' she said out loud in the dark.

Nothing.

She waited. Her mind started to drift. She thought about Alfie, about that time between killing the Beast and the Silver Crown coming for them. That bliss. Just Alfie – naked and hard. Always there for her. Wanting no one but her.

And then she felt something. Knew deep inside that Lilith was right, that she and Alfie were bound together by something paranormal. That she was with him even now, even though he was thralled to the Divine. Even though he had betrayed her, left her to die. She felt everything that had ever been between them. A history. A love story. A soul. She listened to her heartbeat and realised it wasn't the only heartbeat she could hear in the room.

21

With the moon coming and Sabrina's magical assistance, it didn't take long for Leon to get hard again. Sabrina pushed him to the floor and climbed on top of him, facing away from him. Leon had his hands on her tits, stroking and working them. As Leon bucked up into Sabrina, he noticed that they were both watching Alfie, still sleeping.

He seemed to be restless, rolling and moving. His chains clanging against the bars every time he tried to twist too far.

Sabrina put her hands over Leon's on her tits, urging him to twist and work them harder, tightening his fingers on her nipples, fighting her way to another climax.

But Leon was watching Alfie's face, wondering what he was thinking. And then Alfie said something, barely really spoke, but his lips moved and Leon went cold. He knew exactly what word had just formed on Alfie's lips. A word Leon hated and dreaded. A word that made him feel sick inside.

'Iris.'

It was as if Leon's jealousy of Iris was the biggest thing he'd ever felt. More than his loyalty to Alfie or to Sabrina. He hurt inside. Then, in that moment of grief, he just wanted to get away from this place. Rip himself away.

Behind him on the floor was a metal tray that Divinia had brought him his evening meal on hours ago. He slipped his right hand off Sabrina's body and groped on the floor. His fingers found the rim of it in seconds and he lifted it up, moving as fast as he could, and smashed Sabrina around the head.

Sabrina fell on to the floor. Out cold. Leon scrambled out from underneath her and started to drag his jeans back on, looking frantically towards the door. There was no sign Divinia had been alerted by the noise of his attack.

Alfie was still rolling around, muttering a little more loudly now, 'Iris. Iris.'

The only window in the cellar was high and small. 'Wolves escape,' Leon whispered to himself as he got it in his sights and leapt.

22

Iris?

It was Alfie. He was saying her name over and over but she didn't know why or if he knew she could hear him.

She said, 'Alfie,' very softly.

And again, he said, *Iris?*

'Alfie.'

'Iris!' That was loud. Loud and close.

Iris rolled on to her side. 'Alfie,' she said again.

'Iris? It's Vik.'

Iris opened her eyes. Vikram was standing over her. 'Hey,' she said, sleepy and confused.

'Sorry,' said Vikram. 'I didn't want to wake you, but I wondered if you had got any new leads from the witches you saw.'

Alfie cried out. 'Iris! No! Don't go!' He sat bolt upright, suddenly awake. Leon stared at him, frozen and frightened, perched on the tiny window ledge of the high window.

Alfie said, 'She's still alive.'

The door to the cellar crashed open and Divinia stood there. Her eyes moved from Alfie, to the unconscious Sabrina, to Leon perched up high. Her calm quiet gaze settled on Alfie. 'Tell your cub to come down from there,' she said evenly.

Alfie looked at Leon. He looked scared and confused. But he couldn't disobey the Divine when she spoke like that. 'Come down,' he said.

23

Iris sat up, slightly shaken. Something had happened to Alfie, but she wasn't sure what. She looked at Vikram, trying to settle her thoughts. 'Sorry, look, Vik, I'm a little busy. But, yes, the witches fixed me up and I think they might be able to decloak the chip in Alfie's arm. But I need time to try something first.' Iris sighed. 'Except we don't have time. We need to find him before the full moon rises. We need to stop the Divine.'

'Why?' said Vikram. 'What's she going to do.'

'I don't know, but if witches think it's bad enough to intervene . . .'

'OK,' Vikram said, nodding calmly. 'We'll sort it. When can the witches get the chip activated?'

Iris frowned. Vikram looked strangely beautiful. Her room was dark; the big window showed a blue-black London sky. The only real light that didn't come from the cityscape was leaking through the quarter-open door. A little of it fell on Vikram's jawline, lighting the nap of hairs there, making his skin look like velvet. Something about the simplicity of what he had said, the purely expressed desire that whatever the problem was it would be sorted out, made her think of Blake. Blake in the early days of their relationship. Blake way back when.

'Can you come back later?' Iris said. 'I just need to do something before the witches can fix up the chip.'

'Sure,' said Vikram, standing up, 'I'll come back in an hour. The night is still young.'

But it really wasn't. It was getting late. Too late.

* * *

Alfie was still dazed and sleep-headed. Sabrina was walking around holding her head and looking viciously angry. She was staring at Leon. She couldn't believe it. Nor could Alfie when he figured out what must have happened. Leon had hit a witch – *a witch!* – over the head and knocked her unconscious.

Did Leon know she was a witch? Maybe he still thought she was a werewolf.

Divinia was crouched behind Leon roping his wrists together. Every time she wanted Leon to do something she sent it down the line by telling Alfie to tell him what to do.

The Divine used sending it down so naturally. Alfie had always considered it a last resort. It bred ill-feeling in packs to keep using that pull over and over. Or, at least, Alfie felt it did. Clearly, the Divine felt differently. And who was Alfie to question her?

It was clear to see how the Divine could use the lines and loops of power that threaded through all werewolves to bind them all to her will with sending it down.

Alfie's wrists were still cuffed behind his back. His cock and nipples were both hard. Hot and tight. He wasn't sure why.

When the Divine had Leon trussed, she used Alfie to make him stand up. 'Well,' she said, 'I had thought that there was no need to confine you. I thought your loyalty would keep you close to your sire. Obviously that is not the case.'

'Why should I stay here with him?' Leon snarled low. 'He doesn't care about me.'

'I thought you were proud of what a true wolf you were, Leon,' said Sabrina, pushing away from the wall she was leaning on it and coming close. 'That's how it works. He doesn't care about you – but you care about nothing but him. Even my magic hold over you just isn't strong enough to fight the way you feel about him. It's more than just thrall, isn't it, Leon? Does he know?'

And the way Sabrina was smiling, Alfie knew; knew she knew.

'Fuck off,' Leon said.

'He's in love with me,' Alfie said slowly. 'And yes, I know.'

'Tell him to come into the cage, Alfie,' said Divinia. 'Tell him to come into the cage and lie with you.'

Leon's eyes went saucer-wide.

Alfie told Leon what to do and he did it.

As Leon's body shifted in the straw next to Alfie's, Alfie saw the fear in Leon's eyes. The Divine came up close behind them and – after a few careful instructions and the detaching of Alfie's wrist chains from the bars of the cage – got them face to face. 'Well,' she muttered as she started to tie Leon's ankles to Alfie's, 'it would seem you are right, Sab. This one is already hard for his sire. And he's disgusted by it.' She reached up and chucked Leon under the chin. He tried hopelessly to turn away. 'You're disgusted by your own desire, aren't you, cub?'

Leon said nothing. He didn't meet Alfie's eye as the Divine bound them at the knees. She wound more rope around their chests.

Leon was a little shorter than Alfie, only a little. Alfie tried to look into Leon's eyes. He tried to show him something from his sire that would be soothing. But he knew he couldn't soothe Leon now. Leon knew that Alfie had no power. Barely a mind of his own. Alfie was totally thralled to the Divine. Helpless.

Behind the Divine, Sabrina was laughing. 'Make sure their cocks are close together. Let that pup show his sire how he really feels. It's the only way my magic wouldn't have held him. Filthy cub in love with his wolf-daddy.'

Leon snarled and struggled, but that just made his crotch rub against Alfie's. Alfie could see it in his eyes – he was trying so desperately not to get any harder.

Alfie looked past him at Divinia. He felt himself relax as he stared at her.

'Move against him,' the Divine said.

Alfie pumped his hips. Leon's cock was obvious, hard and heavy. Grinding against Alfie's which was still stiff from waking. There was a single layer of denim between them, Leon's jeans. Alfie was still – as always – naked.

'So what now?' the Divine said, looking at Sabrina.

'Oh, let's just leave them like that a while. Nice lesson for that pup to give him no choice but to let his sire know just how he feels.'

The Divine said, 'Sounds good to me. And we need to talk anyway. We have things to plan.'

The two women left the cellar, without a backwards glance.

Alfie's bare chest was tight against Leon's. His flesh was so warm. But Alfie's heart hurt because the Divine had gone. It was so painful for him every time she walked out of the room.

He was only barely aware of the fact that, every time he thought of the Divine's name, he ground his erection against Leon's.

It wasn't until she had gone, and he felt sure she wasn't coming back, that he lay still. Leon's face was right in front of his. He stared at Alfie some more. 'Please,' he whispered. 'Please, sire.'

But Alfie just smiled. 'Divine,' he said. Vague and vacant.

'You didn't say *her* name earlier,' Leon said, darkly.

Alfie looked at Leon's strong-jawed face. 'Huh? Who else is there?'

'Vix bitch. Iris. You said she was still alive.'

24

After Vikram had gone, Iris lay back down. She was sure she had felt something before. But she couldn't be sure if she had dreamt or imagined it.

She tried to fixate on Alfie and felt her mind wander a little. She thought again of magical times they'd spent together. That space they'd shared between her killing the Beast and the Silver Crown coming for them. They'd holed up in Alfie's pack house, buried in his attic bedroom. They had fucked each other raw, unable to stop. Alfie's body had been like an addiction.

As she thought about him, her nipples hardened. She tangled herself in the sheets. She pushed her uniform out of the way and pushed her hands into her underwear.

She squirmed on her narrow bed as she remembered how it felt to be chained down by Alfie, using the magical silver chains he used for sex. There was something sexy about watching him fix her wrists into the magically self-adjusting cuffs and know that he had done this to himself time after time. That he had let other women chain him down. That he hadn't had a choice. That for years the only way Alfie could have sex was like this. That magnificent body of his. His body that had a wolf inside.

Alfie climbed on top of her as she was stretched out taut on the bed. Naked and exposed, her pussy stretched open for him. She couldn't bring her legs together. She couldn't roll over. Nowhere to hide. Her nipples were already hard.

Alfie leant down and tormented her with kisses that

were more tease than anything. The tip of his tongue. A twist of his lips. Then nothing. Riffing on her frustration as he pulled away over and over.

In Cobalt, Iris stretched her legs wide apart recreating the memory. She rubbed her hands over her body, moving where Alfie's hands had moved. Her mind twisted. Nostalgia and ecstasy and regret. Longing. Longing. She wanted Alfie so much. So very much. And she knew he knew it too when she heard him say, *Iris?*

25

'Iris?'

Alfie was squirming against Leon's body. They were still tied nose to nose. When he spoke, Leon started. 'Sire?'

Alfie, is that you? Are you really there?

'What?' Alfie looked around the cage as far as he was able. 'I, uh, I heard Iris.'

'That was me, sire. I was telling you. You said Iris. Before. You said her name.'

'No. No. I heard her voice. I really did. Like she was right here.'

'Alfie, man, are you OK?' Leon frowned. 'This is the most lucid you've been for weeks.'

Alfie looked at Leon. He did feel different, like a veil had been lifted. And then he felt her again. Iris. All over and around him. Iris. He was inside her. Alfie groaned and rubbed himself against Leon.

Leon squirmed. 'Please, man. Don't fucking do this to me.'

But Alfie barely heard. He knew he was lying on the floor of his cage, rubbing himself against Leon, but the fantasy of Iris was so clear. Bracing with his shoulder, he rolled himself over, forcing Leon underneath him. Pinning him on the ground with his bigger body.

'Ow,' Leon yelped. 'Damnit, man, my wrists are tied.'

In his mind Alfie was on top of Iris. Fucking her as she was chained down to his bed in the pack house. He leant down to kiss her, teasing with his mouth. Underneath him, Leon opened up his mouth, needy and ready.

Alfie, said Iris.

'Sire,' said Leon.

Alfie moaned. He bent his head again and kissed Iris. Long this time. No more teasing. He loved kissing. He loved to use his mouth. He thrust into her with his tongue and his cock. She was squirming beneath him. Helpless and taut. He looked at the stretch in her muscled arms. He knew the way these chains worked. They'd held him enough times. They pulled that little bit too tight. They were very secure, but, the way they held, that slow burn under the arms that would grow and grow and become unbearable. He thought of keeping Iris chained to his bed for hours. Going away and coming back to fuck her again. Using his muzzle to keep her quiet.

Possessing Iris like that seemed such a twisted idea. Not Iris. Iris was so free. He thought of her like a bird in a cage. His to take and use over and over. He was coming inside Iris. Quick and hot. God, and the Divine wouldn't be pleased about this. Somewhere inside him Alfie felt the memory of what she was doing to him, saving his semen up for something. She wouldn't want this. This stickiness that was pooling now between his groin and Leon's.

But he stopped thinking about that, the moment he realised he could still hear Iris in his head.

Alfie?

'Iris, God. Is this real? You're alive?'

Blake. Blake rescued me. The chip in my arm.

'Oh, thank God. I'm so sorry, Iris. How are you doing this?'

Witches, Iris said.

Alfie felt strangely scared. If witches were involved anything was possible. There was a moment's pause and then Alfie said, 'Look, Iris, I don't know what you're doing, but I know this is part of a plan to find me. Don't try to find me. I don't know how you've broken into my head right now, but the Divine has me thralled. And messing with werewolf thrall is bad news. And I don't want you coming near me while she has control of me. Please, Iris, I don't want you to see me with her. I'm a werewolf, Iris. I look human but I'm not. Hairy on the inside, Iris? You ever heard that phrase. If you come for me, Iris, I will hurt you. She will make me hurt you. Don't come here.'

Don't think I don't know what you are, Alfie. I know. You don't scare me. And I know if she makes you hurt me, well, I know it's her and not you doing it. Tell me where you are. Or I'll find another way to find you.

'You won't find this place. It's the Silver Crown's base in London. Highly cloaked and warded. Built for the Crown by witches in return for a fix of the Divine's power. Listening to Divine talk about it, you'd think witches would never have had any power if it hadn't been for her.'

Really?

'So she says, she's been juicing them up for years. Then they got all super godlike and turned the tables. Locked her up in a cage – the cage I'm in now – and formed the Silver Crown to keep her incarcerated. But that was years ago. I don't think the witches need her any more.'

Wow. Well, I guess the witches forgot to mention that. Maybe they know where that place is.

'No, they don't. She told me all about it. When Sabrina got in with the Silver Crown, she reformulated all the cloaking so only she could find this place.'

Well, that's OK, we can still trace your chip. It's cloaked but the witches are going to amplify its signal.

'Iris, no. I told you not to come for me.'

Don't be silly, Alfie.

'I won't let you, Iris. I'll have Leon rip it out of me.' Leon looked up. Alfie wasn't sure if he'd been having his conversation with Iris out loud or not.

Inside his head he could hear Iris shouting, *No! Alfie, no.*

Alfie tried not to listen – he felt strangely clear headed and awake. Iris was fading away fast. The chip! He needed a plan. 'So, cub, how're those ropes on your wrists?'

Leon smiled. Alfie had been trying to get out of his own chains – without success – every lucid moment he had. Even with the strength of the Divine's thrall, the wolf's need to escape was still strong. He knew Leon would have been working on those knots ever since the Divine tied them.

He wasn't really surprised when Leon brought one hand, then the other out from behind his back.

'There's a micro chip buried in my bicep, pup. You can see where the cut was made, even though I thought I'd mostly healed it. I need you to dig it out of me. It's deep in the muscle.'

Leon went a little pale. 'I – sire, no. I don't know if I can.'

'Don't worry. I'm not giving you a choice about this, cub,' Alfie said.

26

'No! Alfie, no.'

'Iris? Are you OK?'

Iris opened her eyes to see Vikram standing beside the end of the bed again.

'Um, it's gone two a.m., Iris. I said I'd come back.'

Iris swallowed. She pulled her hand out of her underwear, grateful that most of her half-dressed body was hidden by the tangle of bedclothes. She scrambled into an upright position, keeping herself covered, trying to formulate what had just happened. It felt a lot like waking from a dream.

In fact, she thought, can I really be sure that it wasn't a dream?

'Vik,' she said, her voice sounding odd outside her head, 'I need a phone. I think I know how to find Alfie. But we have to move fast.'

Leon was kneeling over Alfie. He had got most of the ropes off, but Alfie's manacles defied every trick both of them knew.

'Forget them. They're probably spelled,' Alfie had said. 'Now get the chip out.'

In the end Leon had needed to force most of his left fist into Alfie's mouth, while he used his other hand to reopen the wound. He could feel Alfie tense and shaking with pain as he bit down on Leon's fingers, leaving deep marks on Leon's bony knuckles. But Leon was strong, and he had been told what to do by his sire. He forced two fingers down into the almost healed wound and drew out a tiny gore-covered microchip. As he pulled free, instinctively, he ducked his head and licked Alfie's wound.

Alfie sighed softly.

'What can I do with it, though?' Leon said. 'They'll still trace it if it's here.'

'It won't be here.'

Leon gestured wildly around at the cage and cellar that held them.

Alfie smiled. 'I have a plan,' he said. 'Now swallow that chip.'

When Sabrina followed the Divine into the cellar, she was delighted to see Leon lying on the floor of the cage. He was lying on his stomach and his jeans were off. 'So,' she said as she approached the cage, 'you got the ropes off, did you?'

'Wolves escape,' Divinia muttered, as she unlocked and hauled open the cage door.

She marched in and over to Alfie, who was sitting propped against the bars. She dropped into a crouch and cupped her hand around his balls. 'Twice,' she said roughly. 'You fucked him twice, didn't you? You've come twice. What a waste. I knew we shouldn't have left them in the cage together.'

Sabrina saw Alfie meet the Divine's eyes with his big werewolf-gold ones. He couldn't lie to her. 'No. I came when we were tied together. Then I fucked him. Then I sucked his cock.'

Divinia reached around behind Alfie. 'You really can't get free of these cuffs, can you?' she said.

Alfie shook his head.

'No, no. It must have been a shame for you to get to fuck but have to do it chained up like in the bad old days before you got yourself collared like a puppy dog. And you must have had to make him help you take him. How humiliating for the pup.'

Sabrina smiled to herself. Exactly as she had been hoping.

'But you got to come,' Divinia went on. 'Such a waste of your power.' She turned to Sabrina. 'I can't believe you let me leave his cub in his cage. You know I'm trying to keep him chaste until I can start to collect his seed.'

'Oh, it was worth it. You'll still have enough for the potion if we're careful now. And look at this uppity creature. Humiliated by his desire for his wolf-daddy. Perfect.' Sabrina put her mouth very close to Leon's ear. 'You won't try anything like that again, will you, pup?'

Leon barely looked at her as he shook his head and rolled over on to his back. 'Please, Sabrina, I want *you* to be my alpha. Not him. I want your control.'

Sabrina smiled. She really did have a delicate place in her heart for Leon. Witches were renowned for their weakness for cocksure strutting men. Leon under her thrall – she couldn't think of anything more delicious.

She bent down and placed her hand on his forehead. 'Of course,' she muttered, 'the spell will take more easily if you want it.

Leon gritted his teeth. This was the place where Alfie's plan would succeed or fail. He closed his eyes as Sabrina's hand touched his head. He didn't dare look at Alfie, but pictured him instead, thought about how much he loved his sire.

He let the memory of Alfie half an hour ago wash over him: Alfie on his back with Leon astride him. Leon having to guide Alfie inside him and drive himself down again and again, impaling himself on Alfie's cock, working for both of them, until Alfie had roared and come inside Leon.

Then Alfie had buried his face in Leon's groin and worked Leon's hard cock with his mouth, only stopping to whisper parts for his escape plan – or, at least, his plan for Leon to escape. His kissed Leon afterwards, tasting of Leon's come, and whispered into his mouth that this would help him stay strong and loyal.

The last time Sabrina used magic to convince Leon to break his thrall and betray Alfie, she had convinced him first that Alfie was a turncoat, a traitor to werewolf kind. Now, as Sabrina laid her hand on Leon, bending her head to kiss him and scalding his mouth with the violent sweet-heat of her silver tooth, he knew he would die loyal to Alfie.

Leon blinked up at Sabrina as she pulled away from him. 'Queen,' he said softly.

But already Leon saw Divine looking suspiciously at them. Alfie had said she wouldn't like it when she realised what Sabrina had done. Alfie's power over Leon was the way the Divine controlled him. Without the pull of the line, the Divine had no sway over Leon. Sabrina had broken one of her sacred pack lines. Thrall was the heart of the Divine's power; she wouldn't stand for Sabrina's warping it with witchcraft.

Alfie had said, 'Sabrina and the Divine barely tolerate each other anyway. They might act friendly, but Sabrina helped the Silver Crown keep the Divine locked in this cage. Sabrina's messing with werewolf thrall. The Divine is a wolf. She's going to be angry.'

As the Divine straightened up, she said, 'You shouldn't come into my house and mess with the ways of the wolf.'

'*Your* house! Witches built this place for you, Divinia. To protect you. If they hadn't, your own children would have ripped you apart in the hope of inheriting your power years ago.'

'That's not true. You don't understand how it works. Werewolf loyalty. Thrall. You wouldn't play around with it if you did.'

As the witch and the wolf argued, Leon sneaked a look at Alfie. He had his head tipped back against the bars of the cage behind him, staring at the Divine, his feelings for her back as strong as ever. The thought of leaving Alfie made Leon feel sick, but he couldn't disobey a direct order. He had told Leon to run, get as far away as possible.

What Alfie hadn't said, perhaps hadn't considered, but what Leon knew, was that Iris would find him. Iris was going to trace the chip, wasn't she? That was the whole deal. And Leon was looking forward to a few exchanges with that bitch.

27

'Vik, I need a phone. Do you have a phone?'

'Well, yes. I have an MCD.'

Iris looked blankly at him.

'A mobile communications device. Don't you have those? Here.'

What Vikram pulled out of his pocket and passed to Iris looked exactly like an Institute-issue coms set. As Iris dialled Cate's number from memory, she thought how weird this was. Dr Tobias must have got their communication devices from Cobalt. This seemed like confirmation that Cobalt really were the power behind the Institute. Who had started calling these things 'coms'? Coms sets? Was it Blake?

The second time Iris met Blake, he had told her about Cobalt. They had slept together the first day they met – after Dr Tobias had introduced them. And then, afterwards, cocksure and so fucking sexy, Blake had suggested they go on a date. He offered to take her out for a drink while she could still taste his come in her mouth.

The next evening, he met her in the Lamb and Flag. Iris was sitting at a wide oak table in the dark and crowded pub. Blake wasn't late, but she had been ridiculously early. A fact borne out by the shredded beer mats that arced out around her like she was about to bed down for the winter. She was meeting a real werewolf hunter for a drink. She was so nervous she practically jangled.

When he finally appeared, bowling through the swing door of the pub, his collar-length dark hair and narrow face instantly recognisable, Iris jumped out of her seat and waved excitedly.

Blake ducked his head and came towards her looking furtive. He was wearing a brown overcoat layered over a white lab coat and, underneath that, what seemed to be dark-red army fatigues.

As he slid into the seat opposite her, he said, 'OK, nice greeting, so now the whole pub is wondering who we are and what we're doing.'

'What? Are we being all covert? Isn't that a bit, um, unnecessary?' Iris hoped her snippy tone would make him take her seriously. His easy chastisement had been just a little too paternal for her liking. At 22, Iris had felt like an adult – after what she'd seen, what she'd been through – but she knew other people often had trouble treating her as one. Iris alternately blamed her overbearing, overprotective parents and the fact that, with her short dark hair and slight angular figure, she looked more like a teenage boy than a capable grown woman.

Blake held up his left hand deferentially. 'OK, fine. You're right, I was just messing with you anyway. No one cares. Watch.'

Iris stared open-mouthed as Blake stood up and threw off his overcoat, slung it over the back of his chair and shouted, 'Don't mind us, we're werewolf hunters.'

A few people looked around, but most clearly pretended not to have noticed. Iris slunk down in her seat.

'See. No one cares. No one believes in paranormals any more. You can make as much of a song and dance as you like.'

Iris swallowed her embarrassment. 'Right,' she said precisely. 'Now do you want a drink?'

When Iris came back with their drinks, before she even sat down properly, Blake said, 'So, you learnt lycs were real the hard way, eh?'

'I guess.'

'Well, that's the usual way it happens. Jude, the girl

you met yesterday, Doc's other trainee, she has had some awful times with lycs. Won't even say much about it.'

Iris took a sip of her drink. 'And you? Did something happen to you?'

'Nah,' said Blake, leaning back. 'I'm an anomaly, babe. A lyc hunter without an axe to grind. So, anyway, shall I do the big reveal?'

'The big what?'

'The big reveal. I love it when I get to be the one who does this to someone. Shall I tell you the truth about the world? You've found out lycs are real. Want to know the rest?'

'The r-rest?' Iris swallowed. 'Sure.'

'OK. First thing you need to know. There really is magic. Actual magic. Anyone can learn to do it, but witches are the fucking experts. And, yeah, there really are witches. I don't mean like pagans or druids or any of that shit. Not hippy crap. Witches. Great and terrible. It's kind of hot, in a weird way. They're powerful like you can't imagine, practically omniscient. They're tricky fucking bitches. If they're on your side, great; if they're not, well, you'd probably be dead before you found out.'

'God.' Iris thought for a second. Then, feeling a bit silly, she said, 'What about, er, vampires? Are vampires real?'

Blake smiled. 'Ah, that's a weird one. Yeah, they are. But here's the thing, lycs and witches are mythical. Like, officially they don't exist, even though they, obviously, do. Vamps used to be the same, but Vampires got reclassified about twenty years ago – at least in this country – as non-mythical. I mean, only in secret of course. No one's going to announce that. But the powers-that-be accept that they are real. They even fund this sort of clandestine organisation – well, I say clandestine, it's actually part of the Home Office – called Cobalt to keep the peace with them. Vampires don't interact much with humans, anyway.'

'How come vampires were reclassified and lycs and witches weren't, though?'

'No one really knows. The rumour is that the vamps wanted it, set it up. Vamps are immortal so most of their clans are rich as fuck. Like the church, well, except not.'

'Cobalt. God. Real vampire hunters? Part of the government? So what are Cobalt like?'

'Rich is what they're like, bloody rich – compared to us scrabbling out of the Doc's basement. I met them once, Erin and Charles Cobalt, they run it. Greatest vampire hunters in the world – a married couple fighting against the dark.' Blake winked at Iris. 'So romantic. Or it would be if they weren't the freakiest pair of fuckers I ever met. They defeated Darius Cole about twenty-odd years ago – this uber-scary vamp who massed an army and tried to enslave humanity.'

'Yuk. So is he dead now, this Cole creature?'

'Really dead or vampire dead?'

'Really dead, like not here, not going to enslave humanity.'

'No. No he isn't. Cobalt gave him to the Vampire Clan Council and the Council sentenced him to live. I think that's a vamp thing. A vamp punishment. They keep him alive. You know, forever. To suffer.'

Iris shuddered visibly. 'Ew.'

'Yeah, well, it's gross. Vamps are so gross. They fund the people who hunt them. Ick. Perverts.' Blake stopped and took a pull of his pint. He shrugged. 'But, really, it's not actually so strange that vampires would fund them. Humans are probably the best creatures to keep rogue vamps under control. Vamps are really powerful because of the mind-control stuff, but the sunlight thing is a huge vulnerability. Find them while the sun's up and you don't even need a stake. Just open the curtains.'

'That is so weird. Vampires fund the vampire hunters.' She shook her head.

* * *

Back in her bedroom at Cobalt, as she waited for Cate to answer her phone, Iris thought how, when she had that conversation with Blake she had no idea that their werewolf-hunting operation was headed by a werewolf. Dr Tobias himself was the Beast, Iris's nemesis, the wolf she wanted to kill with all her heart. But she wouldn't find out the truth for eleven years.

All that time. All that time.

'Cate,' Iris said urgently into the coms when a voice answered, 'he won't tell me where he is. And now he knows we're tracing the chip. I think he might try to remove it. We need to do the amplification urgently.'

'OK. I'm on it right now,' said Cate. 'It's being done as we speak. Get mobile and try to get a trace as soon as possible.'

28

Thursday, 21 February 2008

Iris was used to orders. She knew the power and efficiency of chains of command. Debate had its place, but so did obedience.

Vikram was driving, as Iris was jacking his MCD into a Cobalt laptop. She was like a machine, snapping from task to task. It all came back to her in a rush. She was trained to do this.

Once, in bed, talking about work, Alfie had said, 'Damn, Iris, sometimes you're so freaking sci-fi.'

And Iris laughed and kissed him and said, 'Well, you're so bloody medieval, werewolf.'

Now she looked at the map on the glowing screen and muttered, 'God, Alfie, come on.'

The three coms sets they had used in the cellar to chip themselves had been Iris's, Blake's and the spare they used to keep in the glove compartment of their truck. Iris knew that the chip that she had put under her own skin, the one Blake had used to trace her, had been the one from her own coms set. But she wasn't sure which of the other two chips Blake had stuck into Alfie.

At least it was all compatible with Cobalt equipment. She typed the codes of both into the tracking program and watched the screen, not really daring to hope. *Alfie.*

It took a while. Vikram drove the SUV in lazy circles, drifting wider and wider.

They were on the North Circular when Iris said, 'Oh.'

'You got something?'

'Yes. I think. But it's moving.'

'Where is it?'

'West. Heading west. It's outside London. Still inside the M25. Pick up the A40.' Iris touched the little flashing set of co-ordinates on her laptop screen. 'But if it's moving that must mean he dug it out.'

'Maybe he's moving.'

'Maybe.' Iris wished she knew for sure, but the only thing she really knew was that this little signal was pretty much all she had left of Alfie that wasn't as intangible as a dream.

The Divine stood staring at Alfie. Her fight with Sabrina hadn't turned to magic – but it had been vicious. Both women were shaking with rage – rage that seemed to amplify ten-fold when they saw that Leon was gone.

Sabrina said, 'He tricked us. This was a plan. *His* plan.' She pointed a perfect finger at Alfie. 'We ought to kill him.'

The fatal magic was already taking shape when the Divine shouted, 'No! We need him. He's crucial.'

Sabrina stifled the spell and a few wisps of it bounced across the cage and hit Alfie. He yelped as it grazed his arm right where Leon had dug out the chip.

The Divine looked at him, peering at the spot. Alfie's body was so scarred and injured that she hadn't noticed this new damage before. She furrowed her brow. 'You dug that chip out of your arm? Why?'

Sabrina said, 'Is there someone you don't want to find you, werewolf?'

Alfie opened his mouth but didn't speak.

'He's losing it,' said the Divine. 'I don't think he's capable of telling us anything. You might be wrong about his planning his cub's escape. Leon was always the wild one. Alfie?'

Alfie looked at her, 'Yes, ma'am.'

The Divine moved closer. 'Did you help him escape?'

Alfie looked blank.

The Divine moved closer still and unlocked the chains on Alfie's wrists. 'Give me a stone or something, Sab,' she said over her shoulder.

Sabrina pulled a large football-sized boulder out of the air and passed it to the Divine, who set it in Alfie's newly released left hand.

'I know you can't escape those chains,' the Divine said slowly, 'but this escape has made me realise I can't get complacent. Smash your hand, Alfie.'

There was a tiny flash. The Divine had pulled the thrall tight, but a voice somewhere inside Alfie screamed at him not to do it. Screamed and screamed as he hefted the boulder in his left hand and brought it down hard on his right.

While Alfie was still howling with pain, the Divine roughly chained his left arm to the bars of the cage and turned to go. 'We don't need your cub anyway,' she said, walking away. 'And soon we will begin the collection ... and your problems will really begin, Beast.'

29

Iris dozed in the passenger seat. Vikram had connected the signal from the chip into the SUV's sat nav. They'd never had sat nav at the Institute. The disembodied voice giving directions was strangely soothing. They had been on the road for hours, sliding down the M5 towards the West Country, through Devon and into Cornwall.

Time was slipping away. It was still dark outside, but dawn was coming.

She thought she might connect with Alfie again, but she only got fragments. He didn't seem to know she was there. He was saying something about his hand. His hand hurt. Pain. That was all she could sense. Pain. But she couldn't fathom what that meant.

She was drifting a little when Vikram said, 'So, this werewolf that is your boyfriend. Not your ex, like you said, your boyfriend. Still. When the Divine took him.'

'Mmm?'

'I found some more stuff in Tabernacle's files. After you killed the Beast, you went on leave. There's a lot written by him about whether or not you should be allowed back. Particularly the fact that you are "sucking Alfie's dick". That's him, isn't it? The unstable wolf?'

'Yes,' Iris said softly, 'yes it is.'

'So you are a sniffer?'

'No. I don't think so. It's not werewolves. It's just him.'

'Did he tell you that you were his life mate? I hear that's what lycs do to seduce women.'

'No, no, nothing like that. He doesn't believe in life mates.' Iris looked out of the window at the street-light-scattered darkness. 'I think I do, though.'

'But you've lost him to the Divine,' Vikram said. 'I've been reading up on that too. She'll have so much hold over him. He's her heir now. Beast cub becomes Ancient Beast. You've killed all the Ancient Beasts, haven't you?'

'I don't know. No one knows for sure. But when she came for him...' Iris felt her throat start to ache. 'Her hold over him seemed very strong.'

'So he can't love you any more. Not while she's alive.'

'And, according to the only prophecy on the subject, if I kill her, I die.'

'Sheesh,' said Vikram. 'The gods don't make it easy for you guys, huh?'

Iris laughed at her own reflection in the black window. 'No,' she said, her voice hollow. 'No.'

She felt Vikram's hand on her back. Straining in the dark glass she couldn't make out his reflected eyes. 'You thought about moving on yet?'

'Well, not exactly. I mean, I'm in the middle of a cross-country dash to save him.'

'You really think the signal's him?'

'I don't know. Look, can we talk about something else. How do vamps have sex?'

'What?'

'You said vamps are drawn to human sex because they don't have sex like humans do. So what do they do? They do have sex, right?'

'They do, kind of, they do this thing called blood rites.'

Iris turned around in her seat to look at him as the sat nav gently told them to turn left.

'They can do all the normal sex stuff. Fucking. Everything like that. But their big thing is biting. They bite at the point of orgasm. Well, the bite is the orgasm really.'

'Weird,' said Iris.

The atmosphere in the SUV was suddenly taut with charge. Iris's mouth was dry.

'Touch yourself,' said Vikram, his hands steady on the

steering wheel. 'I know you want to. This paranormal stuff gets you hot, doesn't it?'

'No,' said Iris, knowing she meant yes, knowing she was wet already. She couldn't fathom why. Vikram was ... Something in the tone of his voice. She didn't know how to say no to him. It was like he knew what she wanted in a dark place inside, and just lifted it forwards. She looked back at the black window again, and gasped at what she saw.

'Go on,' said Vikram. 'I know you need to. Talking about Alfie and now about this. It's in the air. You need to come or you won't be able to concentrate. Whatever you think of me, my orders are to bring Alfie Friday in alive – that's going to be my priority. You don't have to worry about me distracting you from your mission. It's my mission too.' As he spoke, Vikram obeyed the gentle voice of the sat nav and pulled over on a patch of rubbly ground.

Iris slipped one hand down the front of her trousers. Her head was fogged suddenly. She fought to remember what she had realised a moment ago. 'No,' she said, even as she was doing it. 'No, this isn't right. Isn't what I want.'

'What you want is to give in to me,' Vikram said, still soft, still telling her hidden truths.

Iris slipped her fingers into the heat of her cunt, her liquid centre. She thought of Vikram. Of looking out at the dark night. Of her reflection in the window. And Vikram, Vikram hadn't had one. No reflection. As she touched herself, she murmured, 'You're a vampire.'

'Yeah,' Vikram said, super-soft.

'And you used your mind control on me. You're using it on me now.'

'Oh, only a little. Mind control is a wonderful thing, Iris. You think that morphial connector of yours would work without it?'

Vikram sighed and Iris heard a voice in her head: *Iris.*

'Alfie?' He was there, she knew it, strong and real. She looked at Vikram and spoke to him – it was like she was in two places at once. 'Are you doing this?'

'Imagine this is his hand,' Vikram said, as he popped his seat belt and reached over, pulling her hand from beneath her waistband and replacing it with his own.

'But his hands are so big. His fingers are like . . . Oh!'

Alfie's hands were on her then. She felt them. So *real*. Twisting against her hot sticky flesh. He was over her. His body. His face looked surprised, confused as to where he was. And drowning in his own arousal. 'Where are you, Alfie?' Iris murmured. 'Are we following you?'

Don't. Please. Don't try to . . . Alfie said. He was kissing her. Biting at her neck. Her chin. Her jaw. God, she wanted him. The *real* him. Not this. Not just this, this dream, this underwater love. She wanted him hard and real for her. Alfie was flesh, not mind. Alfie was animal. Power and heart and heat and grunt. This wasn't enough. And yet . . .

Sex with Alfie was beautiful. Utterly amazing. But she wanted to be with him. She felt his fingers slip inside her and heard him say softly, *My hand. My hand's broken.*

But it didn't feel broken. Two, three fingers inside her, his thumb on her clit. So good, *too* good. He made her come.

Iris bucked and rolled, in Alfie's arms, and Vikram, on top of her, leant in and broke the skin in her neck. She felt it, but it felt fine and good. He cried out hard as he pulled away from the bite, convulsing too.

Iris sighed and wiped the blood away with her hand.

The SUV was parked in front of some thin-looking trees facing a gravelly track. Across the track was a small wooden hut. 'That's where the chip is,' Vikram said, nodding. 'It's stopped moving.'

'OK,' Iris said, blushing.

'I'm sorry. I had to do that. It seemed like the best way to call him to you. Sex.' Vikram shrugged. 'Werewolves, you know. And reading him in you was the only way I could get a fix on him. He's not in there. Not in that hut. I could sense how close he was.'

'Then what have we been following?'

Vikram reached over the back of his seat, pulled out Iris's crossbow and handed it to her. 'Let's find out.'

30

It was easy. After the event Iris found herself wondering if it was because Vikram could read her mind. But, whether it was that or simply a set of smooth paramilitary moves from two people who worked for the same organisation, Iris wasn't sure.

In quick succession, they prowled over to the cabin in the dark. Vikram kicked the door open, and Iris sprang through it with the crossbow locked and loaded. And Leon, yes, of course it was Leon – the missing piece – fell to his knees with his arms raised next to the bed in the tiny wooden cabin.

He looked at Iris with a sly grin, 'Vixy. How are you? Sire told me he'd left you to die in some hole in the ground.'

'Yeah, well, your sire's spectacularly bad at killing me.'

'Ha. I hear that's kind of mutual. In fact, I hear there was even talk of you two being life mates before ... oh dear, did the Divine Wolf come along and enthral your puppy dog?' Leon grinned with all his teeth showing. 'Nasty!'

'Oh, whatever, Leon. I'm not interested,' Iris said, speaking fast, as though it might cover up the sound of her heart breaking.

'Oh, over him, are you? Got a new man?' Leon jerked his head at Vikram, still in the doorway. 'One who smells like ... ? Damn, dude, you smell like a cadaver ... Oh. My. God.' He turned to Iris. 'Oh, God, seriously? Gross. Sniffer and bloodfucker in one fucked-up bitch? What the hell? Should have known not to put anything past you, Vixy.'

Iris didn't say anything. What was there to say. Deny it? Who cared what this stupid lyc thought. And then she saw Leon furtively glance at the richly patterned thin rug in the middle of the wooden floor. It was only a brief glimpse – but it was enough for Iris to wonder why he did it.

'So,' said Vikram from the doorway, 'are you going to tell us where he is?'

Leon looked at them shiftily again, then another lightning glimpse at the carpet. 'No,' he said firmly.

Iris exchanged glances with Vikram, who made it clear he'd seen the furtive glances too. 'OK, OK, doggie. What's under the rug?'

Vikram walked across the room, keeping his gun on Leon, before dropping it as he moved to check the rug. As Vikram bent down, Leon said quickly, 'Actually, he's dead.'

Iris started. 'What? You mean Alfie? Don't be . . .'

In the next moment, Vikram turned, pulling up his gun, shouting, 'Careful, Iris, he's trying to distract you.'

But it was too late. It had worked. Even as Iris was telling herself that she had connected to Alfie less than ten minutes ago, Leon was bolting for the door. He flung himself through it, diving out of range of the crossbow bolts and silver bullets that followed him.

Iris turned to Vikram. 'You think he meant that?'

''Course not. You were connected to Alfie just then, out in the car.'

'Was I? How can I be sure I didn't dream that? I have been known to, uh, well, imagine things quite vividly.'

'You mean Matt? Your dead brother?'

'You know about Matt? Is that in my file too?'

'Nah. I've had a bit of a poke through your mind, though. Sorry, I know that kind of thing freaks humans out. But, really, we do it all the time. It's no big deal. It just saves time. Anyway, look, stop thinking about that.

Alfie's not dead. The Divine wants him for something. We know that. We're trying to stop that. If you want to find Alfie, we need to get after our best lead. Let's split up and hunt down that dirty lyc.'

31

They had to find him before dawn. If they didn't, Iris would be searching for him on her own. She prowled through the copse over the road from the hut, breathlessly silent, making arcs with her torch.

Something hit her from above. A human something, dropping out of a tree and hammering into her back. The next instant she was on the ground on her stomach, her mouth full of mulch, and the weight on her kidneys was oh so familiar.

She grunted a greeting. 'Blake.'

'Hey, baby.'

'What are you . . . ?' Iris was still face down in the dirt with Blake on top of her. 'What are you doing?'

'Hang on.' Blake shifted his weight so Iris could roll over underneath him, then set himself back down right across the very top of her thighs. She shone her torch into his familiar face.

It was dark silent woodland all around them. Silent and still. Iris thought fleetingly of Alfie. Of that night – God, was it really only four months ago? – that he had come roaring back into her life. A wolf. A wolf on a night that wasn't a full moon, Knocking her on to her back. Leering over her in the dark out at the university parks. Iris looked past Blake's shoulder at the star-spangled sky.

This was all too familiar.

Leon said that Alfie was dead, that she would never get Alfie back now he was enthralled by the Divine. But didn't Leon love Alfie too? Hadn't she always known that?

Alfie was gone. Blake was here. Blake. Right here. Right now.

And he was grinning at her. 'I just wanted to see you alone. I knew you'd follow that signal as soon as it was up. I thought it might be nice to get together without either Erin fucking Cobalt or any *actual* witches breathing down our necks. God, Iris –' Blake paused, sitting back and stretching both his arms wide '– I remember when life was simple and you were the only crazy bitch I had to keep happy.'

'You were keeping me happy? I always wondered what it was you thought you were doing while we were married. You know, I never once thought it might be that.'

'Oh, you weren't happy. I seem to remember bringing a smile to your face once or twice.' Blake's expression changed suddenly, switching gear into something far more serious. 'God, baby, we have to find Alfie.'

'I know. That's what I'm here for. But the chip wasn't him. It was Leon.'

'Oh fuck, did Alfie dig it out of his own arm? I suppose that was probably compulsory for a big dumb hero like him.' Blake shook his head. 'OK, well, did the connector work?'

Iris shook her head sadly. 'He won't tell me anything. He doesn't want me to come for him and he's not very coherent.'

Blake looked intently at her. 'Well, anything. If you spoke to him, he must have given you some clues.'

Iris scoured her brain. 'He's in the base of the Silver Crown. Built by witches, but only Sabrina can find it now.'

'Oh, God, isn't Sabrina the one they killed for being a traitor?'

Iris nodded. 'Iron shoes, last I heard. Other than that, all I know is he's in a cage. A Silver Cage. But where, damnit? London – that's all we know and how sure can we even be of that?'

'Hmm. There'll be a way. Always is. Cobalt have a lot

of money. And you know they're going to pull out all the stops. Frankly, Iris, the only reason they've kept you alive is because you're their best route to Alfie. And look how right they are – you've already got yourself magically connected to him.'

'Why are Cobalt so keen to find *Alfie*? Not the Divine, herself? Alfie isn't this big threat to humans. Why are Cobalt so desperate to get hold of him?' Iris shifted under Blake, who was starting to feel incredibly heavy. It was cold on the ground and Iris could see her breath smoking in the air every time she spoke.

'They want Alfie because he's magic.' Blake reached down and flicked Iris on the chin. It hurt. ''Course, you always knew that, didn't you, wolf's woman? But, look, is it any surprise they turned up at the Institute when they did? They probably have the place bugged and all sorts. They want him because he's unstable. He's the perfect weapon.'

'What? Fuck. A weapon. Why do Cobalt want a weapon?'

'Cobalt are part of the government. Governments always want weapons. That's, like, a thing. Yeah, they're deeply enmeshed with vamps too, but their office is on Whitehall. They're practically part of the military. There's always been dabbling, all over the world, in using paranormals for weaponry. There were all sorts of weird experiments with vamps. God, over a hundred years ago, before the big vampire segregation, some pretty sick stuff went on. In fact, some people think it might have been because of all that stuff that vamps took themselves out of the human world all together. Vamps have psychic powers. The strength of what they can do really varies, but it's unpredictable. There was so much work trying to get a vamp that wasn't psychic. I don't know why. The only other powers vamps have are a moderate amount of additional strength and, of course, the immortality. But really, not great weapons. Lycs were always dismissed, mostly. Only useful at full moon. Pathetic. Unless . . .'

Blake stopped talking and looked at Iris, his head cocked to one side. Iris felt her realisation settle inside her. Nausea. 'Oh, God. Alfie. He isn't bound to the moon. He's a weapon they want to use for . . . ? For what?'

'You can imagine the applications. He sees being close to the skin as a curse, but, well . . .'

'You could use him as an assassin. Send him to your enemy with a hypo of adrenaline to jack up. Well, if you could get him to do what you wanted.' Iris gasped again. 'Which the Divine can. Oh my God.'

'Yeah, well, don't freak out or anything, Iris. Well, maybe do freak out, I would, but I think that might be what they really want *you* for. As well as finding Alfie, I think you might be being prepared to be used as Cobalt's persuasive tool too. That's what I would do, if it were me. Which it isn't, by the way, I'm a one hundred per cent good guy.'

'Really? Well I'm no use for controlling Alfie. Not while the Divine has her claws in him.'

'They don't understand about her. Or even about how lycs work.'

'I don't think I really understand about her. Why does she want Alfie? What's happening, Blake? Why did she take him? What's she going to do?'

'Same as Cobalt, I think. Use him as a weapon. But she probably has bigger plans. Your unstable werewolf assassin idea was great, babe. And if I ever start publishing my own comic books that's our first title, but you know that isn't going to be enough for anyone who's really out to exploit Alfie's power. You need to think bigger than smuggling him into a hotel room and having him go native on some despot. I mean, what you want to do – what you can bet Cobalt and the Divine will both want to do – is find a way to breed him. And the really scary thing is – I think the Divine might succeed. Cobalt getting their claws into Alfie and having a go at some clumsy vivisection – I can cope with that. A whole army of Alfies thralled to the Divine – I'm less happy with.'

'But you can't. You can't breed werewolves. I mean, that's werewolf 101. If a werewolf has a child, the child is human. Or it is so long as the lyc doesn't bite it.'

'There might be other ways. Cloning. Magic.'

'So the Divine's going to breed him? Is that right? Is that what Lilith meant when she said that she would be trying to overthrow humanity?'

'Reckon enough unstable werewolves would do it, don't you?'

Iris shifted again under Blake's weight. Her nose was so cold, and the earth underneath her was freezing. The place where he was sitting on her was the only part of her that was warm. 'Fuck. So that's why the witches want me to find him.'

Blake screwed up his sharp nose. 'Possibly. It's a bit hard to tell with witches. But, yeah, probably. A day until full moon. I don't know what she's planning – but if Lilith says that's the deadline then it is. That's kind of why I wanted to see you, Iris. I wanted to be sure you know you're on the clock, baby. I wasn't trying to sneak up on you.' Blake reached out and touched Iris's cheek.

'You did kind of jump out of a tree on top of me.'

'Nothing wrong with a bit of flourish.'

'And, actually, you are still on top of me.'

'Yeah. I know.'

Iris was still so cold. 'And when I find the Divine I kill her. And I die.'

'The first Beast's heir will pay the price,' Blake quoted.

'So I die. I'm the heir.'

Blake shrugged. 'What do I know?' And he dipped his head down to hers.

Blake's lips were hot, just above her cheekbone. He slipped out the tip of the tongue and licked the salt from the corner of her eyebrow. 'God, Iris, I want to fuck you.'

'It's cold, Blake.'

'Is that really your only objection?'

'Hell, Blake, what is this?'

'I just told you. I want to fuck you. Come on, Iris. Just say yes. I've come all this way. Cornwall. The end of the damn earth. King Arthur was conceived here, you know.' He licked her skin again.

'I thought you came to remind me I was "on the clock". Something I actually already knew.'

'Not really.' He licked around her eyebrow and then under her eye. 'Say you want it, baby. Say you still want me.'

'Last time we were in this situation, you weren't so worried about my consent.'

Blake laughed softly. A single syllable of a laugh. 'This time's different. I want you to want it. Want me. Still. Please, Iris. Please, say it.' His lips were still so close like a promise of a kiss.

Blake, who'd always been there, who'd never changed. Blake who'd followed her here at risk of his life. Blake who probably loved her more than Alfie ever could. Alfie was enthralled to the Divine. It was hopeless. Alfie didn't love her. Blake did. Blake who'd never cheated.

Except with a witch, Iris. It doesn't count if it's a witch.

'Yes,' she whispered, her mouth half against his. She opened her mouth to kiss him.

Blake laughed – a dark chuckle into her slightly parted lips. 'Thank you, Iris,' he said, pulling his mouth away and sitting up and back. He stood up. Iris felt a sudden rush of cold as he moved off her.

Iris looked at him. He'd taken a step away from her and was a shadow in the dark. 'Blake?'

'I can't, Iris, I can't. I'm glad you would have let me, though.'

'What? What!'

'Shush, Iris. Don't.'

Iris shook her head. 'Blake! What do you mean? Why can't you?'

'God, I want to, Iris – but I can't.'

'Then . . . ? What? Then why did you ask me?'

'I just wanted you to say yes.'

Iris was about to say something else, when there was a shout, a cry of: 'Iris. Damnit, Iris.'

A figure came out of the tree and threw itself at Blake in a running dive, bowling him over and on to the ground with his attacker on top of him.

Iris shouted, 'Vik! No!' Certain who the attacker must be. And then, 'Blake!' as she saw Blake swing a punch at Vikram's jaw that sent him over backwards. Blake moved forwards drawing something out of his pocket that flashed in the scraps of moonlight . . .

And then Iris saw no more. Hands came out of the dense forest behind her, one over her eyes, one over her mouth. She was off her feet and being borne away.

They were in the middle of nowhere. It wasn't even dawn yet. And there was only one person at large in these woods that wasn't currently accounted for.

32

Leon threw Iris down on the floor of the cabin and leapt on top of her, pinning her down. She looked up at him, a little stunned. 'What are you playing at, Leon? Didn't you just escape from us an hour ago? I thought wolves were meant to be experts at running away.'

It was dark in the cabin. The gas lamp that had lit the place before was out now. Iris was still holding the torch she'd been carrying when Leon grabbed her. It cast a single beam across the floor. Leon's face was just bone highlights, lit from below.

'If you're trying to imply wolves are cowards, save your breath. I know what wolves are. I know what I am. I don't need to listen to Vix crap.'

'Well, I'm a Vix, Leon, as you know very well, so all I can talk is Vix crap.' Iris rolled her eyes, although it was almost certainly lost in the dark. 'What the hell do you want with me, Leon?'

Leon cocked his head on one side and looked at her for a long moment that was all uncanny and animal. He was in the same position as Blake had been, straddling her across the top of her thighs. 'Wanted to talk to you, didn't I? I'm not an idiot. I knew you'd track me. I was waiting for you in that cabin. Just didn't expect you to turn up with a – oh, God, I just remembered – with a *vamp*. A corpse. Please tell me you're not fucking him.'

'Why the hell would you care . . . ?'

'You're right. I don't. Except that it's totally gross. You know he's dead, don't you? A magically animated corpse. Vamps are zombies, basically. They just make better conversationalists. He reeks. He's rotting.'

'He smells fine to me.'

'That's because you're human, Vixy. Vamps rot slowly, but they still rot. The smell of him'll make you puke. In the end.'

'Did you want anything specific, Leon? Or just warning me against trying for happily ever after with a vamp.'

'You killed Misty. Why are you alive? Why did he let you stay alive? Why have any of us –' Leon lowered his face to hers '– let you live?'

Iris shrugged. 'There's this prophecy thing. Don't blame yourself. I have a destiny.'

'Yeah, whatever,' said Leon and from somewhere behind him he raised Iris's crossbow.

Iris didn't even know he had it, and thought she must have lost it in the dark outside. But suddenly there was the cool tip of a silver bolt against her forehead. 'This isn't about Misty,' Iris said, trying to keep her voice level and cool, as she felt her death touching her. 'This is about Alfie, isn't it?'

'Alfie,' said Leon slowly. 'Do you miss him?'

'It's only been a few weeks,' Iris said, but then, as soon as she'd finished saying that, she said, 'Yes.' And her throat was full of a dull thick ache.

'I'm in love with him,' Leon said lightly. 'That used to be my biggest secret, but right now I don't care who knows. She tried to punish me for it. Sabrina. Punish me for not being able to break my thrall again. I couldn't. I could never betray him again. Not after we'd been together. Not after we'd fucked.'

'What? You and Alfie. When did that . . . ? What?'

'In the caverns while the Silver Crown had us imprisoned. Of course, you wouldn't know. He never got that chance to talk to you about it. About how much he loved fucking me.'

Iris shook her head. 'What?' She looked at Leon. He was still threatening her with a crossbow, but somehow he looked mellow. 'Well, he was never very good at being faithful.'

'Especially not now,' Leon said and his expression softened even further.

Iris felt as if any minute he might crack open a tub of ice cream and they could both settle back and talk about what a faithless bastard Alfie Friday was.

'That's not all. He made love to me then. And then he saved me. He took the Silver Crown and ascended to Ancient Beast not because they tortured him, but because they were going to torture me. And then, well, we've been locked up together all this time . . . He does love me. He does.'

A tear slid down Iris's cheek. She knew exactly what Leon was talking about. Leon lowered the crossbow and kissed her.

Her mind was loose and empty. It felt like every time she started to pine for Alfie another man moved in to confuse and comfort her. But this was the most surprising yet.

Leon. What the fuck? As she felt her mouth opening up to his, Iris's mind was full of Alfie. Alfie and Leon, that was so arousing. She remembered being locked in the pack-house cellar with Blake and Alfie, that moment, after they had both fucked her to near unconsciousness, where she had seen them kiss each other. Her pussy throbbed hard at the memory.

And then she thought of Alfie's big hard body and Blake's tight wiry muscular one. She thought about something that had never happened. She thought about Alfie fucking Blake. Alfie's big hands, his thick fingers, moving over the sharp angles of Blake's body. Turning him over. Thrusting inside him. Blake softening like that. Blake being used and invaded. Liking it.

Leon moved his mouth. He licked Iris's cheek and then bit her chin. It shattered the fantasy. Iris was suddenly aware of what this was. *Who* it was. 'Alfie fucked you?' she gasped, still bleary, confused by it.

'Yeah. At first we were locked up with him for days, with nothing much else to do. How do you think we spent the time?'

'I thought he was thralled to the Divine?'

'Yeah, well, she liked that at first. Let him. Then it changed. Now she has him in these spelled irons. He can't touch himself. She comes in and touches him, but doesn't let him come. She wants to build up his jizz for something. I don't know . . .' Leon was breathing heavily as he spoke, clearly turned on by the memories. Memories of seeing Alfie turned on, close to orgasm. Iris knew how hot that was. His big body arching, going taut, his nipples hard, his mouth open. 'Just before I escaped. That was the last time he fucked me. God, he's a vicious fuck. Hard, isn't he? Nasty with it.'

Leon found Iris's cunt through her trousers and stroked the seam of fabric that covered the seam of her.

Iris pressed herself into his touch, thinking of Alfie. The way Alfie liked to fuck. Hard. Animal. Wolf inside. She was sure he would have been even rougher with Leon.

She thought of their two snarling mouths. Alfie. Leon. Savage. Kissing for dominance. She was bucking in Leon's hands now. 'What did he do?' she whispered.

'He fucked me. Then he took my cock down his throat. God, he's so good. He's defined by sex. After him, what is there? What can there ever be?'

Iris moaned. 'He fucks so hard. Like he can't help but fuck hard. He's just so big. Big. Bad. Wolf. Each of his fingers inside me feels like an entire cock. I like his hands in me. In my cunt. In my mouth.'

Leon rolled off Iris and she moved on top of him, kissing his chest. Leon was moaning. 'When he pushed up into me . . . God. He was like a lost part of me. I wanted him so much. For so long. I waited . . .'

Iris was on the brink of tears. She licked at one of Leon's nipples. 'He came inside you?' she asked.

Leon met her eyes, his own gold-tinged ones glittering a kind of understanding. 'You want to see if you can still taste him?'

Iris nodded. Leon rolled over.

She took his jeans and underwear down, battling against them, clumsy with lust. Eager, frantic, she ran her tongue over the curve and the line of Leon's arse. Moving along, and down, and dipping inside. She twisted her tongue against the tight little ring of his anus. He moaned with pleasure and her mind was full of Alfie fucking him. She forced her tongue inside.

He tasted like darkness and moss. Iris's torch had gone out now. But the sky outside was navy blue not black. Dawn was coming. She didn't know if she imagined it or not, but suddenly, in that magical space, not night, not day, she felt him. Alfie. The scent of him all over her as she pushed her tongue into Leon.

But he wasn't here. Iris was crying. It was too much. Everything was splintering, falling apart. Alfie had told her once that after she had rejected him he had tried to fuck her out of his system. Now she felt like she was doing the same. Except – just as Alfie claimed had happened with him – every fuck just reminded her how much she missed him. After a few moments she moved off Leon and got on to her knees, supporting herself on the side of the bed. 'Fuck me now, Alfie,' she whispered.

Leon climbed up and moved over her, covering her back with his body. He was fucking her before she even thought it. Not Alfie. Leon. And then he was at her ear. Nasty. 'You're never going to see him again, though, bitch,' he snarled.

'Tell me where he is, Leon,' Iris sobbed, her voice muffling as she buried her head down in the bedclothes.

'You're never going to see him again. He's my sire. You're nothing. Nothing. He never loved you like he loved me. Wolves are for wolves. Everyone knows that. You were there when the Beast got him. If you were even worthy, he'd have taken you then. If the Beast had bitten you that night, think how different it would have all been. The two of you could have headed up a pack. But you weren't bitten. You're not a wolf. Not worthy.' Leon grunted, thrust hard and came.

Iris didn't know where she was for a second. Then there was Leon. She could feel him now. His body over her, smaller, tighter than Alfie's. How could she have ever fooled herself?

He was still panting.

Almost everything Iris knew about fighting was about finding the gaps. The perfect space to attack. The off-guard moment.

She rolled around underneath him and punched him hard in the face. He went back and hit his head on the floor.

And then he didn't move.

33

Blake was standing over Vikram, his sword point jabbing at Vikram's throat. 'Dawn's coming, vampire. Or shall I just take your head off? Save you from a burning?'

Vikram sighed. 'Oh, God, OK. Damn, is there anyone who can't figure out I'm a vamp from one look at me? I thought I passed quite well. I haven't fooled anyone.'

'Try Alfie Friday, when you find him. He can often be fooled over what day of the week it is.'

'Huh.' Vikram gave a sly, shaky grin. 'Friday, huh? Iris is your ex and she's Friday's woman. I'm not surprised you don't like him much.'

'I like him fine. Me and him, we're best pals. We get together for a beer some nights and talk about how best to make Iris scream for her mama. Just saying he's kind of meaty all over.' Blake shrugged and watched the point of his sword jolt against Vikram's skin.

'Iris is a bit of a hoodlum, isn't she? You like strong women, do you?'

'Well ... Like with like, you know. I like women who can match me. I screwed a witch once,' Blake said, 'tied her down to her bed and stuck my dick in her mouth then fucked her hard and made her tell me how much she loved it.'

Vikram snort-laughed. 'Yeah? You expect me to believe that with you standing there with all your limbs and your head on the right way round. You do something like that to a witch – you don't walk away. Not recognisably human.'

Blake sniffed. 'Yeah, well, this is a rather unusual witch. Anyway, I've got some good news for you, vamp.

I've decided not to kill you. I'll let you live, even give you enough time to get back to your big car before the sun comes up. But I do have some conditions.'

'Anything.'

'One.' Blake jabbed the point of the sword into Vikram's crotch. 'That filthy dick of yours – or any part of your cadaverous body – never touches my wife again. She doesn't need *another* dirty paranormal lover boy.'

'I never had sexual intercourse with –'

'Shut up now.' Blake lifted the sword and slashed it diagonally across Vikram's face. The razor-sharp blade split the skin, just missing his right eye and left corner of his mouth. 'Duelling scar. Nice.'

Vikram whimpered, terrified. He didn't even move his hand up to his face.

'And don't think I can't feel your vile psyche powers in my brain right now, because I can. And I'm not telling you a damn thing. You might be a vamp, but right now you work for me, unless you want me to cut this off. What'd happen if I did, vampire, if I chopped your dead cock off? Would it grow back?'

'I really don't know,' Vikram said, his voice sounding twisted.

'I should check that out.'

Vikram went pale.

'Oh, I don't mean on *you*, dead-boy. I just meant I ought to know that. I should look it up. There must have been experiments. But, anyway, the other thing. You need to give Iris these.'

Blake pulled a sheaf of papers from his pack and dropped them on to Vikram's stomach.

Vikram *oofed* as they landed and Blake dropped on to his knees next to him. 'Hang on a minute,' he muttered, pushing his crumpled brown overcoat out of the way and whisking a scrappy pen from the top pocket of his white coat. He scrawled something on one of the pages.

Vikram brought his hand up to his face and poked at the slash Blake had made across it.

'Great,' said Blake, as he straightened up and turned. 'So give them to Iris, OK. See you then, Vik.'

Blake started to walk away, listening to the sounds of Vikram sitting up, clutching at the papers as they slid down his chest into his lap, before scrambling to his feet.

'What are all these?' Vikram called after Blake.

Blake didn't look back. 'Divorce papers.'

'What? Do you want me to say anything?'

'Tell her I'm sorry. The whole thing was a mistake. I should never have got in her way. She has a destiny, you know. And, for all the prophecies that are written about her, not one of them includes me.'

34

Iris looked around as the cabin door burst open. Vikram stood there, his face bleeding.

'Are you OK? Your face . . . ?' she said. 'Is Blake with you?'

'Blake's gone. There was a bit of a scuffle. He gave me this. He got away.'

Iris felt her shoulders drop. 'Did you hurt him?'

'God, no. I see you got the lyc.'

'Oh,' said Iris, 'yeah.'

Iris looked at Leon, who was lying on the bed, still unconscious. She'd managed to haul his jeans back on to his unmoving body – better not to have captured a naked werewolf, not with her growing reputation. He was still breathing, that was all she knew – can't kill a werewolf that easily.

Iris was holding her crossbow casually at her side. As Vikram approached the bed, she raised it to cover him.

Vikram pulled a silver dagger from his belt and pressed the silver blade of it to Leon's cheek.

'Ah!' Leon seemed to jolt right up into the air.

Vikram sprang back. Iris repositioned the crossbow so the bolt was aimed right at Leon's heart. All three of them were panting.

'He won't say,' Iris said softly. 'He says he'll never tell us where Alfie is.'

Vikram seemed to ignore her, not even looking round. 'What are you doing here, werewolf?'

Leon shrugged. 'Alfie told me to get away. He knew you were trying to trace that chip in his arm. I ate it and ran away.' He shrugged again.

Iris felt sick. 'Why?' she said and her voice sounded strange, plaintive. 'Why did Alfie do that?'

'I was meant to get the chip as far away as I could. Out of the country even.'

'But you didn't. You came here. You wanted us to be able to follow you.'

'He wanted *me* to find him,' said Iris. 'He wanted to kill me.'

Leon was staring at Iris. He blinked. 'Yeah, well, sorry about that. Seems I really don't have the knack for killing werewolf hunters. Not like you do, Iris.'

Iris felt herself bristle, but kept it together, feeling Vikram's questioning eyes flick on to her for a second as he turned his head. 'Just tell us where he is. We know it's somewhere in London. Tell us.'

'You're never going to see him again, Iris,' Leon said, manic with glee.

Iris felt her bottom lip tremble slightly. Leon was her last hope. And Leon, she was so very certain, would rather be killed by her than let her be reunited with Alfie.

'So you'd let him die?' snapped Vikram. 'You'd let your sire die, werewolf?'

'Die? I'm not letting him die. The Divine will keep him as her consort. Don't you know what he is? He's ascended now. He's not your cuddly boyfriend any more, bitch. He's an Ancient Beast. The only one alive. Burning with power. And he's close to the skin. You think she'd kill him? She's taking him as consort for when she calls the wolves and they arise. He's what she needs. And she's what he needs.' Leon narrowed his eyes at Iris. 'They're happy. And I'm a good cub. I'd do anything to keep my sire happy.'

'No!' Iris sprang across the room. She leapt on to the bed and straddled Leon. She pushed the bolt of the crossbow into his throat, and he screamed out as the silver touched him. 'Tell me,' she said, shaking. 'Tell me where he is, motherfucker, or I will kill you right now.'

'Iris.' It was Vikram's voice behind her.

She felt his hand on her shoulder and turned. 'Don't try and fucking stop . . .' Her voice trailed away. Vikram looked strange, scared. 'Iris,' he said again, his voice weaker, 'the sun's coming up.'

Iris looked back down at Leon, still pinned under her thighs, looking confused. Boiling and bristling, she shoved her left hand into her pocket and pulled out a tranq dart. She shoved the point of it into Leon's side without a thought and he slumped in seconds.

She turned back to Vikram who was looking at her wildly. 'This place isn't light-proof enough,' he garbled, fear on his face. 'You've still got a few minutes. Ten, maybe, even, before I flame up. Get on the MCD to Cobalt and tell them to send a helicopter for you and Leon. There isn't time to drive back. I'll meet you back there.'

'A helicopter? Fuck. They'd really send a helicopter?'

'I think Erin Cobalt will decide this warrants it.'

'OK,' said Iris. 'What about you? How are you going to . . . ?'

'I have ways to travel you wouldn't understand.'

'Vampires can teleport?'

Vikram smiled. 'Not exactly.' And, without a pop or a fizz or anything at all, Vikram was gone, and in front of Iris was a small bat, hovering in the air precisely where Vikram's face had been.

35

The Divine opened the door of the cage. She had Alfie's food and the bowl she always used to wash him. As she bent and began, she said nothing about his crushed hand. But after she had washed his face she leant in and kissed him delicately.

Alfie moaned. He wanted her so much. His desire was endless. She let him kiss her as he wished, deep and greedy, struggling against his chained wrist.

The Divine curled her fist around his eager hard cock. He gasped, greedy at the touch.

At first he thought it was her usual morning tease, but as he got close, she whispered, 'It's time to start gathering, cub.'

Alfie tipped his head back and rolled it against the bars. She'd said this before, made him think she was going to let him come and then changed her mind. And, just before he reached the point of no return, her hand stilled on his cock.

'Sab,' she said coolly, 'attach the device.'

Alfie opened his eyes a crack. This was new.

Sabrina was standing just outside Alfie's cage. He was so entranced by the Divine he hadn't noticed her. She held something Alfie hadn't seen before – a tangle of plastic tubing.

Sabrina rounded the cage and sauntered inside, before coming to a halt between Alfie's bare spread legs.

'Put it on him,' said the Divine.

'OK, OK, you're not *my* alpha, Divinia,' Sabrina muttered.

The thing in Sabrina's hand was something like a

condom and a cock ring. The ring was hinged, which was lucky, Alfie was so hard she would never have got it on him otherwise. A little polythene pouch, bigger and looser than a condom, covered his entire cock.

Behind Alfie, the Divine said, 'Good. Now move back so I can finish him.'

The Divine's hand covered Alfie's cock again, gripping him over the pouch. She hissed, 'You're my consort now, Alfred. You may call me Divinia.'

Her hand stopped moving and Alfie rolled his head to the side to look at her through the bars. 'Uh, Divinia,' he gasped.

'Do you want me to let you come now, Alfred?'

Alfie was panting, tugging at the cuff behind his back. 'Uh, uh-huh.'

'Well, you can. You will, I promise. But I need something from you first.'

Alfie panted. 'Anything. Anything, just let me come. God, how long have I been locked up in here like this?'

'First,' said Divinia, 'I want you to say you never loved her. Say that you never loved that human woman.'

'Huh?' Alfie was thralled tightly to Divinia, but, even so, even with that, even after he'd chained her up in the cavern and left her there, this was difficult. Because he knew, even as Divinia was his heart and his centre now, he *had* loved Iris, once upon a time. He'd be lying. He bucked in her fist and she loosened her grip a little, so he felt nothing.

'Come on, Alfie, say it. Say it and I'll finish you. You know it's true, anyway. A beautiful strong wolf like you could never have truly loved a filthy human.'

And, oh, that, that made so much sense. 'Yes,' he whispered. 'I never loved her.'

'Again,' Divinia said, her hand feeling like home as it moved on his cock.

'I never loved her,' he roared, just as Divinia brought him to his screaming desperate peak and the wolf came rushing up to meet him in his orgasm, held back only by the powerful magic of the Silver Cage.

By the time he was lucid, Divinia had removed the device that had collected his semen. She was turning to leave the cage. 'See you in thirty minutes, Alfred.'

'Thirty minutes?'

Divinia smiled. 'Oh yes, today we will see how my wolf can perform.'

Iris felt like she might be about to go crazy. A bat? A helicopter? And now she and Vikram were sat on a fat red sofa in a narrow dark room.

The sofa faced a dark window – a two-way mirror – and through it they could see Erin Cobalt and Leon in the interrogation room. Leon was sat bolt upright, naked, his wrists cuffed behind the chair back. Erin was perched on the small table in front of him, one leg up on his chair, the pointed toe of her shoe resting gently on his vulnerable crotch.

Vikram leant over in the darkness. 'This is the room they used to interrogate Darius Cole. The famous rogue vampire. You can still see the marks on the wall.'

Iris looked where Vikram was pointing. Against one wall was the shape of a human figure, a shadow imprinted of a man standing with his arms raised, manacled above his head. The rusted manacles still hung there. The reason his figure was still visible was because all around him the paint and some of the stonework was corroded. As if he had been doused in some terrible chemical and the only bit of the wall that had been protected had been the part where he stood.

Iris swallowed. 'But why is . . . Why would holy water be so corrosive?'

Vikram laughed. 'We're beyond all that claptrap at Cobalt. Charles Cobalt, Erin's husband – he's dead now – came up with the idea that we could get a priest to bless any liquid. He needn't even know what it was. Nitric acid worked best. It used to take about a week for Cole's eyesight to recover. Then they'd do it again.'

Iris shuddered. Cobalt weren't like the Institute. Would Blake do something like that? She'd always thought that Blake was capable of anything – but this just seemed so *barbaric*.

Iris looked back through the smoky glass at Leon in the black-walled room. Behind Erin on the table were several spools of silver wire and three large bottles made of brown glass, the standard way of storing the photo-sensitive silver-nitrate solution. Both were interrogation methods of Blake's. Iris stood up. 'I'm not going to watch this.'

'Don't you want to find out where your boyfriend is?' Vikram sneered a little on the word 'boyfriend'.

Iris shook her head. She wanted to say that she didn't – not like this. But she really wasn't sure if that was the truth. She wanted to find Alfie so much it burnt inside her. But what Erin was going to do to Leon . . .

Iris stood up. 'Page me on my coms, uh, my MCD,' she said as she walked away.

36

Upstairs, Iris leant against the front desk in the large echoey, honey-wooded reception area of Cobalt. Here, like everywhere else, no expense seemed to have been spared. It was good to talk to her ex-werewolf-hunter trainee Pepper. Even if it was strange to see her sitting behind a desk. A sedentary job hadn't changed her though. She still had the same hard squat body, short-short hair and softly butch face.

'I know you think I'm a coward now,' Pepper was saying. 'But I couldn't hack it out there. Not after what happened. When you and Blake left me alone with that lyc, I nearly died. It left me scared of the dark, you know. Lost my nerve.'

'I know, Pepper. I'm sorry. A lot of bad stuff went down that night.' Iris didn't know quite how to tell Pepper everything about that night. Especially how being in a hospital bed might well have saved her from a far worse fate.

'Is Blake all right?' Pepper said out of the blue.

'I think so. I'm sure he'll be back.'

Pepper smiled when Iris said that. Pepper had always had a little soft spot for Blake. Even at her first interview she'd given him far too many coy little glances. And Blake, being Blake, had teased and ignored her for as long as he could before giving her one quick salacious wink that had almost made her fall off her chair.

That same night, in bed, Blake had floated the idea of a threesome – him and Iris and Pepper. But it had never happened. Blake had always been a distinctly monogamous man – witches notwithstanding.

And now, Iris could see, Pepper missed Blake almost as much as she did.

'I saw him when he brought you back,' Pepper said.

'Really? What happened?' Iris wondered, not for the first time, if Cobalt really were after Blake's blood or if it was just a paranoid delusion.

'Well...' Pepper began, her face brightening, about to deliver something juicy.

But, before she could say anything else, Iris's coms set started bleeping. She flipped down the mouth piece. 'Yeah.'

It was Vikram. 'Get down here.'

Erin Cobalt was striding up and down the corridor outside the interrogation room. 'You,' she barked as soon as she saw Iris. 'Why did you leave your post? You're our werewolf expert.'

'I'm sorry, I –'

'Never mind. You're here now. OK. What's summoning?'

Iris felt her heart flip. Summoning – the ability every werewolf had to call his sire to him. The ability Iris had once been desperate for Alfie to use to call his sire, the Ancient Beast that killed Iris's brother. And now, if Leon had agreed to summon Alfie...

'Well?'

'It means he can call Alfie. If we take him to where he was bitten. Camden, I think. Is he co-operating? He tried a trick by offering to do a summoning once before.'

Erin looked slightly confused. 'Oh.'

'What?'

'That doesn't sound...? Hmm. Maybe he didn't say summoning. I'll go check.'

'Why? What did he say.'

'He said the Divine. This great mother wolf – that's who's with the unstable wolf, isn't it?'

Iris nodded.

'Well, he seems to think that she is going to summon wolves to her. She can do that at full moon, apparently. That's tonight, isn't it?'

Iris nodded again.

'So she's going to summon these wolves and imbibe them somehow. Give them a power. A potion?' Erin flicked her head at the door of the interrogation room. 'He's gibbering a little. Maybe I misunderstood. I'll go check.'

Reluctantly, Iris followed Vikram back into the viewing room. She didn't see how she had any choice. Through the glass she saw Leon, far limper in his chair. His chest was covered in the specific sooty chemical burns she remembered seeing on Alfie the time Blake had tortured him with silver-nitrate solution. She swallowed.

Erin approached Leon briskly. She put her foot on the railing under his chair to steady it, lifted his head with one hand in his hair and then slapped his face with the other. 'Summoning,' she said tersely, her voice coming into the viewing room through a loud speaker, 'is a way of a cub calling his sire.'

'I know,' Leon said in a harsh whisper.

Erin slapped him again. 'So what are you talking about, werewolf?'

In the viewing room, Iris whispered to Vikram, 'Leon knows a lot about werewolves. More than me. We need to listen to this.'

Vikram just nodded.

Leon said, 'This is an older rite. Maybe the original source of summoning. It's a legend. One of the great stories. The Divine will return and unite us. She will use the threads that connect us – the bonds that link through summoning – to reverse it and call the wolves to her.'

'And then what?' said Erin with an eyebrow flicker. 'You take over the world?'

Leon looked more relaxed suddenly, cockier. 'Naturally.'

Erin balled her hand into a tight bony fist and

punched Leon so hard the chair he was sitting on went over backwards. There were a few seconds of near silence as Erin slipped off the table to examine Leon on the floor. 'Iris,' she said, turning, looking at the mirror, 'can you get the doctor down here?'

Iris flipped her mic down again and quickly told Pepper to send a doctor. Then she got up and paced behind the bright-red sofa. Lilith had said something about the Divine uniting all the wolves and destroying humanity. Leon would love that, wouldn't he? Leon would never give away the location, never let them stop his dreams from coming true.

Somehow, while she was pacing and thinking, she kicked a bag lying on the floor, Vikram's black leather satchel. The papers inside it spilt on the floor. Cursing, she reached down to stuff them back.

Vikram leant over the back of the sofa. 'Oh,' he said, 'actually, Iris . . .'

But Iris had already seen the sheaf of papers. Divorce papers. For Blake Tabernacle and Iris Instasi-Fox. Iris swallowed.

She had lost Alfie and now she was losing Blake.

She didn't look at Vikram. She started leafing through the papers. Right in the middle was a note: Blake's tight sloping handwriting. 'Vikram,' Iris said, 'I need to put this stuff in my room. I won't be a second.'

Iris dashed up the stairs and ran down the shiny-linoed corridors to her room in the medical wing.

She sat down on the bed and pulled out the note, hoping it might have some kind of explanation for Blake's behaviour. Why he was on the run, why he wouldn't – or was it couldn't? – have sex with her.

That he still loved her.

Iris

You already have the most important information about how to find Alfie. You told me. I'm not writing it down here though, because I have to give this note to corpse-boy. Go to the library. They must have one. They took all my damn books. It's all in there.

Blake x

And take care, baby. Remember you don't have to fuck every monster you meet – OK.

37

'Where's the library?'

Pepper looked up from the magazine she was reading. Iris glanced at the pages showing pictures of soldiers and combat. 'What? There isn't a library.'

'There must be. Blake said . . .' Iris stopped talking as Pepper's face brightened at the word 'Blake'. 'Uh, I mean, Blake's books. Where would Blake's books be?'

Pepper shrugged. 'I don't know anything about Blake's books.'

Iris sucked her top teeth a second. Stupid Blake's stupid instructions. Unless they did have a secret library and Pepper didn't know about it. She said, 'Where's Erin Cobalt's office.'

'Uh, on the secure floor. Same as yours.'

'Same as mine?' 'Um, Pepper, do you have a key for my office?'

Pepper smiled. ''Course I do.'

Following Pepper's instructions, Iris took the lift to the secure floor. As she emerged, a sign on the wall listed her name and Erin's among others she didn't know. The corridor was quiet. Whoever the other Cobalt operatives were with offices on the secure floor, they didn't seem to be at work today.

There was no sign of Vikram's name on the secure-floor sign. His office must be somewhere else. Perhaps that had something to do with him being a vampire.

She found the door with her name on it and opened it. And there, inside, piled floor to ceiling, was everything they must have taken from the Institute.

Iris almost sobbed when she saw it. Coms sets, uniforms, computers, weapons – all of it so familiar it made her ache.

And books. So many books. Blake's entire library. Carton after carton. She had no idea what she was looking for. She sat down on one carton, with another full of dusty volumes open in front of her. She really needed some help. She closed her eyes. Somehow she could feel him already. Like the connection was close. It was too easy.

'Alfie? Are you there?'

Hmm. Huh?

'Alfie? Are you OK?'

She broke my hand.

'What?'

She broke my hand. Because of Leon. Smashed it with a stone. She made me do it myself. Thralled me. Made me crush my own hand. Oh, oh, please, not again. Worse than the witches. Not again.

Iris thought of Alfie's hands. She adored his hands. So many times he'd knelt over her and pushed his hands into her mouth, finger by thick finger. Her insisting that she ought to suck off each of them in turn before she sucked his cock. Taking each one for longer than the one before, each one deeper and wetter, as Alfie panted over her, watching her mouth at work. Until he was screaming – desperate for that mouth on his cock.

'Alfie,' Iris said, trying to push away all the images that were swimming in her head of Alfie's warm thick fingers, Alfie's crushed hand, 'where are you?'

In the Silver Cage in a cellar. Oh, Iris, my hand hurts and she has the other one cuffed to the cage bars. She keeps making me ... Don't try to rescue me. I can't imagine what she'd do to you.

'Sure, baby, sure. Alfie. Is anything happening tonight? At full moon?'

Iris. My hand. Did I tell you the other one is cuffed to

the cage. Yes, full moon tonight, Iris. My blood is so hot. She keeps making me come. It hurts. My hand is broken.

He was rambling. Alfie often seemed to get more incoherent, less rational, as the moon started moving towards him. Maybe being an Ancient Beast hadn't changed that. A Silver Cage – why did that seem familiar?

'Alfie. I have to go. Are you going to be OK.'

But all Alfie's voice in her head said was: *The moon, the moon,* over and over.

Iris opened her eyes and picked up the first of Blake's books. She flipped to the index – no mention of the Silver Cage. She tossed it aside and took the next book. Nothing. The next. And the next.

She went through three crates of books before she found it. When she pulled out a decrepit old book called *The Sacred Silvers*, she didn't need to check the index. On the cover was a Silver Cage. And a Silver Collar, some Silver Crowns and some Silver Chains. Iris's mouth went dry. This must be what Blake had wanted her to find.

38

According to the book, werewolf lore claimed that there were several sacred silver objects that could control werewolves. The most famous was the Silver Collar, which could stop a werewolf changing from man to beast or from beast to man. Iris paused a moment on that line. It had never occurred to her that the collar might be used to stop Alfie changing *back*.

She dismissed that for the moment and read on. There were also twelve Silver Crowns that were used by the Ancient Beasts as part of their ceremonial rites. That was why they were called the Silver Crown. There were also some Silver Chains and a Silver Cage.

Iris knew most of this already. She read on, hoping to find something that would help her establish where this Silver Cage was. Surely that was what Blake was getting at.

She started skimming through some dull stuff about how the objects were meant to have been made by the Divine Wolf herself. How the collar was the most mysterious and no one really knew why it had been created.

And then she found it. Not the simple solution she was looking for, but near enough. The silver objects were believed to have a unique trace, to give out a unique signal. Something like a magical radioactivity, something *traceable*.

Iris reread the passage about the trace over and over. As far as she could see, all she needed to do was figure out what the trace signal was. And to do that she needed at least one of the other items.

So where is the Silver Collar?

It had been on the floor where the Divine had thrown it while Iris was chained up in the cavern. She remembered staring at it glittering in the last of the light as the final candle guttered and died. But what then?

She remembered Blake picking up the collar and the crowns. She had been lying on the floor in the recovery position and Blake had gone round taking all the crowns off the Beasts and then powdering the bodies. Hadn't he said something about there only being ten collars and Iris had murmured something about Alfie still wearing his. And Blake had said, even so, there ought to be twelve.

But, if Blake had them, well, she had no idea where Blake was.

Iris thought again about Blake saying one crown was missing. Iris had killed ten Beasts. Tobias was already dead. And the twelfth Beast turned out to be the Divine herself. So Blake had picked up ten crowns. Alfie had one on his head as he left. Maybe the missing crown was Dr Tobias's, the Ancient Beast Iris had already killed. He hadn't worn it for work as director of the Institute and he definitely wasn't wearing it when he died. In fact, Iris had never seen him wearing such a thing. So where would it be? Still in his house in Oxford – the one that he had left to Blake?

39

Vikram met Iris in the underground garage. 'Iris! I was just tracing your MCD. You weren't picking up. You need to come back downstairs.'

But Iris could barely comprehend. 'I know,' she gasped, pulling out of Vikram's grip. 'I know how to find him. I have to find him. But I need to go to Oxford.'

Vikram nodded at one of the black SUVs. 'I'll drive.'

Two hours later, they parked up outside a rambling old house in the Summertown district of Oxford. This leafy sprawl of wide pavements, tree-lined avenues and adventure-book houses was popular with Oxford's academics and, it seemed, its 'secretly actually a werewolf themselves' werewolf hunters.

'So the missing crown's in there?' said Vikram, who Iris had briefed on the drive down.

'I really don't know. All I know is Blake has ten crowns and Alfie has one. One is missing. That could be Tobias's. But I can't be sure. The one Alfie's wearing could be Tobias's. That would make sense too. But this seems like our best bet.'

'Do you want me to come with you?'

Iris looked up at the house – the house where she had become a werewolf hunter. The house where Blake had first fucked her, pushing her down in a disused bedroom. She could smell the musty sheets on that bed, still feel the way Blake fucked. Fast and tight. She hadn't been the woman she was now, hadn't been able to hold her own physically against Blake then. Then he had overwhelmed her, pinned her down, smothered her mouth with his. He had fucked her demons away. If only briefly. And promised her that together they would destroy everything that scared her. And Blake had always been there for her, from that moment on. While Iris had quickly overtaken him in ability with reflexes and fighting skill, he had been the one at her back. The tracker. The scholar. The watcher. Always there. Blake. She felt half lost without him.

And then she remembered that this was his house now. That Tobias had left it to him. Had he been back here? Maybe?

She turned to Vikram. 'Wait here,' she said. 'I'm going in alone.'

Alfie opened his eyes. She was back already.

As Divinia picked her way across the cage towards him, he pulled himself up into a sitting position. His left hand was still chained to the bars behind him, his right hand too injured to be of any use.

'How are you feeling, Alfred?' she said, crouching in front of him.

Alfie moaned something. His mouth felt like it was full of dry sand.

'Oh, I know, I know.' She touched his face. 'One more time and then we'll see about getting you something to drink.'

As her hands moved down his body, Alfie tried not to scream. Her fingers were soft and firm, forming a tight well around his cock. He sighed in spite of himself. Surely there was nothing more he could give her. How many times had it been so far? Too many. She had said something, hadn't she, about him being able to do this as many times as she wanted with the combination of the moon so close, her thrall over him, the abstinence she'd enforced. Her touch was like a kind of music.

Oh, but it hurt now. Even as his ecstasy began to build, he could feel a tight ache in his balls, which turned into a stabbing emptiness.

'There's nothing,' he whispered, his dry throat rasping. Had she said she'd give him water? 'There's nothing left.'

'Don't be silly. Your body obeys me. It will give me what I desire. It can do nothing else. Don't you dare think of her, werewolf. Your woman. You think she's alive, don't you? I know you lied to me when you said you'd never loved her. You just wanted to spill your filthy seed. You still have feelings for her, don't you? Even though you have the honour of being with your Divine. I saw the gold in your eyes turn grey when I made you chain her up. I think the only way I held you in my control was because part of you aches to control her. Part of you wanted to fulfil that command. But you never can. You'll never control that one. Oh, her connections to you are so twisted and varied. She killed your sire. She's your life mate. She's your first true love, your sworn enemy. She'll be here. She'll want to stop us. Do you think she'll kill you in the end, that woman of yours? Either way it's bound to be interesting.'

Alfie couldn't resist the way the Divine was milking his cock. She had slipped her other hand slowly and sinuously over his balls and was pressing on his taint. Then, as she squeezed tighter with her fist, making him moan as his sore cock got yet harder, she slipped two fingers into his arse, twisting around, jamming against his prostate, magnifying his painful climax as he came into the collection device she had slipped on to his cock.

Alfie was panting. The Divine looked unimpressed as she held up the translucent sack. 'Barely a teaspoon full,' she said, eyeing the bluey-milky liquid. 'You don't get any water in return for that. We've still nowhere near enough for the potion.'

Alfie was still speechless, rolling his head against the bars, as the Divine turned and stalked away.

40

Iris knew Tobias's house well. It was set in a large garden, stretching away green and damply lush behind the house. Even at the front the house was set well back with generous space and, best of all, it was sheltered from the busy Banbury Road by a high boxy hedge. Iris didn't have Blake's skills at breaking and entering, but this place was a burglar's wet dream.

Iris chose a window round the back and put it in with a deft elbow; then she used her sleeve to protect her hand as she reached in and found the catch. She didn't even think about alarms until she had both feet on the carpet of the familiar dining room.

The soft bleeping early warning made her heart sink. How could she have forgotten?

She dashed out of the dining room, along a short hallway and into the lobby by the front door. There was the alarm on the wall. A white box with a light flashing red on the front.

She trawled her brain. The code. It must be in her head somewhere.

Way back when she had been a trainee werewolf hunter, they had trained here. She had come here every day and worked and worked in the vast basement. Worked until she could hit a pinprick of a target with a blade or a bullet. Until she could dive and roll and kick and beat any of them hand to hand. But none of that told her the alarm combination. She'd never let herself in, never been here when there wasn't someone else in the house.

She had memories of Tobias turning to that box and

pecking his long fingers on the panel, but she'd never paid any attention to that.

Had there been any time she'd seen it? Any time she'd seen anyone else turning off the alarm?

Oh.

Yes.

One night on a full moon sweep not far from here. They'd left Jude burying a hound's body and chased another out into open country. Panting and screaming with exertion they'd eventually had to let it go.

They'd both thrown themselves on the ground to try to get their breath. And then Blake had been on top of her, as flushed and sweat-sticky as she was.

'It's when you're like this,' he'd said through ragged breaths, 'nothing in your mind but how much you want to kill, that I most want to be inside you. Feel that dirty heat and hate.'

Iris didn't reply. She knew the lust burning into her from his eyes was reflected right back. She pulled her dark-red combat fatigues down and shifted, opening her legs under Blake's hard narrow hips.

Iris moaned, thrust her hips up on to him, bringing him deeper, harder, home. She arched her back and rolled her head, showing her neck to him, and he dipped. He pushed his head into the well, pressed his tongue to her skin in the almost pitch dark and then pulled back, startled. 'Fuck!'

'What?'

'Iris, you're bleeding. Your neck.'

'What? Well, it must just be from the fight.' Earlier that evening the hound Jude was now burying had sprung from the trees and slammed into Iris's from behind, flooring her.

Blake was still inside Iris, He swirled his hips making her moan. 'Claws or jaws, Iris?' And then, with a smooth soft motion, he drew his silver gun from his shoulder holster and held it to Iris's temple.

Iris felt a vicious rush of fear like a shock wave. Her eyes were tight on Blake's. The two of them had played all sorts of games with guns since then, but this had been the very first time Blake had held a gun to her head. It felt strangely normal.

'Claws or jaws?' Blake said again, fucking her now, harder than ever inside her.

Iris couldn't speak. All she could feel was the gun on the side of her head and Blake's cock inside her. Both steel hard, invading. Blake came with a cry and then pushed his face back into the wound at her neck, slipping one hand between her legs and stroking her clit, keeping the gun tight in place with the other. After Iris had come he said, 'OK, I have some kit at Tobias's house that can test for lyc saliva in your wound. You're not going to run, are you?'

'Why would I run?' Iris said, staring up at his wild hard face.

'Because, if it turns out that lyc bit you, I'll have to shoot you.'

So they'd gone back to Tobias's house, found the kit and Iris had tested negative. But Dr Tobias hadn't been at home; he was at a meeting in London, Blake said. And so, he unlocked the door with what seemed to be his own key, and the alarms started that soft bleeping. He pushed Iris up against the wall, still holding the gun on her, kissing her hard, back into the pseudo-William Morris wallpaper, and with his free hand he jabbed at the keys.

Iris was remembering this right now as she stood in that same hallway, looking at that same wallpaper: Blake pressing the keys, Iris rolling her head, idly looking at the numbers he punched. At that moment, when she'd been watching, Iris thought she might well have been bitten. And she knew that, if she had been, she would far rather Blake shot her than become the thing she hated most in the world.

But still she had watched him jab the keys. She *must* know.

She felt as if her brain would break she stretched it so hard trying to recover that memory from nearly a dozen years ago. But she dredged up something: four numbers that were her best hope. She flipped open the front panel of the white box and the keys she pressed made eerily familiar electronic tones.

The bleeping stopped.

Iris began to wander through the house full of ghosts. She'd eaten in this dining room, rested on this sofa, browsed in this library. Here was the bedroom where she'd once overheard Jude and Dr Tobias fucking. Blake had told her once that he'd slept with Jude too, about a year before Iris joined. He'd said, 'Jude's a crazy bitch in bed. But not in a good way, baby. Not like you.'

Iris wondered then, as she climbed the stairs to the top floor, if Blake had ever slept with Dr Tobias. It was an odd sort of out-of-nowhere thought, but their relationship had always been strangely overly close. Dr Tobias had been closer to Blake than to her or to Jude. Blake had had his own key to the house. Iris had never had that. Then Tobias had left the place to Blake. And Blake had known Tobias was a werewolf, an Ancient Beast. He had known Tobias was the wolf Iris most wanted to destroy in all the world, the creature that had killed her brother. And he had never told her.

And Iris realised that she was standing outside the room where she and Blake had first had sex, the spare bedroom full of junk. The kind of place where Dr Tobias may well have stored his Silver Crown.

41

In the bedroom Iris pushed the spike of nostalgia out of her head and started to search. She emptied out box and after box. Most contained paperwork. There were only a few artefacts. Dusty junk. Nothing that looked anything like the twisted metal wire of the Silver Crowns.

A piece of paper with the Cobalt letterhead caught Iris's eye. She picked it up. It was a letter about the suggestion that Cobalt should fund the Institute's running costs. One short paragraph explained that, now one of the werewolf-hunting team was dead, Cobalt would be far more likely to consider the application favourably.

Iris swallowed. Jude had died just before they had secured the funding that had moved them to the new building, died in the wolf-jaws of Dr Tobias's wolf-self. She knew Beasts were fully aware of themselves when they changed. She knew Dr Tobias had deliberately killed Iris's brother in order to seduce Iris into becoming one of his team of werewolf hunters. But it had never occurred to her that Tobias would have killed Jude – one of his own – in order to get the funding deal from Cobalt.

'Fuck,' she whispered. 'Jude.' She tried to find some more information about the dealings with Cobalt. She had tipped out box after box of paperwork, and they were strewn over the bed and the floor. Tears were pricking her eyes. Tears that were for Alfie as much as they were for Jude. And tears that were for herself as much as either of them. 'The crown's not here, is it?' she said to herself, still not crying, but kind of close.

'No,' said a voice behind her.

She turned, knowing already. 'Blake!'

'Hi, Iris,' Blake said, his voice soft and low, 'you seem to have broken into my house.'

'Yeah, well, I was looking for . . .'

'I know what you were looking for. And you're right, it isn't here. I think the Silver Crown – the Council of Ancient Beasts themselves – took it. Or he made arrangements. It isn't here. It probably is the one they put on Alfie's head.'

'Oh.'

'But that's not the point really, Iris. The point is what on earth you are doing here searching for a Silver Crown that was pretty unlikely to be here, when you had all the sacred silver you needed to fix the trace signal back at Cobalt.'

Iris's eyes went wide. 'What?'

When Blake had carried Iris out of the tunnels under Oxford, tipping the landlord of The Bishop to use the entrance at the back of his pub, no questions asked, she had been close to death.

His first thought had been the John Radcliffe Hospital. The place the Institute always used for injuries that were beyond their basic skills. But Iris was grey, her breath rasping; her shoulders weren't lying right and the abrasions on her wrists were horribly infected, as was the incision on her bicep where she had put the chip into her own arm.

Blake knew Iris. Knew her body, her mind, what she was capable of. And he knew she might not make it through this.

That was why he decided to take her to Cobalt. He knew how much money they had. The facilities – the cutting edge of medical science. Things that were untested and unlicensed. Plus magic. They'd have magic.

When he walked into Cobalt's reception with Iris like a baby in his arms, he'd known he was walking into the lion's den. Pepper, at reception, said, 'I'm sorry, sir,' as she pulled a gun on him.

'It's OK, Pepper,' he said. 'I know you've had your instructions.'

And then Blake found that being handcuffed to a chair in a dirty basement room that reeked of one purpose and one purpose alone was made so much worse if the woman approaching with the familiar gleam of torture-lust in her eyes had a bandage across her face from an earlier head butt.

Blake nodded at it. 'I'm sorry about that.'

'What? This?' Erin Cobalt touched the fabric swathing the nose that Blake had felt crunch under his cranium. 'I quite understand, Mr Tabernacle. You had to go and find Iris. You brought her back to us. All very procedure.'

'Procedure? This place? Really? What's with the *Midnight Express* chic then?'

'Well,' said Erin, squeezing herself into the gap between the small metal table in front of Blake and his knees to perch there, 'I just thought I ought to check what information you have that we might need.'

'Before you kill me?'

'Well, we could hardly do it afterwards.' She reached behind her back and grabbed the item Blake had already seen on the table before she came in. A bunch of wires attached to sticky pads. Blake knew there was also a large box on the table covered with dials. Erin leant forwards and ripped open Blake's shirt.

Blake fought to keep his breathing even. As she began to stick the pads on to his chest, she said, 'Does electricity work on werewolves?'

'It hurts them,' Blake said evenly. 'But it won't kill them. And nothing hurts them like silver anyway.'

'Hmm, yes, vamps are similar. You can hurt them with things that would hurt a human, but nothing makes them squirm like holy water, crosses, light boxes.' She reached behind her and flipped a switch without even looking at what she was doing and Blake's entire body turned to pain.

When she flipped the switch back and the pain stopped, everything was different. Blake could feel the sweat covering his body, running down his brow and into his eyes. He was scared. Erin had more power over him than he could stand. He inhaled hard through his nose. 'So you decided against torturing me with sexual arousal then?' he managed.

Erin lifted one foot from the floor and planted the toe of her pointed shoe right in Blake's crotch. 'Whatever gave you that idea?'

She slipped the shoe further and lifted his balls. Her hand crept back behind her to the machine and Blake felt his breath getting heavy. A second later he couldn't feel her foot jammed into his crotch any more.

'Jesus. Fuck! Damn!' Blake shouted as the pain subsided enough for him to speak.

Erin smiled. 'And I thought you were a fan of torture.'

'This isn't torture,' Blake said, grimacing.

'Oh really? You want me to turn it up?'

'That's not what I meant. It isn't torture because you haven't fucking asked me anything.'

'Oh, right, sorry. I thought you knew. I want the unstable lyc. Where is he?'

'I don't know where he is. I thought he'd be with Iris. In fact, if you want him I've already brought you your best chance of finding him. Iris. Fix her up and I reckon she'll be pretty motivated by that insane puppy love of hers.'

'Huh,' Erin said and Blake flinched, assuming his unsatisfactory answer would earn him another blast of electricity. But it didn't. Erin just said, 'She doesn't know where he is any more than you do.'

'No. I didn't say that. I said she'd be pretty motivated to find him.'

'And you're not? You're not finding this situation in any way motivating.'

Blake inhaled again. 'It's not the same.'

Erin shrugged. She reached behind her again and Blake didn't bother to hide his flinch. But she didn't touch the electro-box; she brought out another item Blake had forgotten lay on the table – a wooden stake. Erin placed the blunt wooden point against Blake's chest.

'I'm not a vampire, Dr Cobalt,' Blake said softly.

'You'd be surprised what a stake through the heart will kill,' Erin deadpanned. 'It's an incredibly painful death for a human. It's happened by mistake too many times. I haven't done field work for a long time. But back in the day I had easily enough strength to drive this right into your chest and fix you to that chair. It's the bluntness that makes it hurt so much.'

'That isn't torture either,' said Blake. 'That'd kill me. There's a skill to real torture. And it's mostly about *not* killing your victim.'

'Very true, but you're boring me now, Tabernacle. Tell me how to find Friday. You know full well sleeping beauty upstairs doesn't cut it. Give me something concrete or I decide there's no further use for you here.'

Erin moved her foot out from under Blake's balls and ran the sole of her shoe over his cock. It stirred a little. He didn't exactly get hard but he felt a rush of blood there. God, this was a frightening woman. He had no doubt at all she would kill him. And in exactly the horrible brutal manner she had just described. He knew when he brought Iris back here that he was risking something like this, knew almost exactly how it might play out. But Blake, being Blake, had always thought he'd find a chink. A way out. He said, 'The Silver Crown, the Council of Ancient Beasts that Iris killed – you know about them, right?'

'I've read your report.'

'It seems likely that Alfie is an Ancient Beast himself now. That he ascended somehow. Iris was muttering something in the truck about it. The Silver Crown all wear Sacred Silvers. I don't know if they are magical or just totems, but they are part of the cache of Sacred Silver objects that werewolves revere. Iris killed ten Beasts – eleven if you count Tobias. I collected ten of their Silver Crowns from the caves along with Alfie's Silver Collar. That's a sacred silver too. If I'm right about where Alfie is – who's taken him – the Sacred Silvers could help. They're your best chance.'

'You have ten crowns, the unstable has another. Where's the twelfth?'

Blake shrugged. 'Good question. But a better question would be where are my ten?'

'Where are *your* ten?'

'I walk away,' said Blake. 'You won't see me again. You have Iris. I walk away. In return for the crowns.'

Erin's throat moved as she swallowed. 'Fine. Tell me where they are.'

'Oh, I don't trust you.'

'Well, you're not leaving until I'm holding the crowns.'

'I told you, I don't trust you. But I do trust my ex-soldier, Pepper. I'll take Pepper to them. Do we have a deal? The Silver Collar's with them too. That's your bonus prize.'

'Fine,' said Erin tightly.

42

'And that worked?' said Iris, full of wonderment.

'Yep. Took Peppy down to the car park. She was in radio contact. They were happy. And it's not like Pepper can't handle herself. I showed her where I'd hidden the crowns and collar under one of their bloody black Mercs. Then I took the truck and got away. Nothing more than a few gross burns on my chest.'

'But Cobalt have the crowns and the collar. Fuck.'

'Yep. And it seems they haven't even figured out what use they are. How to trace with them. Stupid bastards. When I saw they were sending you all over the place for Alfie, I thought maybe it had fucked up, that Alfie didn't have his crown any more. But then when you said he was in the Silver Cage. Oh, man, how incompetent are Cobalt? No wonder I got clean away.' Blake paused and held Iris's gaze with something very familiar. 'But isn't that enough shop talk, Iris? Can't we discuss your love life? I mean, damnit, Iris. A vampire! You necro-bitch!'

'What? Oh, God, you fought him in the woods, didn't you? Well, I don't know what he told you, but fuck off, Blake. It's none of your business. Anyway, this is hardly the time to get jealous – we need to get back to Cobalt and get those crowns. Also, though, if we're talking love lives, isn't it time you told me what's going on with you and Lilith?'

'Lilith?'

'She was sitting on your lap. I know you two were together once before. The source of all your bleats of "it isn't cheating if it's with a witch" –'

'It isn't!' Blake interrupted.

Iris kept talking. 'And then, suddenly, divorce papers. So is it a love thing? With a witch? Really? You?'

'Well, it's nice to feel we've both moved on from lycs,' Blake snapped.

Iris looked down a second. It seemed like the wrong thing to say – the wrong time and the wrong place – but she had to say it. Without looking up, she said, 'I haven't moved on from lycs, Blake. You know that. And nor have you. You haven't moved on from me.' She couldn't keep her feelings inside, not here, not in this room. The room where they had first kissed, first fucked.

'Oh damn, look at me, Iris. Isn't it obvious I'm not hung up on you any more? Haven't you figured it out for yourself? I'm . . .' He stopped and swallowed. 'OK, I'm magically bound to a witch. Lilith offered me her binding and I took it. That magic is – oh, God, there are no words for how powerful. If I put my dick inside you now, it'll most likely go black and drop off. So, looks like I'm over you whether I want to be or not, doesn't it?'

Iris shook her head. 'I don't know why you're doing this, Blake, why you let Lilith . . . God!'

'No,' said Blake sharply. 'Nor do I.' He shifted, cocking his head and wriggling his hips. 'Tell you what, though, now I can't fuck whomever I please – and I want you to understand that by "whomever I please" I pretty much mean you – I kind of understand how it must have been for Alfie all those years. If all it took was a set of magical manacles to get out from this curse I'd probably go halfway around the world to find them too.'

'Oh, God,' Iris gasped. 'The chains. The chains that are part of the Sacred Silvers – they're his chains, aren't they? The ones Alfie uses. Surely we can find the chains. Last time I saw them they were attached to Alfie's bed in the pack house in Marston.'

'That's right, baby. Smart thinking.' Blake grinned.

'You knew that. Oh, fuck. You knew that all along. You're kind of getting into this thing where you know it all already and drop me cryptic hints, aren't you? Is that what fucking witches does? Make you act like one?'

'Iris,' Blake said slowly, tilting his head down and looking up at her, 'are you *trying* to rile me?'

Iris shrugged. 'Maybe I am. I've missed you, Blake. You can't fuck me. I get that. But we can still fight can't we?'

'And you really think this is a good time for a fight. Aren't we in a race against time?'

Iris thought of everything that had happened in the run-up to this moment. How het up and twisted she felt inside since Blake ran his rough tongue over her lips in the woods the night before. She needed something. She wouldn't be able to do her job without it. And if this was all she could get from Blake now . . .

She nodded. 'Yeah, I do.'

It was immediate. Blake exploded out of the doorway. But it was too pat a move, obvious. Iris dived and he skidded on the rug by the bed.

Iris was sitting on the floor looking at him. She sprang to her feet, but Blake recovered quicker than she would have thought and yanked one of her legs, pulling her back down. He managed to get up and straddle her lap, pinning her arms to her sides. With Iris and Blake it always came down to his advantage of strength over her advantages of technique and speed. He moved his face into hers. 'You know,' he said softly, 'I have no idea what this witch-binding thing will let me get away with. I don't even know if I can kiss you. But I know I can do this.' His tongue darted out and flicked over hers.

Iris sighed as her pussy flooded with slick wet heat. Oh, Blake could still light her fire.

But she didn't let his clever suggestive tongue distract her for long. The grip of his left hand on her right wrist was his weakest point. She yanked up sudden and hard, forcing her hand free with a head rush of taut friction. She used her elbow fast against the side of his head, knocking him sideways and down on to the rug. Iris scrambled over him on to the bed and he grabbed her foot as she moved, trying to pull her back down. She kicked out and heard him yelp as her foot made contact with some part of him.

But where to go? She climbed up on the bed.

This bed, the bed where Blake had once overwhelmed her so easily. She let herself drop into a prone position on her back, coughing as the dust from the long-abandoned linen billowed up all around her.

When it cleared, Blake was kneeling up on the floor and looking at her. 'What sort of move is that?'

Iris flashed her eyebrows. 'It's a "what you going to do", Blake? Fuck me? You know you can't. Lilith owns your dick now.'

'Yeah. OK. I'd rather you didn't go on about it.'

'Not go on about it? Oh but it's too funny not to go on about.' Iris lifted her hips and started to shuck down her combats. Blake – the man who had once fucked her while holding a gun to her head in case she had been bitten by a werewolf – powerless without his cock. She kicked her way free of her clothing and slipped both hands between her legs. 'God, you know, Blake, your not being able to fuck me makes me kind of hot.'

Blake climbed up on the bed and lay down next to her. 'Just when I thought you couldn't get more perverted.'

Iris laughed as she brought one hand up to her mouth and moistened her fingers. She moaned aloud as she reached back down and drew her slippery fingertips over her clit.

'I don't suppose,' Blake said, 'that you could see your way clear to signing the divorce papers before you bring yourself off thinking about my misfortune.'

Iris opened her eyes. 'I have,' Iris said, 'they're in my bag.'

'Right,' said Blake. 'And now you really are going to make me watch you masturbate, are you?'

'I'm not making you do anything.'

'This is my house, Iris.'

'Well, you could help me out. If you like.'

'I don't think I can.'

'Not even with your tongue. I thought it was your cock she owned.'

Blake made a face. 'That's just a metaphor. She's a witch. I can't be unfaithful. She never got over the way I fucked her that time. No matter what they say about turning them down, I really should never have screwed a witch.'

'You didn't just screw a witch, you screwed *the* witch. Lilith. God, Blake, have you any idea how powerful she is?'

'Of course I fucking have. I'm not some clueless civilian.'

'But why, why did you?'

'She wanted me to. And she's a witch.'

'Why you?'

'She wanted someone who could be a man for her. She wanted someone who would hold her down, force his dick into her mouth, play the bad man. You know I've always been good for that, Iris.'

'I know. God.' Iris sighed and twisted her fingers over her clit again. The thought of Blake and Lilith together like that was weirdly hot.

'Oh, you like that, do you, baby?' Blake whispered.

'Maybe. Kind of. God, and she let you do that? A witch.'

'It was all her idea.'

Iris sighed heavily. She was close to orgasm and Blake would know that as well as she did. 'Well, you must have been good.'

'I was *too* good. She wanted me back. Permanently. And now she's got me.'

'Perhaps ... And she's just going to force you? To what? To be her sex slave?'

'I think she's going to force me to force her to be *my* sex slave. Possibly. It all gets rather muddy.'

'And you don't have any choice?' Iris gasped.

'Oh yes. Well. I had to consent. It's all very romantic – witch's binding. I consented.'

Iris stilled her hand, holding herself on the edge of orgasm. 'You . . . ? You did?'

'Yes. It's that kind of a deal.'

Iris felt her throat prickle. Blake was what? Blake was leaving her? Giving up? She shook herself, reminding herself again that it was over, that she and Blake were history. But, somehow, with Alfie in the thrall of the Divine and now Blake betrothed to a witch, she just felt like everyone, everything was leaving her. She had never felt so alone, so powerless.

Blake turned and pulled her bag up on to the bed. He yanked out the divorce papers and smoothed them out on the ancient bedspread. 'Well,' he said, 'this all seems to be in order.'

'So now you marry her? Is that what it's called? Marriage. You'd be married to a witch? Does it matter that she's unconscious?'

'Nah. And it is kind of a marriage, I think. You could call it that. You signing the papers was actually the final stage. The other rituals are done. That's why I couldn't kiss you in the wood. I'm already bound to her. This is just a formality, makes it permanent. The part where you have to relinquish your claim to me.'

'So once I signed you were . . .'

'Permanently. Yes.'

Iris started to stroke her clit again. She was still on the edge. 'And you can't ever, uh, be with anyone else. Oh, God.'

'Yeah. Even beyond death, apparently. Which is nice. Can't even fall on my sword.'

'Blake, oh. I wish you could touch me. How can you fight me and not touch me now?'

'Witch rules, Iris. Stop thinking with logic.'

'But no one. Not just me. No one else. Ever again?'

'Why not? It's not actually that much of a problem for me, Iris. I actually quite like monogamy. Simple and clear. I find it rather relaxing. You're the one who has trouble making decisions.'

'I made my decision, Blake. I chose Alfie.'

Blake spoke through his teeth. 'Really? Look at yourself. You should be out rescuing him right now and you're trying to get me to push my tongue into you.'

Iris moaned. 'Yeah,' she panted. 'And it's killing you that you can't.'

'Maybe.' Blake shrugged and Iris had no idea what he was thinking.

'I just still don't see why.'

'Why what?'

'You said you *had* to consent to it. I mean, I understand that she's a witch and everything, but the whole consent thing would be meaningless if she could just threaten you into it, so why? Why did you agree?'

'Why did I agree to marry Lilith and give up my joyous life pining after you? The woman who enjoys stroking her cunt right in my face and taunting me about how I can't have it. You see what you've done to me?' Blake knelt up on the bed, his erection suddenly unmistakeable.

Iris shifted. She was so turned on she was incoherent. 'Um, yeah. Well, no, I mean, God, Blake, so what's in it for you?'

Blake moved closer. He lifted one leg and swung it over Iris's body so he was straddling her. But he was careful that not one inch of his body touched hers. For one spare second he glanced down at Iris's hands, still buried in her pussy. 'You think I didn't get something in return?'

'What?'

'What does one usually get from witches?'

'Well, magic.'

Blake smiled. His face was so close to hers. Breaths and kisses. 'So, had any use for any magic lately? Big expensive magic? Out of the reach of mere mortals kind of magic?'

Iris gasped. Her body flipped. She felt like she was made of goose bumps. 'The morphial connector. Alfie. The whole witch intervention. That was you? That was what she gave you in return?'

Blake moved closer. His face was very close to Iris's. Their lips were almost touching. He nodded.

'Blake . . . No. Even so. You can't do this. Not for me.'

'Already done.'

'But how can I . . . ? How . . .'

'How can you ever repay me?'

Iris nodded.

'You don't need to. I owe you, Iris. I knew about Tobias all that time and I never told you. I married you and I kept the biggest secret from you. I understand that. This is me repaying my debt. But, if you want to give me something in return . . . damn, Iris, right now I would really like to watch you come.'

Iris looked down. Her fingers were still frozen on her clit. Blake was still far too close to her. He'd given his soul for her. Was this his redemption? He was holding the divorce papers. She'd signed her name Iris Instasi-Fox Tabernacle. It had felt odd because her usual signature didn't include Blake's last name, but, somehow, she thought he'd like it.

At one point – way back in the day – she and Blake had got business cards. Dr Tobias had them made up when they had 'got professional' as she liked to think of it. When they'd moved to the new building, taken on some new staff and even stopped nearly killing themselves trying to make their own magical cover spells. The cards had been something of a point of bemusement for Blake and Iris. They weren't exactly sure who they were ever supposed to give them to, what with the whole covert operation thing, and they were hardly going to hand them out to lycs before they silvered them.

The only useful purpose Iris's business cards had managed to serve was to finally destroy her marriage to Blake, when he realised that she actually wasn't going to have *his* name put on them. She had argued that Iris Instasi-Fox-Tabernacle was more than a mouthful and a typesetter's nightmare, which was when he had suggested that she drop a few of the more unwieldy syllables. And she had. She packed up most of his belongings from her flat that day.

But it had taken until now – ten months later – for her to actually sign him out of her life.

Iris swallowed hard and drew her fingers over her clit. Spelling out her name again. IRIS – INSTASI – FOX – TABERNACLE. She stared into Blake's eyes, barely finishing the last letter of his last name as she started to come.

Blake, still with his face close to hers, made a soft grunting noise, somewhere between pain and arousal.

'Are you OK?' Iris said a moment later when she had recovered. She could feel his breath on her face. She was still buzzing.

'Yes. Fine. It's probably psychosomatic, but just looking at these papers and watching you – oh, God, you looked beautiful doing that, Iris – it's like I can feel the magic settling. You know, binding me to Lilith. You know where it's going to be housed.'

Iris looked down Blake's body. Under his dark-red army fatigues, he looked as if he had an erection. The fabric was loose there, but Iris knew Blake's body so well.

Blake caught her chin and lifted her face back to his. 'Oh, that's not the magic, Iris. That's still you.'

'Uh-huh.' Iris flashed her eyebrows. 'Don't give me a line, Blake. You've just taken a witch's binding. What's the point?'

Blake was still holding her chin. He rolled his eyes. 'I

just watched you come, Iris. I know that was hardly a new experience for me, but you still had an effect. And now I just wonder what it really means. If I'm completely bound to Lilith now, what would happen if I . . .' He leant forwards and kissed Iris on the lips. It seemed to last quite a long time – maybe a couple of seconds – before there was a loud sound somewhere between cymbals and thunder and Blake was flung very hard across the room. He hit an old bookcase with a crash and paper-work and books began to rain down on him as he sat there, dazed.

Iris watched him struggle to regain his composure.

'Ah, right, so that's what happens. Completely worth it.'

43

It had become a reflex. When she approached the cage, Alfie rolled his body up into a foetal position as best he could with his left hand chained to the bars and his right hand smashed.

But she wasn't coming for him. Not for his sore soft cock or his aching empty balls, balls that felt like they had been turned inside out. She had Sabrina with her. Sabrina hadn't been there since that first time when she fitted the device.

Ever since then, Sabrina hadn't been present for the times when the Divine forced Alfie's cock to some version of hardness with her tongue and throat and hands and then brought him to ever more painful, screaming tearing orgasms, while he begged her over and over not to make him come again. 'Please, no. Please, no.'

So, if Sabrina was here, this was going to be something else.

'You are the wolf,' Divinia was saying, although Alfie only realised a moment later that she was talking to him. 'You are also the man. And you are unstable. You are a creature beyond, now. You can change outside the moon and you are man-conscious, rational in your wolf form. You are like nothing the world has ever seen, werewolf.'

Alfie looked at her. He couldn't speak. He felt so far from sensational. He was so weak.

'Of course, moon is coming. I know you feel it. I'll have to take you from the cage then. Let you change. And then you'll know. Feel the power of the Ancient Beasts. The fully conscious wolf. Not an animal, an unearthly creature. You'll have your army by then. Be my consort. You'll thank me for all I've done.'

Alfie was still just looking at her. He felt like he wasn't really in his body. He was up on the ceiling, disjoined. Watching her from afar, not really here.

'Shit,' Sabrina shouted. And she sprang, rushed across the cellar, unlocked and hauled open the door. She grabbed Alfie by the shoulders and shook him. 'Divinia, we're losing him.'

Divinia was still standing by the doorway. 'Oh, Sabby, he can't die. He's a werewolf.'

'He can still slip away from us. Catatonia. Insanity. Fuck!'

Divinia shook her head. 'That won't make any difference. The magic will still work. I can still take his powers.'

'You need him for the line,' Sabrina said. 'Your thrall is strongest over him. Your heir. You need him or you'll never hold control. Even with the spell. What is the use of creating a race of all-powerful creatures if you can't command them?'

Alfie saw Divinia's eyes light with a kind of mania, but the scene in front of him was fading away.

'Woah, it's batman!' Blake cried as he flung open the passenger-side door of the black SUV. Over his shoulder Iris saw Vikram scream and flatten himself against his tinted window on the driver's side, panting and staring wide-eyed at the stream of sunlight.

'Fuck, mate,' Vikram shouted. 'That stuff burns me.'

'Yeah. I know. Must be terrible for you.'

'Just be more fucking careful,' Vikram said sulkily as he braced himself, while Blake climbed into the SUV, hunching up so Iris could squeeze in next to him. 'Sorry,' Blake said patting Vikram's thigh. 'I didn't know you were in here.'

Iris made a scoffing noise as she leant out and pulled

the SUV door closed, seeing Vikram relax. 'I told you he was. Only about a minute ago,' she muttered.

Blake didn't really respond. He just made a soft sort of noise like, *hmm*, then said, 'You know, Iris, I still can't believe you're fucking a vamp.'

Iris rolled her eyes as Vikram started the engine and said, 'Where are we going? Did you figure it out?'

'Not quite,' said Iris. 'We need to go to a house off St Clements. I'll give you directions. Just get on to the main road.' She turned back to Blake. 'I'm not really fucking –'

'I mean,' Blake interrupted, 'what do you call someone who is a bloodfucker and a sniffer. It's bizarre, Iris.'

'Well, what do we call you?' Iris snapped. 'Witch fucker?'

'Witches are humans, Iris. There's nothing strange about my relationships. You know what would interest you, Iris? I've got some books somewhere among the ones *that bitch* stole about some experiments they did in less enlightened times. They took vamps and got lycs to bite them. Or vice versa. You know. Cross-breeding. Most of them died, although there are rumours about . . .' Blake tailed off.

'Oh, God, Blake, will you please drop it,' Iris said, then directed Vikram to turn left on to Marston Ferry Road.

Vikram did as she asked, then said, 'Rumours about what, Blake?'

'Huh?' said Blake. 'Oh. Oh right. Nothing.'

44

'Oh, hi. I wondered if anyone would ever come and see me,' said a familiar dark confident voice.

Alfie sat up. He was ... Where was he? Nowhere. A world of white and wispy grey. Even the ground he was sitting on didn't appear to be ground at all. 'Lilith?'

'Hey. Alfie, right? We've met once before. Say did you ever think about that modelling work offer?'

'Um, not really.' Lilith was sitting right next to Alfie. She was wearing a tight, fitted black suit. The fabric of the jacket and short skirt was quilted and tweedy with oversized gold buttons. She wore sheer black stockings and gold high heels.

Alfie was naked. 'Are we ... ? Where are we? God, this is like being inside a cloud.'

Lilith swung her legs that dangled in front of her as if she was perched on an invisible ledge. 'Yeah. If you want. I mean, obviously, we're not. That would be crazy. Inside a cloud! We're, er, well, somewhere in your mind. Or my mind. Best think of it as your mind.'

'And you're what? A figment of my imagination? 'Cause I can't see why I would imagine you. I hardly know you.'

'You're not imagining me. Your imagination doesn't have the capability to dream up a fabulous suit like this. I'm unconscious too. A spell backfired. That's why we're both here. Our, you know ...' Lilith tailed off a second, coughing, and in the middle of the coughing seemed to say 'souls', then she ahemmed a little more and continued. 'Uh, yes, *those*, are not in our bodies. So we've ended up here. Does that make any more sense?'

'Not really.'

'Well, OK then. We're inside a cloud.'

Alfie laughed. 'Oh, good. I thought so.'

'How's your hand?'

Alfie lifted his right hand, which was covered in blood. Two of the fingers seemed to be at strange angles. They both looked at it like it was some kind of alien creature. 'Hmm,' said Lilith. 'That'll take some fixing.'

'If someone showed that to me, I'd say it was an amputation.' Alfie said calmly.

'Really. You could be right.'

'My balls hurt far more though. My balls and my cock.'

Lilith glanced down and Alfie spread his legs for her, wincing. Alfie's genitals looked pretty normal. Lilith bent her head and inspected them. Then she reached out, grabbed his cock and squeezed it gently. Alfie moaned. 'Well, let's hope this isn't an amputation job too,' she whispered.

'Uh-huh,' was all Alfie could manage.

She caressed his cock a few times. Alfie squirmed.

'You know,' said Lilith softly, 'last time you came to see me you were having trouble with sex too. You remember what I did?'

'Yeah,' Alfie said, his voice cracking as he tried to deal with the burn of her hand on his sensitive cock. 'You had twenty-seven witches fuck me. You thought it might make me forget about how much I loved Iris.'

'Oh yes,' Lilith whispered. 'A little tease of mine really. You took them all though. Twenty-seven witches. And here, now, moon coming. You should be OK with this.'

'But she never stops,' Alfie moaned. 'I don't even know how many times she's made me come today. Over and over. I've been begging her. Begging her not to make me come. Can you imagine that? But she won't listen.'

'She wants to make a potion of your seed, Alfie. She wants to make all wolves like you, able to change practically at will. Lycans are so vulnerable. Not human. Sub-human even, most of the time. Even in your human bodies you're more like animals with your power struggles and your pack living and your base desires for food and sex. Oh, you're hard to kill, but really you're so vulnerable in human society. Living on the fringes, struggling to make ends meet, exploited for sex and strength by all kinds of itinerant humans. But if you could change *any* time – oh, imagine the power. The respect you'd get then. And if, like you, you could have the kind of clarity and control over your wolf that an Ancient Beast has ...'

'Can she even do that?' Alfie said, more evenly this time. Her hand on his cock was starting to feel different. Nice, even.

'Yes. If she manages to make the potion. It's controlling what she creates that will be the tricky part. But she has a lot of power over wolves. Thrall, line, alpha. She's like the ultimate alpha. But it's you that gives that to her.' Lilith slipped off the invisible ledge they were both sitting on and knelt at Alfie's feet. 'You are the only Ancient Beast now. Iris killed them all as you ascended. The power of a Beast cub to ascend if his sire was killed has always been known but never used before. And then it turned out to be you and you were unstable. That's a huge amount of power.' Lilith still had her hands on Alfie's cock. She gave it a particularly slow and loving stroke, healing. 'Close to the skin. And then there's Iris. The bonds between the two of you make you more powerful than ever.'

'Me? Me and Iris? She's not even a lycan.'

'No. But she's close enough. It's woven into her now. Wolf's woman. Warrior wolf. Oh yes,' Lilith said and she lowered her head and swallowed Alfie's cock right down to the root and then up again. She looked up at him. 'I shouldn't do this. I only secured a witch's binding with your friend Blake a few hours ago, but this doesn't count, does it? What with us being on a non-corporeal plane and all?'

'A non cor – You mean inside a cloud,' Alfie said dreamily as Lilith sheathed his cock in her throat again. Then he added softly, 'Blake . . . ?' But coherent thought was leaving him.

Lilith was a witch. Perhaps that was the best explanation for why this felt so good when it should have been more pain and fire. Or perhaps it was something to do with the non-corporeal inside-a-cloud thing. Alfie, really, was beyond caring.

Lilith was healing him. He knew that for certain. His balls, which had been so tender and goddamn empty, began to twitch and tighten so pleasurably. He had almost forgotten how good this could feel. The Divine had turned his greatest pleasure, sex, something he had once taken untold risks to pursue, into a torture. But not anymore. He gasped and jerked his hips into her face, moaning as he wondered obliquely if this was OK. She was a witch. But they'd been here before. He'd had his cock in a willing witch's mouth before.

He ran his uninjured left hand over his chest, tweaked and flicked one nipple a little and thought, suddenly and overwhelmingly, of Iris. Her hot mouth on his cock. Iris – lost and found and lost again. The first time she'd ever sucked him. In his shared student house, Iris's hot uncertain mouth. He was slimmer then and so eager. He came so fast, thrusting down her throat, hands in her hair. And with that memory his orgasm began to rise past the point of no return. And even as he hit his peak he realised that, of all the pain Divinia had wrought on him, nothing was as bad as taking him away from Iris.

Before he knew where he was, Lilith picked up Alfie's injured hand and brought it to her mouth. He winced as she licked the skin, letting the blue-white semen in her mouth glide over his skin like a balm. It healed him. He couldn't believe what he was seeing. But, as he stared at her mouth, her tongue flickering over his bloody ruined flesh, it re-formed, knitted and healed.

When Lilith finally pulled her head away to inspect her magical work, Alfie still couldn't believe it. 'We should test that works,' she said softly and got up from the floor, repositioning herself straddling Alfie's lap. She drew his hand up and under her short stiff designer skirt. He found the wide band of her lace stocking tops, her suspenders and then her hot damp pussy. No underwear.

Alfie gasped and Lilith leant forwards. 'Yeah, I know,' she whispered in his ear. 'It's like you've died and gone to heaven.' Then she sat back and looked at him.

Alfie knew his mouth was half open. 'But I haven't . . . !'

Lilith just laughed. 'Oh, of course not, silly puppy.'

With Lilith's hands guiding his Alfie slipped his rebuilt fingers inside Lilith. He knew he had big fingers. Big and thick. But Lilith squirmed and thrust, demanding he work three of them inside her.

Moaning and gasping, her head falling down onto his shoulder, she urged his thumb to find her clit. And then, as he twisted and moved his hand she screamed and sobbed her way to a fast rising wave of orgasm. More than one. The ends of each melting into the start of the next.

A second later Lilith sat up. 'Thanks for that, butch.'

Alfie cleared his throat. 'Uh. Yeah. Thanks for sorting out my hand.'

'Oh, no problem. It might not cross over. Hard to tell whether magic I do here will still be effective on the other side of the veil. It might not feel better until I wake up.'

'Oh. Do you know when you're going to wake up?'

'Hard to say. I'll be there when I'm needed.' Lilith met Alfie's eyes with her deep-brown ones. She suddenly looked uncharacteristically soulful. 'I don't know when. But you have to go back.'

'I do?' Alfie felt a sudden surge of nausea. 'God. Can't I stay with you?' And then his eyes went wide as he remembered a crucial detail. 'Sabrina said it wouldn't work without me. The magic will work but without me to pull through the line she won't have the power to control the creatures she creates.'

Lilith looked hard at Alfie. 'But the spell will still work. She'll still be able to create her race of uber-wolves. That, without her able to control them, would be a hundred times worse than anything she has planned. You have to go back.' Lilith touched Alfie's chin. 'She'll pull you back with magic if you don't. Or she'll try to and that might fracture your sanity all together. Better if you go willingly.'

Alfie found he was nodding his head, although he didn't know why. And Lilith was growing faint, smoky, ghostlike.

45

Iris, Blake and Vikram sat in the SUV across the road from the house Alfie had rented for him and his pack when he first came to Oxford in search of the Silver Collar. This was the house where Alfie had changed so suddenly on the doorstep and bitten Aurelia. The house where Iris had cornered Alfie in his attic bedroom and pressed two guns against his chest. The house where Iris and Alfie had finally realised what their insistent feelings for each other meant. And, of course, it was the house where the Silver Crown had brought them when they captured them and locked them in the basement to await their fate. It was, in short, a house with more than a couple of memories. More significant and poignant to Iris than Dr Tobias's rambling manor. She swallowed.

Blake said, 'OK, I reckon the back's our best bet. We got in through the back once before.'

'No need, Blake,' Iris said softly. She was rummaging in the pocket of her combats for her key chain. She drew it out, sparkling. 'I still have a key.'

'Oh, cute!' said Blake. 'Alfie gave you a key. I never knew you were that serious about him.'

Iris opened the door of the SUV, slipped out on to the pavement and turned to look at Blake. 'I am deadly serious about him, Blake.'

Alfie opened his eyes. His hand still hurt. His cock was still sore. His balls still throbbed.

Divinia was stood over him. He swallowed hard and looked up at her. She smiled a terrible smile. He felt her thrall rush over him like a terrible living death, the power she had to command him. To suck him deeper into obedience or to let him dance away from her, held only by the lightest thread – but a thread she could use to yank him close again whenever she pleased.

Divinia said, 'As I was saying to Sabrina, the power I have to call all lycans to me, like a reversal of summoning is only the beginning. I can use that to create a link through you. With the power of the Sacred Silvers. The Collar, the Crown, the Cage, the chains. A thread that binds us all. A connection that will let your power ripple through them all. All Beasts. All close to the skin. Tell me, Alfred, don't you think it's a wonderful idea?'

Alfie shook his head. 'Why? Why ever would you want to do this?'

Divinia laughed. 'You don't even know who you are, do you? *What* you are.'

'I guess I do actually. Maybe. I'm coming to realise.'

'Do you remember me, Alfred?' Divinia said softly. 'We've met before.'

'I don't think.'

'I can be in any wolf. Take them. Control them. The Silver Crown didn't hold me all the time. I have tested your power once before. You remember Hera.'

'Hera in Brazil, who gave me my chains.'

'Yes. She tested you first, didn't she? Used your power. The wolves who guard the Amazon gateway are a rare breed. Every month they save the earth from destruction by those terrible creatures that leak through the gate, the Carci. But only werewolves can kill Carci. So every month at full moon when the gate opens they protect it. But if anything slips through – like those triplets – they are powerless for twenty-eight days. And then you came along. With your power to change when you needed to. Unimaginable.'

Alfie looked at her. 'Well, I guess. In fact, Hera did say something about that.'

'It was all foretold. That you would slay the triplets, find the collar, that your woman would be the warrior that freed me.'

'Iris didn't free you.'

'She destroyed the Silver Crown. They were holding me. I gave them power and they contained me. They used to use this cage to dampen my power. The silver is spelled for more than just holding your form.'

'So why did they let you out?'

'Sabrina. She controlled me with witchcraft. She was my portable prison. Until your woman helped me out there too.'

'What?'

'She led a coven to Sabrina. Powered her down. Set me free.'

'But you and Sabrina are in this together.'

'Ah, Sabrina. She is a tricky one. Now she knows that she and I have common goals, yes, we are working together. She is a useful ally. And so are you.'

'I still don't ... What do you want?'

'You know it, werewolf. I need your power. The power to change outside the moon, to flip, to have the wolf close to your skin. To be the Beast. What if every were-wolf had that power? We are so vulnerable – a silver blade or a silver bullet. If every wolf could change whenever he wanted ...'

'I don't change whenever I want –'

'Shush, werewolf. You don't understand. I will draw them to me. Just before the full moon rises I will have my maximum power. The moon herself draws her strength into me to show my true form. I can use that power to call the wolves. Turn the power of summoning around. Draw every wolf to me and give them a taste of you, my prince, of your power. Let them all taste you. Draw them tight to you with thrall. And let them be part of what you are and at your command.'

'Why?'

Divinia looked slightly surprised. 'So we can rise. So wolves can rise. It was written.'

Alfie rolled his eyes. 'I'm starting to get awfully tired of things that are written.'

46

Iris led the way with Blake behind her. The sun meant Vikram had to stay behind in the SUV. Blake didn't say much as Iris led him upstairs, which was odd, as Iris would have thought this was a prime position for smart remarks.

On the first-floor landing he said, 'So, you reckon Alfie's still got tenancy of this place.'

'I think he might have. It's not been a month yet. He might not even have missed a rental payment.'

'Well, that's good. The last thing we need is for the landlord to have come round here and cleared the place out.

'Yeah,' said Iris vaguely, 'we've been lucky. Lucky with Tobias's house too. Imagine if he'd left it to some long-lost child of his and we hadn't been able to get at any of his stuff.' She walked halfway down the hall to the narrow doorway which hid the flight of steps leading to the large attic bedroom that had always been Alfie's.

Blake followed her. 'Actually, Iris, there's kind of something I should tell you about that . . .'

Iris turned with her hand still on the open door. 'Yeah?'

'Oh, well, maybe now's not a good time.'

Iris shrugged and started up the stairs. And the nostalgia came over her like a wave.

If the spare bedroom in Dr Tobias's house had been a trip to way, way back in her past, climbing the stairs to Alfie's bedroom was like a return to yesterday. To memories still so fresh she could taste them.

This bed. This room. She'd let Alfie chain her down to

this bed. Just to prove she trusted the man with the wolf inside. She'd used his same magical chains to hold him when she made love to him without the magical collar that kept him from changing when he reached orgasm.

Matthew – her dead brother's ghost – had been here when she did that. Remembering that, Iris realised that she hadn't seen her over-friendly ghost for quite a while.

Of course, the chains were special. Every bit as magical and powerful as the collar they'd treated as sacred. Somehow Alfie seemed to think of them as a lucky find.

She was frozen at the top of the stairs, unable to think of anything but Alfie's stubble-surrounded lips on hers.

Iris?

At first she thought it was Blake, but then she realised it was Alfie. Alfie in her head. She'd made a connection through the conductor.

Blake, standing a couple of stairs below her, looked at her quizzically.

Iris held up her palm to stop him saying anything. 'I'm connected. I'm connected to Alfie again.'

Iris just about made out Blake nodding before she closed her eyes. 'Alfie?'

Iris, damn, you have no idea what she's planning. This is going to be bad. Terrible. And I have no idea how I can stop her.

'Alfie, calm down. You need to tell me where you are.'

You can't come here, Alfie sort of screamed.

'OK, OK. Just tell me what you know. Leon said something about summoning.'

Just before moonrise she can use summoning to pull lycans to her. It's like you saw when I summoned the Beast. It'll pull the lycans through the air.

'OK,' Iris said softly.

And then she's going to use some kind of potion that she's made from me. It'll change them. Make them all close to the skin like me. All conscious when they change. They'll be an army of monsters under her control.

Iris swallowed. 'How – how many?'

Who knows how many she'll be able to call. Depends how strong the lines are. Hundreds. Maybe thousands.

'Right. Well. I have a plan to trace you. The collar, the cage and the crowns are all Sacred Silvers. So are the chains you had on your bed. If I get hold of one of the items, I can trace the others, follow the signal they give off and find you. And when I find you – I don't know – there must be a way to stop it.'

You can't kill her. You'd die.

'That's not important.'

Iris, no!

'I'll fix it, Alfie. There has to be a way.'

God, Iris, I miss you so much. My hand is broken and my cock hurts so much, but I'd still give anything to lie with you right now.

'I know. I know. I'll be there soon.'

You won't, Iris. You can't find me.

'I can. The Sacred Silvers, the chains. I'm in your bedroom right now. That's why I think our connection is so strong.'

The chains? You're in my bedroom looking for the chains . . . ?

'Yes, I . . .'

And then Iris saw it so clearly. Alfie, sitting on the floor in a sparkling Silver Cage. He was naked and his legs and torso still bore the burn marks from the torments the Silver Crown had subjected him to. And she saw what he was looking at. His left wrist, tangled up and chained to the bars of the cage, by an all-too-familiar metal cuff and chain. She knew even before he said, *Iris, the chains are here with me.*

'The chains are with Alfie,' Iris said, opening her eyes, looking across Alfie's attic room, seeing the bed. There were no chains attached to the legs any more.

'Fuck it!' said Blake.

47

They trooped back down the stairs. 'It's like you said,' Iris said to Blake. 'Breeding him. She's going to reverse summoning just before full moon. Draw the wolves to her then she's going to use a potion that I'm pretty sure she's made from Alfie's semen to change them all and make them like him. Unstable, human conscious in their wolf form.'

'Jesus,' said Blake. 'That's the most horrible thing I've ever heard.'

'I know. An army of Ancient Beasts. Able to change any time.'

'Not that. A potion made of Alfie's semen. Gross!'

'Oh, did you say you were going to tell me something?' Iris said as she followed Blake through the door on to the landing.

Blake turned. 'Tell you something?'

'Yeah. Something about Tobias. That house. His leaving it to you.'

'Oh, yeah. I was ... Iris, are you OK.'

Iris realised her mouth was hanging open in sudden shock. She was looking past Blake down the landing where the door behind him had opened up. At first she thought the figure who stood there was a ghost.

She was so pale, long limp hair like straw, tall and curvaceous. Her face was the colour of milk, and she was wearing a lilac dress, utility, a nurse's uniform. Iris recognised her.

'Pearl?' Pearl was one of Alfie's pack. Somehow it hadn't occurred to Iris that any of them would still be here. Of course she knew what had happened to Leon.

But it wasn't until this moment, staring at Pearl, that she thought for a second about the rest of the pack Alfie had left behind.

Pearl said, 'Have you come to take more of his things?'

'Whose things?' said Blake.

'She must think we're whoever came and took the chains. You think that was the Divine?' Iris whispered.

'Could've been,' Blake hissed back. 'If she'd got Alfie locked up somewhere – why not?'

'Are you doctors?' Pearl said, her voice sounding shaky.

Iris said, 'Pearl, I'm Iris. Iris from the Vix.'

'You were locked in the cellar. How did you escape? I thought they were going to kill you.'

'Well, they didn't,' Blake said.

When Iris looked at him, she saw he had pulled his gun and was holding it loosely at his side. 'Don't, Blake. Look at her. She doesn't know what's going on.'

Blake sniffed. 'Is your line to Alfie intact?'

Pearl blinked. 'My what?'

'Zac bit you, right?' said Blake. 'Is Zac here?'

'He's – he's in the bedroom,' Pearl said.

'It won't work,' Iris said, looking at Blake. 'The line passes through Leon. And Leon's at Cobalt.'

'We could get him to summon Leon.'

'But Leon won't summon Alfie. If there was a chance of that, Cobalt would have made him. Leon wants the Divine to carry out her plans.'

'Can't summon Leon anyway,' Pearl said. 'Zac got bit by him in Texas. And we can't move him.'

'Can we speak to Zac?' said Iris. 'I mean to both of you. There's some rotten stuff going down.'

'Iris,' Blake hissed. 'They're lycs. Not on our side.'

'The chains are gone. It's over. Right now they're all we've got, Blake.'

Pearl said, 'I don't know. Zac's not well. I don't want Vix near him.'

'I know how you feel,' said Iris. 'But Alfie's in trouble. He's your pack alpha, right? Please. I know you hate us. I know you hate Vix. But we have to stop the Divine.'

Pearl shook her head slowly. 'I don't know.'

Iris saw it out of the corner of her eye. She went to say, 'Blake, you don't need to –'

But too late. Blake was pointing his gun at Pearl. 'Come on, darling. I've not forgotten you. Let us see Zac.'

And then, from behind the doorway, where Pearl was standing, a soft American drawling voice said, 'Let them in, Pearly. I want to hear this.'

48

The bedroom at the back of the house was a tiny, strange wood-panelled room. On the bed lay Zac. Only the top part of his body was visible under the thin white sheet, but he seemed to be naked.

Iris had met Zac before. He was a young black American guy, and Alfie had explained more than once that he was Leon's cub, bitten by Leon. And he had a cub of his own, Pearl.

'You're Vix,' said Zac, his voice sounding laboured and low. 'What do you want?'

Iris spoke carefully. 'I know you're a good guy, Zac. I know you know it doesn't have to be you versus us. Alfie understood that. I think you do too.'

Behind Iris, Blake said, 'That's one hell of a chest wound.'

Iris looked at Zac's chest. The red furrow on his chest was visible through the sheet, not so big, but it was surrounded by nasty blistering.

'Yeah,' Zac said, looking at Blake.

'Is that why your girlfriend asked if we were doctors?'

'My girlfriend is taking care of me just fine, thank you.'

Iris was looking at Blake now, resting in the doorframe. He reached under his overcoat into the top pocket of his white coat and pulled out his familiar packet of tobacco and rolling papers. He began to roll a cigarette. 'That blistering, I can see it through the sheet – it's silver isn't it? You were stabbed by a silver, blade, mate. You're a lyc – you ought to be dead. How come she saved you? Could it be anything to do with that beauty?' Blake pointed at a large white machine next to the bed.

Pearl said, 'Yeah. So what if it is? Nothing to do with you two.'

Blake had the cigarette rolled and he flipped it into his mouth. He spoke with it stuck to his bottom lip. 'I'm just interested. If you've done what I think you've done, well, wow, you're the smartest motherfucker in this room and I want you on my team.'

'Really?' said Pearl sharply.

Blake pulled a scrappy book of matches from his pocket, bent the cover back and struck the entire thing against the door frame. The whole row of cardboard matches lit up, a little fireball in his hand. It danced orangey magic over his face as he drew it in and jabbed the end of his roll-up into it.

Iris shook her head at this not unfamiliar piece of showmanship. 'What is she meant to have done?'

'She cleaned his blood. Got all the silver out. That right, doll?'

Pearl nodded.

'It's a type of cancer treatment, right? Blood filtering or something. Amazing.' Blake was talking to Iris now. 'To kill a lyc you need to get silver in a wound that would be fatal on a human. She took the silver out of his blood and the stab wound didn't kill him. Never seen anything like it. Never read ... What beats me is where you got that machine.'

Pearl shrugged, tugging at her grubby lilac utility dress. 'I'm a nurse – *was* a nurse. I knew what favours to call in.'

'Ha!' Blake said in an explosive exhalation of smoky breath. 'Knew what dicks to suck more like.'

'Actually, I didn't have to do that. I have friends. Not that I wouldn't have. To save Zacky's life.'

'Either way, sweetheart, it's a stroke of fucking genius.' Blake reached into his pocket and pulled out a pen and a notebook, still smoking his roll-up by moving it around his mouth. 'So how did you keep him alive while you were getting the machine?'

Pearl cocked her head. She was looking more confident by the minute. 'I gave him some basic meds,' she said. 'It seemed like a lycan body treated silver as a cross between an antigen and a virus. I gave him a big dose of anti–viral drugs and some anti-allergens. Talked the nearest chemist into it.'

'Fuck. OK, baby, you have got a job when we get this mess sorted, which, er, may never happen. Actually, we should tell you about that. Big old coup's coming. Humans versus lycans. I reckon you too can look forward to being on the winning side though, baby.'

49

Blake explained about the Divine and Alfie to Zac and Pearl. 'I don't think she can summon every werewolf – I'm not sure how far down the line her power will reach. But you two are part of Alfie's pack. It's bound to reach you.' Meanwhile, Iris looked at the equipment in the small room. The machine was still pumping Zac's blood in and out of his body. Pearl explained that there still seemed to be some silver seeping into his body from the wound, so she was testing it periodically.

When Blake finished talking to Pearl, he turned to Zac, still with his hand on the machine and said, 'I need to know everything you can tell me about summoning.'

Iris said, 'Why do we need to know about summoning now. We already know about summoning.'

Blake shrugged. 'Maybe there's something we don't know. Always learning, Iris. Always learning.' He tapped the side of his head and turned to Zac. 'So, look, when you get summoned, can you take stuff with you through the pull. Objects? People? How about your clothes?'

Zac said, 'I don't know. I've never been summoned. When Leon came through, he came through naked. But I think he already was naked.'

'When Alfie summoned Tobias, he came through fully dressed,' said Iris.

'Could you give us a demo?' said Blake idly.

'A demo?' said Zac. 'How?'

'Well, minxy here is your cub. Where'd you bite her?'

'In the cellar downstairs.'

'So how about she goes down and summons you so we can see how it works?'

Zac looked horrified. 'Summoning is a sacred werewolf rite. I would never ask Pearl to do it just to call me to her? Anyway I'm pretty sure you can't take objects. I think you can't take anything. If Alfie summoned his sire, well, that would be different. Alfie's sire is a Beast . . .' Zac started to cough.

'OK. Hang on a minute,' said Blake.

He grabbed Iris by the arm and pulled her out of the room on to the landing. 'Are you thinking what I'm thinking?'

'Kind of yeah, kind of no,' said Iris. 'I am thinking that when the Divine does her reverse summoning thing just before moon rise, it'll pull these two to her, and, if we can find some way of following them, we're laughing. But, you know, Blake, I know you, and what I'm *not* thinking is about how to strap a bomb to one of them.'

Blake rolled his eyes. 'Yeah, yeah, baby. Wouldn't work anyhow. Too risky. We don't know where they're going to end up. Mind you, I reckon your self-sacrificing little brain has got some idea about getting them to bite you and turn you so you get pulled through as well.'

'I considered it,' Iris said. 'It wouldn't work. I need a wolf-form bite and the Divine is going to summon them before moon rise.'

'And you'd be fucking thralled by the Divine when you got there. You should have heard the way you were rambling about the power she'd had over Alfie, making your big loyal puppy chain you up in that cave. If there's one thing that would be like raising a bloody white flag, it would be trying to switch sides.'

'Well, you'd know,' Iris muttered darkly.

'And what's that supposed to mean.'

Iris moved close to Blake. 'Dr Malcolm Tobias. Remember him? The Ancient Beast, the most dangerous werewolf in Oxford, the creature who killed my brother deliberately in order to recruit me to his werewolf-slaying taskforce. A purely selfish operation that was about keeping away the warrior wolf destined to kill him and all the other Ancient Beasts, all the members of the Silver Crown. And you knew. You knew what he was all along and you never told me. What was that all about, Blake? I understand you've taken this binding to Lilith for me supposedly as a way of showing you're sorry about it all, but what you've never really explained to me is why.'

'Why?'

'Why you were so loyal to Tobias in the first place.'

Blake bristled. 'There are things you don't know, Iris.'

'Evidently.'

'And this isn't the time. Look, can't we just concentrate on one super-powered werewolf at a time? Look, they're going to get pulled through to the Divine – we need to follow them somehow. What if we tagged them? Like we did to ourselves when we were in the cellar here. Have you got a coms set?'

Iris dug in her pocket. 'I have but it's Cobalt issue, an MCD – almost the same as a coms, but the back's welded on. No way of getting the tracking chip out. Have you got a coms?'

'I'm playing how not to be seen, remember.' Blake shook his head, slow and thoughtful. 'Fuck it. We're going to have to do the bomb.'

'Blake, do you even have a bomb?'

But suddenly they both started as, downstairs, the doorbell rang.

Alfie was lying on the floor of the cage. His left wrist drawn up and chained to the bars behind his head, his right wrist still lying useless. Lilith's magic had not crossed through the veil.

Sabrina was using some more of the Silver Chains to attach his ankles to the other side of the cage, drawing him out – a tight and familiar sensation. This was how sex had been for him once, for years.

Through the door to the cellar, which had been left open for once, Alfie could see the room beyond. There were two chairs drawn around a fire and a cauldron from which strange steam was rising.

Divinia was pacing outside the cage, muttering angrily, 'There's not enough. Nowhere near enough for the potion.' She jabbed a finger at Sabrina. 'And it's your fault. Your stupid game to humiliate that dumb cub. We wasted two emissions for that.'

'That wouldn't have made any difference. Your thrall isn't tight enough. That's the problem.'

'My thrall isn't the issue at all,' Divinia said, bristling.

Sabrina bent down and took Alfie's face in her hands. 'You still thinking of your girlfriend?' she cooed.

Alfie didn't say anything. He was beyond spent now.

'You want to see her, baby? I showed her to you once before, remember?'

Alfie recoiled at the memory. In the caverns of the Silver Crown, Sabrina had taunted him by making herself look like both Iris and Misty. 'Please. Don't do that.'

But it was too late. Sabrina's face melted and Iris's appeared before him, smiling. So real.

'No,' he moaned. 'I know it isn't you. Iris!' He expected the Iris in his head to answer, but there was nothing.

Then Divinia shouted, 'Don't you dare! He doesn't need her to please me. He bends to my will.'

Alfie heard the cage door open and Divinia was over to him, yanking Iris away from him as her face morphed back into Sabrina's.

She closed her fist around his cock. 'Come on, werewolf, cub, wolf, man, pup, give me more. Your body needs to obey me.'

Alfie groaned.

As she increased the pressure and the speed of her hand, Divinia said to Sabrina, 'Can't you make some magic on him. Increase his yield somehow?'

'Not really. I mean, I can, but then that will upset the

potion. You can't use magically procured ingredients to make magic. It gets complicated.'

'You witches always have an excuse,' Divinia said sourly.

'Oh, like I haven't done anything useful? I've located the other sacred objects for you. They're not even all that far away. Ten more crowns and the Silver Collar, right?'

'Oh yes, yes,' Divinia said, sounding brighter. 'I have the chains, the cage and two crowns, but the potion will work far better with *all* the Sacred Silvers.'

'Two crowns?'

'Oh yes. Alfred had one with him and the other one I already had.'

'I don't know why you didn't bring the others with you from the caverns.'

'I didn't think to. I didn't know then what my magnificent new cub would be capable of.' Divinia stroked Alfie's chest with the hand that wasn't tormenting his cock. 'Close to the skin,' she whispered. 'So rare and precious.'

'So do you want me to go and get them then? The other Silvers?'

'Yes,' said Divinia, as Alfie suddenly screamed in pain and convulsed in her hand as he came. 'And hurry.'

50

'I should get that. It's probably Vikram.'

'If it is, you'll be looking at his charred remains.'

'Well, I should get it anyway,' Iris muttered, turning and heading down the stairs.

Behind her Blake muttered, quite audibly, 'Er, why, exactly?'

When Iris opened the door, she found Cate stood on the doorstep, looking as serene and uncreased as only a witch could. 'Hi,' she said, her voice as smooth as her perfectly pressed paisley-print skirt. 'I just thought I ought to check on you. Morphial connectors can be a little wearing.' Cate cocked her head. 'Not feeling unhinged at all, are we?'

Iris stared at Cate in disbelief. 'No more than circumstances would dictate,' she said, her voice sounding dry and hollow. The sight of Cate, so cool and easy, made Iris realise how red her face was, how hard her heart was banging, how dirty and sweaty and messy she was as she stood on the doorstep.

Cate said, 'Are you sure you're OK, Iris?'

'Well,' said Iris, 'in a couple of hours the Divine Wolf will reverse the power of summoning to spirit I don't know how many werewolves to wherever she is. Then she'll use some kind of potion that I strongly suspect is made from Alfie's semen to change them all into Ancient Beasts with the power of being close to the skin. Beasts who can change practically when they want and who can control their wolf bodies with the rational minds. And they'll all be thralled to her. And she's going to try to overthrow humanity. And Alfie is thralled to her tightest of all. And, if I find her and kill her, her power will dissipate through me and it'll kill me.' Iris took a deep breath. 'But you're a witch. You already know all this.'

'Yes, Iris, I do. I think we'd better get Blake down here.'

Iris turned and called up the stairs and Blake came clattering down. 'Hey, Hecate,' he said. 'Have you seen Lilith? How's my witch-girlfriend in a coma.'

Cate shrugged. 'Still in a coma.'

'Right, right. And I don't suppose, what with her being all sleeping beauty and all, there's any way I can get out of . . .'

'Of the binding?'

'Well, yeah. Even if just for a bit.'

Cate grinned. It was more of a soft smile but by Cate's normal standards of expressions of facial mirth it was a Cheshire-cat beam. 'Well, the short answer is "no, obviously not".' She made a mixed-up face. 'Well, there is one way. But that would only work if another woman could prove a prior claim to your loyalty.' Cate gestured at Iris. 'Um, Iris, I don't suppose you still have any kind of . . .' She stopped and thought. 'You're not still married, are you?'

'Signed the papers this morning.' Iris grinned back at Cate.

Blake scowled at them. 'It really isn't funny, you two bitches.'

Iris batted his complaints away. She turned to Cate and said, 'So can you help us?'

Cate looked slightly blank. 'Help you how?'

'Help us find Alfie, find the Divine, kill her, save the world.'

'Oh,' Cate rolled her eyes, 'you don't need my help for that. You'll find them fine.'

'We're out of options,' Iris said, her voice jarring with a desperate note.

'Oh no. No, you're not. Come on.' Cate turned and began to walk down the front path.

Iris called after her, 'We need to bring Zac and Pearl with us.'

'We do?' said Blake.

'They're all we've got.'

Cate turned, and just smiled.

Iris dashed back up the stairs, dimly aware that Blake was behind her. She pulled her gun. 'You two have to come with me,' she said as she burst into Zac and Pearl's room.

Pearl's face was hard. 'I'm not moving him.'

'Yes you are. It's full moon tonight and you're were-wolves. I'm bringing you both in.'

Behind Iris, Blake said, 'Is this really necessary, Iris? There is some other stuff going on right now.'

Iris turned. 'Yes, it is. But God knows what'll happen to him when he changes after all the stuff she's done to him. He needs to change under observation at Cobalt. He's a potential threat. We need to get him in the SUV, or –' she turned to Pearl '– or I shoot you both. And I will, you know. I've killed over a hundred lycs.'

Behind Iris, Blake muttered, 'Human-form lycs?' But Pearl and Zac were already raising their hands.

Outside, Iris and Blake helped Zac and Pearl into the back, and Cate got in after them. Iris and Blake followed.

'Are you going to tell us where to go?' Blake said.

Vikram was still sitting in the driver's seat. He turned. 'Is everything OK? You get the chains? Who are all these . . . ?'

Cate met Vikram's eyes. 'Witch,' she said, hissing like a riled cat.

Vikram drew back a little. Witches and vampires just didn't mix. 'Ah,' said Blake, 'no need for introductions then. Also, Mr Animated Cadaver, you might like to meet this lovely dog and bitch couple we found. He's feeling a little peaky.'

Vikram nodded at Pearl and Zac, as Pearl helped Zac to lie across the backseat with his head on her lap.

Iris said to Cate, 'So where are we going? You said we aren't out of options.'

'Oh, you're not. You'll get there. But you also need to know this. In order for the Divine's power to dissipate safely through whoever kills her, you need to kill her inside the Silver Cage, OK. That's important. She doesn't know it, but that's what the cage is for. Ironic, really. She built it herself. The cage will dissipate her power safely in a way that won't upset the bonds of thrall that run throughout werewolves. But, well, the one downside is that whoever kills her will probably take the brunt of the power through their body. The recoil will probably destroy whoever wields the killing blow.'

'The heir,' said Iris. 'The heir will pay the price. So who's the heir? Me or Alfie?'

'Oh, that'll be clear enough when the moment comes,' said Cate smoothly. 'Just make sure whoever it is kills her inside the cage.'

'But we don't know where the cage is,' Iris said, almost whining. 'Look, Alfie said he's in some kind of place that witches built for the Silver Crown. Doesn't anyone know where that is?'

Cate shrugged. 'Only Sabrina.'

'And Sabrina's dead.'

'No, she's preserved in case we need her knowledge.'

'Great,' said Blake, 'you need her knowledge right now.'

Cate shook her head. 'I can't access her without Lilith.'

'Arrgh,' Iris screamed. 'But Lilith made herself unconscious precisely so she could help me find Alfie.' Iris stared at Cate, full of fire. 'Just get out of here,' she shouted. 'Get away from me. Unless you're going to help me properly, stay out of my way.'

There was an audible intake of breath from Vikram, Blake, Zac and Pearl. And then Cate said, 'You have all the answers you need now, Iris.' She turned, and calmly got out of the SUV.

51

A couple of hours later, Iris, Blake, Vikram, Zac and Pearl were all sitting in the SUV, on a shady back street just around the corner from Cobalt's building, with Vikram showing Blake how to use the tracing program on the laptop.

Iris fished out her MCD.

'Fuck,' Blake said as he saw it. 'I forgot you had that. They'll know we're here.'

Iris shrugged. 'They'll know in a second anyway. I know they'll be waiting for me, Blake. That's why I'm tooled up as if I'm ... As if I'm you or something.'

Iris had spent the journey up from Oxford ferreting for every weapon that was stashed in the SUV and strapping it to her body.

'You know, Cobalt want to find Alfie too. I'm sure it won't come to that. When you explain...' Vikram began.

'Vik, I've been AWOL all day. And Erin Cobalt isn't the most understanding boss. Frankly, I'd rather take what I need by force than work with her again.'

Blake snorted.

Vikram turned back to the screen. 'OK. I've got you,' he said.

Iris looked over and saw a small flashing point moving on the laptop screen. Her.

'God, Iris,' said Blake, 'don't fucking die.'

Iris laughed. Once. Short and sharp. 'Oh, Blake, that's the nicest thing you've ever said to me. Anyway, not a worry – destiny, you know, I've got to live long enough to die killing that queen bitch. I just have to go in and find one of the crowns or the collar. And, like Vikram said, maybe Cobalt will help me. I am actually just doing my job. On the other hand, no harm in being very, very armed in case they've changed my job description while I was away.'

As Iris turned to get out of the SUV, behind her Pearl said, 'I'll come too.'

'What?' said Iris, turning, looking at Pearl's pale generous face.

'I'll come too. You need back up. Zac's too ill, Blake's too high on their death list, Vik can't get out of the car. It has to be me.'

'Can you shoot?' said Iris.

'Is it hard?'

'I reckon that one can handle herself,' Blake said. 'How long did you work for the NHS, sweetheart?'

'Three and a half years.'

'You work in A&E much?'

'Plenty.'

'Then you're probably the toughest one here. Take her,' Blake said, turning to Iris. 'She's Pure's cousin. She's right. You need someone.'

Two combat boots and then two white rubber clogs hit the pavement as Iris climbed out with Pearl behind her. Iris pulled a gun out of her belt and two knives out of each sock and handed them to Pearl, who put them in the deep pockets of her uniform.

'You sure about this?'

Pearl nodded. 'You say Leon's in there being tortured?'

'Er, yeah. He's Zac's sire, right? Part of your pack? You want to get him out of there?' Iris said, hefting her crossbow on to her back.

'Not really,' said Pearl. 'But, if he's suffered really badly, I'd like to see it.'

Iris didn't ask anything more. She led the way out of the side street and round the corner and there was Cobalt. Somehow, even with its white walls and sparkling windows, it seemed to loom just as much as any of the dark castles in which its prey would have lived.

Iris led Pearl past the noise and clang of the nearby building site and up to the front door.

Blake watched Iris go. Then he turned and watched the dot marked II (who else in the world had the initials II?) moving across the sketchy map.

'Fuck it, killer bitch,' he whispered. 'I hope you're right about your destiny.'

'Blake?' Iris's voice was a crackly whisper through the speakers. 'Did you say something?'

'No, no,' said Blake. 'Where are you?'

'I'm in reception. Pepper's, er . . . Hi Pepper.'

Blake couldn't make out what Pepper said and then Iris said, 'Are you sure you're OK? You're bleeding. Your forehead's bleeding.' A pause and then. 'Right. OK.'

There was another pause. The sounds of Iris's footsteps and then: 'Blake, OK, Pepper seems odd. Vague. It's very quiet here. There's hardly anyone around and . . . *Arrgh!*'

'Shit, Iris. What? What?'

Vikram leant over. 'We've lost her. Change frequency. Quick. Quick.' Vikram started jabbing the keyboard.

Blake shouted, 'Iris! Iris!'

Then Iris's voice came back. She was breathing hard. 'OK. It's . . . I'm OK. Someone just came around the corner with a pen, kind of, in his eye. God. What the hell has happened here? Blake, everyone's wounded. Walking around as if it's all fine. Blood and bruises. It's, God, I don't know, not right. People seem to be . . . I don't know, like they can't see. People are walking into the walls.'

'Get out of there, Iris.'

'No, Blake, no. It's fine. Look, I need to get the Sacred Silvers. No one is bothering me. It's like they don't notice me. This is fine. It's good.'

'It's magic, isn't it? Don't pretend you can't tell. It's bad magic, isn't it?'

Blake was about to say something else, but Vikram pulled the headset from his face. 'Leave her alone, Blake. Let her do her job.'

'Why?' Blake looked at Vikram. 'What do you care? What even are you? You don't work for Cobalt? Cobalt doesn't employ vamps. What the fuck are you playing at?'

Vikram shrugged. 'I'm just an interested party. Not sure which side I'm on, but I'm keen to see Iris do what she needs to do. I'm here for her, to help her and, right now, she needs you out of the way.'

'Oh fuck off, blood boy. I know what this is, you're jealous. Jealous of how Iris feels about me.'

'Well, you'd know jealous. You're defined by how much you want her,' Vikram said.

Blake could feel him, spider-crawling through his mind. 'Get out of there, you filthy corpse,' Blake shouted, shaking his head, but he couldn't shake Vikram free. 'Fuck you.'

'Empty threat from you these days.' Vikram shook his head as if disgusted. 'Witch's pussy boy. I bet you wish you could fuck. You wish you could fuck almost anyone else. Just because you can't. Even me.'

There was something mesmeric about the way Vikram was speaking. Blake inhaled sharply through his nose, trying to clear the fog. 'Don't you dare try that psych stuff on me, vampire.'

'Kiss me, Mr Tabernacle,' Vikram said in a soft voice that seemed to pulse a little like a heartbeat.

'I can't, it'll ... Oh, for fuck's sake. No!' But even as he realised what Vikram was doing – taking an easy route to putting him out of action – Blake could feel his body responding. God, it was so fucking *wrong*. Was this what the dirty little bastard had done to Iris? Blake felt his cock stir in Lilith's binding.

'The last person to kiss me was Iris,' Vikram said in that same gentle pulsing rhythm of a voice. 'And I know how you feel about her. I know exactly.'

Blake screamed inside, but he leant forwards and caught Vikram's lips with his own. The coolness was strangely pleasant. The taste and scent of Iris was almost certainly imaginary. But Blake had a good imagination. Always had. A sharp burn of pain intensified and shot through his body, as a low explosion of sound crashed around him. And he felt his body pulled and thrown backwards, away from Vikram, and into the back windscreen of the SUV.

52

By the time Iris was walking down the steps to the basement, she'd had a number of disturbing encounters with the uncanny employees of Cobalt. They were moving jerkily, zombie-like. Most were injured, but Iris quickly discovered that this was not because of any malevolence going on. The injuries were being caused by the creatures' mindlessness as they walked into walls or stumbled out of windows. This was – as Blake had said – magic. Nasty magic.

'Are you OK?' she said to Pearl. It really was strange how much she looked like her dead cousin – one of Iris's werewolf hunters who had died facing down the Silver Crown with her. Iris was hoping she could be relied upon to fight like him too.

'Not really,' Pearl said hollowly.

'Me neither.'

There were two doors in front of Iris. One led to the main interrogation room, the other to the viewing room. Iris took the second one. She skirted the fat red sofa and stopped and peered through the two-way mirror.

Some of the lights were off in the room where she had last seen Erin go to work on Leon. The lightbulbs were mostly smashed in the room now. Several cords hung down from the ceiling with just dead jagged glass at their ends. The lack of light made it harder to see what was in the room, and at first she thought it was empty.

'There's no one in there,' she said, a note of panicked relief obvious in her voice.

'Yes there is,' hissed Pearl. 'The back wall.' She sounded terrified.

'What?' Iris felt herself jolt with adrenaline as she looked to where Pearl was pointing. Then she exhaled with relief. 'No, no, that's just a mark on the wall, from where they threw nitric acid at Darius Cole.'

'It's moving,' Pearl said, close to tears.

Iris stared at the shape on the back wall. It was hard to make out. But then, like an optical illusion, it suddenly snapped into place. It wasn't the shadowy shape of Cole burnt into the wall. It was Erin, chained into the manacles, barely conscious.

'Oh, God,' Iris said in a soft dull whisper.

Sometimes, when Iris used her body it was all very rational, planned and neatly executed. Fighting and hunting werewolves, training, taking Blake down in the hallway and dragging him, still dazed into the bedroom to push his face down into her cunt.

But, sometimes, Iris wondered who was in control, who was making the decisions. Times like these when she was running, exploding with acceleration, leading with her shoulder hunched to protect her head as she leapt, leaving the ground, smashing through the two-way mirror, flipping in the air and landing in the interrogation room on both feet, in a hail of shards.

Erin twitched, barely a movement.

Iris rushed over. Close up, Erin didn't seem too badly injured, but her eyes had that same vacant stare that every other Cobalt employee now seemed to have.

'Erin? Dr Cobalt? I need the Sacred Silvers you took from Blake. The collar and the crowns. Where are they?'

'Huh?' said Erin. Her head rolled on her neck like it was made of jelly.

Behind Iris, Pearl suddenly said, 'Where's Leon?'

Iris sort of batted her away. 'Not now, Pearl.'

Then Erin said, in a high faraway voice, 'She took him.'

'Who?' said Iris. 'Who took him?'

'The witch. The witch that was here.'

'What witch?'

Erin's voice was still ethereal and deranged. 'She came for the Silvers. I had them here. Down here. She knew. But when she came in and saw Leon – he was unconscious – she went crazy. "*Hers*," she said. Said that he was hers. That's when she cast the spell. She said she'd make us all sleep for a hundred years. But just the brain . . . just the brain.'

Iris had both hands on Erin's face. 'Did she take them? The Silvers?'

'And did she take Leon?' said Pearl, behind Iris.

'Yes. She took them. And him too.'

'What . . . ?' Iris gulped, barely daring to ask. 'What did this witch look like?'

'Dark hair. Very beautiful. A silver tooth. She kissed the werewolf and the sting of it seemed to revive him.'

'Fuck! Sabrina! I knew those witches had messed up.' Iris hit the wall right next to Erin's face with her fist. It hurt a lot but the pain was good, clarifying. 'You lost them. The Silvers. Sabrina took them. Fuck!'

Iris turned and stalked across the room, the shards of mirrored glass crunching under her combat boots. 'That's it,' she said. She turned around as she reached the wall and started to pace back. 'That was my last chance. Now I have no way to find Alfie. It's – what? – an hour until moon rise. She'll draw the wolves to her, do her magic, raise her army. And I don't get to stop her. It's lost. It's all lost.' She shook her head like she couldn't believe it. 'I lost. It can't be right. I am meant to be there. I'm the heir. I'm *meant* to stop her!'

Suddenly Erin said, 'Well, aren't you going to go after her?'

'After her?'

Erin sounded suddenly more lucid. 'Yes. Chase her. Make her reverse the magic she's cast on us. She might still be here. There's a security terminal in the wall.' Then Erin's head slumped down on to her chest as if the effort of that had been too much for her.

Pearl darted forwards. 'Are you OK. Did you say her name was Erin? Erin, are you OK?'

'Forget it,' Iris said. 'She's just so hardass, she's fighting the magic that's shutting down her brain. That little lucid moment has completely drained her.'

'More than that,' said Pearl, touching Erin's neck. 'She's dead.'

Iris flipped open the cover in the wall-mounted computer terminal. She shook her head but didn't say anything. Erin Cobalt had had it coming. Hadn't she? Maybe. How different was she really from Blake? Did Blake have it coming?

She cleared her head and entered her password into the terminal. She had no idea how the system worked but that got her through security. She began sifting through images: various parts of the Cobalt building, horrific sights, people who had injured themselves in various ways. Then, when the image of reception flashed up, Iris went cold.

'Oh, God, Pearl.'

'What?'

'Reception's on fire.'

'Oh,' said Pearl, almost as if she didn't register.

Iris flipped down her coms mic. 'Blake! Are you there, Blake?'

'Still nothing?' said Pearl, leaving Erin to come over to look at the screen. 'Maybe there's no signal down here?'

'No signal? This is Cobalt. I'm sure they're fully connected. No, it must be a problem their end. Oh damn. We need to go out through the car park. It's the floor above this one.'

Iris flipped open the panel on the coms and got an outside line; she dialled the emergency services quickly and barked Cobalt's address.

As she hung up, Iris glanced at Erin. 'You sure she's dead?'

Pearl nodded. 'Quite sure.'

'OK. Then we head for the car park. Let me just check it's clear ... Oh! Oh my God! She's right there!' Iris jabbed the screen. An image of the underground car park had just flashed up: Sabrina and Leon in the underground garage. 'Come on,' Iris said, making to leave.

As she began to pound through the corridor, she felt Pearl at her heels.

Up one flight of stairs and they were in the car park. Sabrina and Leon were making their way towards the big hydraulic doors that led up to street level. Leon was leaning heavily on Sabrina, damaged.

'Stop,' shouted Iris, 'stop or I'll shoot him.' She had Leon right in the sights of her crossbow.

Sabrina turned. God, but she was beautiful. Leon, conversely, looked awful. Close to death. His face and torso were a mass of burns and bruises, his ruined face contorted into a grin that was half grimace. 'Hey, sweetheart,' he said weakly. And Iris thought he was talking to her for a second.

Then Pearl said, 'Hey.'

Leon's voice was scratchy, weak and sardonic. 'So, is it fun for you? Seeing your sire's sire fucked up like this?'

'No,' said Pearl. 'I thought it might be, but it isn't. Where are you taking him?' The last sentence was to Sabrina.

'Somewhere safe,' said Sabrina. 'And you better get out of my way, Fox, if you want to stay alive.'

'Why're you walking?' said Iris. 'That spell drain you a bit? Were you so angry you didn't hold a reserve of power to get out of here?'

'It's not that,' said Pearl, 'magic would accelerate the damage done to him. She must really care about him. Maybe she cares enough to ...' Pearl raised her voice. 'Hey, listen, I can help him. I saved Zac, Leon. Tell her. Tell her how Zac should have died. I saved him. I know how to heal fatal silver wounds.'

'Zac's alive?' Leon said gruffly. 'Yeah guess he must be or you'd be my cub now, sweetheart.'

Iris watched as Leon turned and said something too quiet to hear to Sabrina.

'OK,' said Sabrina, 'you can help him. Come with us.'

'Give Iris what she wants first,' said Pearl.

'What does she want?'

'I want the Silvers,' said Iris. 'The collar and the crowns.'

'I can't give you those. Leon, you need to make the wolf girl come with us.'

'I can't make her. She's part of my pack but I'm not her sire. I can't send it down the line without Zac here.'

Sabrina looked back at Iris. No one moved.

Blake and Vikram were still fighting in the back of the SUV. Vikram was cowering in the driver's seat as Blake, once again, brandished his sword. 'You dirty dead...' he growled and made an extravagant swooping movement with the sword, but, at the end of the last metal-pirouette, it flew out of his hand and across the back of the car. 'Oh damn,' Blake said, scrambling after it before Vikram could stop him.

But then he saw what he'd done. 'Oh.'

'What is it?' Vikram sneered, leaning over the driver's seat.

'Zac. The lyc. The sword hit him. God, it looks like his body couldn't take it.'

'You can't kill a lyc with a...' Vikram was saying, but Blake was looking at Zac's body, prone on the back seat, his face the colour of ash.

'You can if the blade is silver.'

Pearl felt it. It was like her heart being ripped out of her body. Zac was gone and she knew – right in the centre of that utter pain and sudden loneliness as she was orphaned – that the gap had closed and that Leon was her sire now. She had no idea how this stuff worked. Did Leon know what had happened?

She wasn't sure. And maybe it would have been OK if she had kept quiet. But she couldn't. She just couldn't. 'Zac,' she said. 'Oh, God, Zac.' Her achingly trembling face erupted. Tears were streaming so hard she could only just see the grin spread across Leon's bruised and bloody face. He knew. 'Come with us, baby,' he drawled.

Pearl had no choice but to obey him.

As she slunk across the car park and followed Leon and Sabrina towards the hydraulic doors that Sabrina was opening with a subtle bit of magic, she half noticed Iris sinking to her knees and starting to cry too.

Blake was watching the fire engines gather outside Cobalt. 'Oh shit, look, one of us has to go in.'

'No,' said Vikram, 'wait. I'll find her MCD first. No point in either of us running blindly into a building that's on fire – that's bad for me – or full of people that want you dead – that's bad for you.'

'Iris is in there!'

'Let's just be sure.' Vikram pecked at the keys some more. Just as Blake was about to increase his threat level, Vikram said, 'Ah, got her. She's in the car park.'

'Great,' said Blake, his hand on the car-door handle.

'No, stay there,' Vikram said, revving the engine. 'We can drive right in.'

As soon as the SUV bumped down the ramp into the underground car park, Blake saw Iris, on her knees on the concrete, her palms flat on the ground in front of her like she was vomiting.

Vikram swooped the car around in an arc so Blake could fling open the side door as they passed her, grab her around the waist and pull her inside.

The SUV wheeled around and slid back out of the door, past the building site and around the corner back into the little side-street hideout.

Blake had Iris on the back seat curled on his lap. He was tapping her cheek. 'Come on, baby. Stuff to do.'

'What's to do?' Iris moaned. 'There's nothing left.' She sat up. Frowning like something was confusing her. 'Where's Zac? What happened to Zac?'

'He died. There was a fight.'

'You fought Zac? He was barely alive. And where's his body.'

'I powdered it. Remember? Sent it to another dimension with that powder we used to use?'

'Of course I remember. So that's what happened to Pearl. Zac died and the hole closed up and she was thralled to Leon. Oh fuck. Oh, Blake, I nearly had them. Sabrina took them. And she walked away.'

Iris was garbling, but Blake could sort of make out what must have happened.

'And now,' she said, 'there's nothing left. Nothing we can do. Where's Vikram?'

'What?' Blake looked up, surprised.

'Did he go somewhere? Wasn't he driving?'

'Yes.' Blake creased his brow. 'It's still daylight. If he'd got out he'd be toast.'

'He can change into a bat,' said Iris. 'I think he can move a bit more freely when he's in that form. He got back from Cornwall in daylight.'

'He did? I didn't think vampires could ... Iris, Iris are you OK.'

Iris could tell Blake was raising his voice, but it was sounding fainter and fainter. Iris glanced down at her body to see it fading away.

53

Iris sat up. She looked around at a smallish patch of rubbly wasteground. Piles of breeze blocks and bricks littered the place and the ground was pitted and muddy. The puddles had the greyish tinge of cement powder. The sun was low in the sky.

She was alone. Well, not exactly alone, there were people everywhere. Sitting on the ground or wandering around. All equally bewildered. She couldn't see any sign of Blake.

What happened?

Looking over to her left, she saw a huge crane stretching into the dusk-streaked sky. Beyond that was the road, a busy familiar-looking road. There were dazed-looking people everywhere.

'This is the building site next to Cobalt, the new wing. I could see the place from my bedroom window.'

'Yeah,' said a voice beside her, 'weird, isn't it? We're just on the other side of the road.'

Iris turned, not really surprised to see that Vikram was sitting a few feet away on a wooden palette. 'Vikram. Where are we?'

'We're here, where we were trying to get. The summoning's happened. It pulled you through.'

'Me? Why me? I'm not a lyc.'

'No. But the magic is clumsy. You're the warrior wolf, wolf's woman. You're close enough to Alfie that it worked on you too.'

'Oh, God.' Iris shook her head. 'After all that? I just got summoned here anyway. And I always would have been ...? This destiny thing is weird. How long do you think the witches have known that I would...' Iris trailed off, thinking about how much witches annoyed her, then she said, 'And how did you get here? You vanished just before me. How come the magic worked on you? You're a vampire, aren't you?'

'Yeah,' Vikram sighed. 'But it's complicated. I'm here to help you.' He looked back at the road. 'How come no one's looking over here. Hundreds of people on a building-site. Can't they see us?'

Iris shrugged. 'Must be a cloaking spell. Witches use them a lot. Sabrina could have done this easily. We can see out to the street, but from outside the cloak it must just look like the empty site.'

'Is Sabrina another lyc? Damn,' said Vikram. 'Weird. But how come they can do magic. Lycs can do magic? I know she's the Divine Wolf and everything but the idea of lycs doing magic scares the shit out of me.'

'Sabrina's a witch.' Iris squinted at Vikram. 'What are you?'

'Like I say, it's complicated.'

'So where are they?' said Iris. 'Where's Alfie? The Divine? Where's my bloody destiny?'

'Alfie said he was underground, right? How about we look down there?'

Vikram was pointing at a small raised platform of concrete breeze blocks that seemed to be a natural point of focus in building-site debris. In the middle of it was what seemed to be a trap door.

Vikram and Iris made their way through the crowds of dissolute-looking human-form werewolves to the platform and pulled the door open. No one took any notice.

'Why are they so dopey?' Vikram hissed, looking around as Iris peered down into the dark at the long flight of steps.

'Thrall, I think. The Divine must be close and her thrall is amped up. They don't know what to do. They want to obey her but she hasn't told them to do anything yet. Come on.' Iris started down the steps.

After the long flight of steps came a long corridor. 'It can't be . . .' said Iris, after a moment. 'Alfie was so near Cobalt all along?'

Still slightly freaked out from being so near the building full of fire and quasi-zombies, they kept walking, until they came to another small flight of steps that led down through a stone alcove into a small room with a dead cold fireplace and a rocking chair. At the back of the room was a wooden door, slightly ajar. Iris approached the door using every bit of stealth she had, Vikram, undetectably silent, right behind her.

And then, suddenly, all she could see was a brightly sparkling Silver Cage. Iris exhaled when she saw the figure inside it. 'Oh, God. Alfie.'

Vikram turned; under his breath he said, 'Wow. He certainly is kind of beasty looking. Who are the women? I guess one is the Divine.'

'Yeah. The tall woman with short hair is the Divine.'

'Really, she looks so normal.'

'The other one, the one that looks like one of Charlie's Angels, is Sabrina. A nasty piece of witchy-work who likes to help werewolves. Or at least hinder humans. Or something. She's bad news either way. The messed-up guy in the jeans with all the hair sat with Pearl is Leon – he's Alfie's cub.' Iris pointed to the pair of them, slumped against the wall, dumb with thrall. Right next to them was a cauldron, its contents warm enough to steam.

'Right,' said Vikram. 'Alfie's line.'

'Yeah. Maybe that's part of her plan somehow. We know she has all the Sacred Silvers, and Alfie – the Ancient Beast. His line. All the other wolves outside. That cauldron must contain her potion. God. Maybe it's too late.'

While Iris said all this, she couldn't stop looking at Alfie. He had a dirty piece of white cloth wrapped around his hips and his right hand was bandaged up to the elbow. The marks and scars she had seen on his body before were still there. His left hand was chained to the cage with one of the Silver Chains. He didn't look too bad – not as damaged as he could have been – but seeing him was enough to make Iris feel weak and distracted.

Iris looked from Alfie to Vikram, then back to Alfie and whispered, 'I have no idea what to do now, really. I worked so hard to get here – not knowing I was just going to get pulled through anyway – and I never really thought about what I'd do.'

'You've no plan?'

'Well,' said Iris, 'I wouldn't say I have no plan exactly. It's just not a very good one. In fact, it might even be sort of fatal.' She took a deep breath. 'But I always knew that.'

54

Iris burst through the door into the cellar. Vikram was with her. She felt him at her heels and then by her side.

She sprang and landed panting in front of the Divine and Sabrina.

'Oh, God,' said the Divine, her voice weary and sarcastic. 'It's you. You *are* alive, just like he thought. That'll teach me to try an ironic death.' Her features changed in realisation. 'Oh, don't tell me my magic pulled you through, wolf's woman? How disgusting.'

'Yeah,' said Iris, 'I'm kind of hard to kill.'

'Well,' said the Divine, 'let's make it cleaner this time. Stick her in the cage.'

Iris didn't react. Sabrina made a noise like a soft laugh that somehow became a whirlwind of magic that picked Iris up and bowled her straight into Alfie's cage. The door magically clanged open and then shut tight again.

She landed on her hands and knees, only feet from where Alfie was chained to the bars.

The Divine said, 'There is still half an hour until moon rise. That's always a fun thing to do to a wolf's woman who's starting to think she's too important.'

Iris looked over her shoulder at the Divine who was walking towards the cage.

She started to walk around it, trailing a hand on the bars as she moved. 'But we don't need to wait for that with your wolf, do we, Iris? Although –' the Divine paused, mugging as if in thought '– he won't actually change while he's caged, will he? But I don't think that will be a problem.'

The Divine was standing behind Alfie now, just the thick silver bars between them. She reached out and unlocked Alfie's single manacle. Dumbly, Alfie lowered his unrestrained arm. The Divine bent down and pressed her lips close to his ear. But her words were clearly audible. 'Kill her.'

Blake had pulled half of the wires out of the high-end electronic console set into the dashboard and had finally managed to override all the security log-ins.

He jabbed at the keys: Iris's unique initials II – that must be enough to ID her on the system.

A map flashed up on the screen in shades of winking green. GPS co-ords whirled. And then up it came: Iris's location. Satisfied he could work the machine, Blake cross-referenced the position with Vikram's.

That was strange.

Iris had never won a fight with Alfie. He was just too big, too strong and overwhelming. All the clever moves she knew, all her speed, all her sparky tricks – they counted for nothing up against Alfie's sheer brawn. He could simply best her.

Most of the time she thought that was incredibly hot.

Not so much right now.

As Alfie sprang from a crouch, heading right for her, Iris dived, her brain rushing with calculation about his injured hand. She rolled and clanged against the bars at one corner of the cage, as Alfie hit the opposite wall of the cage. He looked dazed as he stood up, awkwardly without the use of his right hand.

Iris scanned the room for something that might help her. The cellar had one high window. And through it she could see the dark-blue crane from the building site high in the sky.

Oh, Alfie, you could have told me about that. If I'd known you could see that crane . . .

She looked at him. Alfie stared back at Iris, his eyes full of anger. And he moved.

Iris locked eyes with him, inhaled and raised both her arms in surrender. Alfie charged into her, barrelling her back into the barred wall behind her. He landed on top of her and twisted her down to the floor. He got her arms locked under his big thighs and sat up straddling her.

He cradled his injured right hand in his left, making a huge double fist. He raised his arms up above his head and looked down at Iris.

'Alfie,' she said and her voice sounded soft and weak. 'Alfie, please. You could have told me about the crane.'

'I didn't want you to come here, Iris. This is why.'

'I know. And I understand this time. The last time you were trapped by thrall and it made you betray me, I didn't understand. But now I do. I know this isn't you. Even after you left me to die in those caves, I still came for you. Hunted you down. Found you. I know this isn't your fault.'

In her head, then, Iris heard Cate's voice. Cate saying, *His feelings for you are still there. Even if the thrall has control of him. He still loves you or this connection wouldn't work. Use your power. Use your love for him. The more you open your heart to him the stronger your connection will be.*

Iris said, 'If you kill me now, Alfie, I forgive you. I still love you.'

Alfie's face changed. It happened quickly and so slowly. Anger became release, then love. Nothing but love. And he dropped down, covered and protected her with his big body and kissed her.

Outside the cage, the Divine screamed in rage as Alfie's lips met Iris's.

Alfie pulled back from the kiss and looked over his shoulder at her, laughing. 'Oh shut up, Divinia.'

Iris stared at him as he turned back. Her hands were

still trapped under his arms. She wriggled them but couldn't get free. Alfie made a low growling pleasure noise. 'You're not thralled to her?' Iris whispered.

'No. I think Lilith has decided to be uncharacteristically *involved* in this situation.'

Alfie ducked down, pecking at her face in quick kisses. 'Lilith?' said Iris. 'I thought Lilith was in a coma.'

'Yeah. That kind of worked out for the best.'

Through the kissing – the perfect moment – several things exploded all at once. The Divine screamed in rage again and raced around the cage, intent on the door. At almost the same moment, across the platform, Vikram who had been standing dumbfounded all this time, launched himself at Sabrina.

The Divine stopped and turned.

Iris pulled herself up from underneath Alfie into a sitting position and yelled, 'Vikram! No! She's a witch.'

Vikram shouted something that Iris thought was probably, 'I know!'

Sabrina raised her hands and hit Vikram with a bolt of energy shouting, 'Never mind what I am, you stupid girl, don't you even know what he is?'

The energy bolt bounced off Vikram, leaving him unscathed, and jetted across the platform. The Divine yelped and leapt out of the way and the energy fizzled and hit the door of the cage. The Divine snapped round. 'Watch it, Sab,' she screamed. 'You just fused the door shut.'

Sabrina groaned. 'Give me some back up,' she yelled, reaching out and looking like she was sucking something out of Divinia from across the room. Bolstered, suddenly looking almost taller, more imposing, she rolled her eyes, then whirled around in a ball of fierce energy. She hit Vikram with something Iris could tell was vicious strong magic. It bowled him up in the air and held him there, imprisoned in a ball of fizzing crackling power.

'There,' said Sabrina, visibly panting. 'That should hold the little fucker for a while.'

The Divine shook herself. 'Fucking freak-cub. I don't know what he's even doing out.'

'Didn't you know?' shouted Sabrina. 'If he's your cub, shouldn't you be able to feel it if he's out of his prison?'

'Not with that one. He doesn't work like a proper lycan, the little runt. He's not even feeling an ounce of thrall. It's disgusting.'

Iris looked at the Divine. 'What? He's your cub. That'd make him an Ancient Beast. A cub of the Divine.' She shook her head. 'But he's a vampire.'

The Divine turned. 'Yeah. That's right. Don't you know about him? You knew there was one missing, right? You only killed eleven Beasts. They had to use me to join the circle as the twelfth Beast, but that's because of him being so, so *wrong*. He's practically a myth. The Ancient Beast that was bitten by a vampire. Some kind of fucked-up experiment. He's not supposed to be out and about, though. Seems witch-built prisons aren't what they were.'

Sabrina shrugged. 'You can say that again.'

The Divine turned back to the cage door. 'Now get this open,' she snapped at Sabrina. 'Then you go in there and get him off her. Then kill her.'

Sabrina poised herself to hit with another spell. Iris was reeling – almost nauseous – from the weight of the knowledge about Vikram, but somehow she managed to focus on the immediate danger. She pulled her gun from her shoulder holster and held it to Alfie's head. 'No.'

The Divine cocked her head. 'Oh, what?'

'I'll shoot him.'

The Divine laughed. 'No you won't, baby. You'd be doing me a favour. He's broken his thrall somehow. He's useless. But if he dies Leon will inherit his power. Reform the links.'

'Maybe. You sure? You sure the link won't be too weak

then? They get weaker every time they reknit, don't they? You want to risk it? Zac's dead. Your chain of power is already looking wobbly.'

The Divine smiled a tight-lipped smile. 'There is no way...'

'She doesn't need to,' said Alfie. 'I've still got something you need.' With his uninjured left hand, he fisted his cock. 'You need one more ejaculation, don't you? The last splash.' He drew his hand up and down his hardening cock. 'You need me alive for the potion to be complete.'

Iris smiled. She twisted under Alfie and heaved him over on to his back. He was still holding his cock as she slipped down his body to nestle between his legs. 'Or maybe, I can make sure the potion is never complete.'

'No, you don't, you bitch!' As Iris closed her lips around Alfie's hard hot cock, the whole cage reverberated as Sabrina threw a jolt of magic at the door.

'Fuck,' said Alfie. 'This cage is magical. So it won't be easy. But who knows how long it will hold?'

Iris exhaled and let Alfie slip deeper into her throat. The feeling was amazing. After so long without him, it was perfect to possess his pleasure like this. To feel him pulse inside her. But this wasn't about enjoyment. This was about one last mission. One last quest. One last race against the clock. *Make him come.*

Alfie started to buck and gasp underneath her.

Iris knew everything about his responses. Every gasp. He was close. So close. She tasted the precome, slippery salt on her tongue.

The cage rocked with another zap from Sabrina and then another and the door clanged open. Iris sat bolt upright, sudden and instinctive. The Divine herself stalked into the cage. She grabbed Iris, lifting her right up into the air. Iris turned and kicked out, but the Divine just flung her, tossed her right up into the air through the cage door and down on to the floor near the open door into the next room.

Then the Divine turned to Alfie. He was on his feet and gave her a defiant look, but the Divine grabbed him, her reactions super-lightning fast, and locked both fists around his injured hand. Iris winced to see it.

Alfie bellowed in pain and dropped to his knees in front of her. 'There's more than one way to control you,' the Divine said. Her voice was low and deep. Iris wondered if she could really hear her so clearly or if this was the morphial connector. The Divine squeezed Alfie again. 'Finish it.'

'No!' Alfie screamed, half sobbing as she squeezed his ruined hand again.

'Finish it,' said the Divine, her voice deeper still. Alpha.

Iris felt the hairs on the back of her neck stand up.

'No,' Alfie sobbed, and Iris could hear his hand crunching.

'Fine,' said the Divine. She stepped over his body with one leg and straddled him. Taking one hand off his injured hand, she dug in her pocket for something which she seemed to slip over his cock. Then she lined herself up and began to lower herself on to him.

'No!' Alfie went to lash out at her with his left hand and Sabrina, blurry fast, took one hand from the magic holding Vikram and shot a bolt of power right through into the cage. It hit Alfie's left wrist and slammed it up against the barred wall at his back, fixing it there. Alfie was helpless as the Divine took him.

He was so close. Iris knew it. He screamed out again. This time: 'No! No!'

The Divine was starting to move on his cock. Up and down. Fast and cruel. Iris knew that move would make Alfie orgasm in moments.

And in moments Alfie cried out and came. The Divine cried out too in pure triumph. And then Iris watched in horror as she stood up and removed the little pouch from Alfie. The last splash a white residue inside it.

I'm the heir. I have to kill her. I have to kill her now while she's in the cage.

Iris was on the floor right next to the open door to the room beyond. She struggled to her feet, pulling her crossbow from her back.

And then something tugged at her waist and pulled her back down to the ground.

'Oh no, you don't.'

Iris turned. 'Blake!' He was crouched just on the other side of the door.

'Hey, baby. Don't think I don't know what you've got planned.'

'Yeah, sure, you're super smart. I have to kill her while she's in the cage.'

'No, you don't, Iris. Not you.'

'How did you even get here, Blake?'

'You have a Cobalt coms. An MCD. I have a Cobalt van.'

'I have to kill her, Blake. Now. She's in the cage.'

'It'll kill you.'

'I know. The heir will pay the price.'

'I'm the heir,' said Blake. 'Not you. I'm the heir. The house in Summertown that Dr Tobias left me? I'm the heir.'

'Blake, what? He just left you his house.'

'You still wondering why he did that?'

'Not really. Not right now.'

'I'm his son, Iris. Dr Tobias is – *was* – my father.'

'Oh for fuck's sake,' Iris said. 'What?'

Iris knew Blake. All the lies he'd ever told her. But she knew now he was telling her the truth. She was staring at Blake and she couldn't think what to say.

'You know it's true, don't you, Iris? It's me. I'm his heir. I'm his son. I know I never told you. Should I have done? Where to begin?' Blake shook his head. 'That's why he left me his house, left me everything. I'm his son. I'm the heir. I pay the price.

Iris shook her head. 'You can't, Blake. You can't be the one who kills her. You'll die. You can't die. You live.' Iris was insistent. This was one thing she'd always believed in. The immortality of Blake. Blake forever. She'd accepted Jude dying. She could believe in Alfie's death or even her own. But not Blake. Never Blake. Blake didn't die.

In the cage, the Divine was still crowing over Alfie. Iris turned back to Blake. 'Blake. Fuck it. There isn't time for us to argue about this.'

'I know. That's why it's me, Iris. I'm the one around here who needs a redemption. And, besides, Lilith has me by the balls. I'm totally fucked.'

'You're not fucked. You're just married to a witch.'

'And that's not fucked?'

Blake started to get up. Iris grabbed his hand. He looked back at her. 'Blake ... Please?'

Blake shook his head. 'Just tell me, Iris, did you ever love me? Even for a minute.'

'Blake ...'

'Was it always only ever him? Was there even a second when – when I could have been the one?'

Iris started to shake her head.

'Just a *second*, Iris.'

Then Iris said softly. 'Yes. Yes there was. I did love you once. I loved you when you said you'd kill it for me. When you said you'd kill the Beast.'

Blake looked solemn. 'I was lying when I said that, Iris. Dr Tobias – the Beast – was sitting right next to you. And I knew it. And I had no intention of killing him. He was my father.'

'I know.' Iris's head still spun if she tried to think too hard about that.

'So maybe after this you'll forgive me,' Blake said,

turning away and pulling out of her grip. He ran for the cage.

As Blake ran, not thinking, images flashed through his head. Women. Fucks. His life in fucks. Backwards. Iris on the bed in the Summertown house when he couldn't touch her. Iris in the woods. Lilith handcuffed on the floor. Sabrina in the pack house. Iris and Alfie in the basement. Iris in South Park. Aurelia at the office, sucking him off under his desk. Pure. Then Iris. Iris, Iris, Iris. Iris cuffed to the bed. Him cuffed to the bed underneath her spread thighs. Lilith – that one time while he was married. Unfaithful doesn't count if it's with a witch. Then Iris. More Iris. The wedding night. Courting. The first time he'd fucked her. Jude that time. Other girls. Back and back.

And then he was in the cage. The Divine was approached the cauldron of potion with Alfie's last splash in her hand. Blake had his silver sword. Would it kill her? Of course it would – destiny – maybe it was the only thing that would do the job safely. He brandished it through the air with a swish and a flourish – smooth moves he knew would kill him – and the Divine's head flew off and landed on the straw-covered floor.

It was the recoil – her power slamming into him – that threw him hard against one barred wall of the cage. He heard the crack as his head hit the bars. And then it all went dark.

55

In a medieval castle that really didn't exist enough to be anywhere in particular, somewhere on the third floor, in a bedroom hung with tapestries over dark wooden walls, in a four poster bed with delicate white linens, a woman wearing a white silk shirt, expensive underwear and a pair of stockings sat up too fast. 'Oh, about time too!'

Lilith took a couple of seconds to realise she was at home. 'And, really, I am so bored with this.'

She reached up and pushed her hands through her hair and the fuzzy tangles became smoothly conditioned tresses. She sighed with delight as she felt each cuticle slip into place. When she looked up, the room was different: light and contemporary, Chrome and off-white and blonde wood. She was high up, a penthouse apartment. When she looked out of the big plate windows that covered one wall, she saw the Thames. London landmarks: the Eye, in the east St Paul's, winking at her in the dusk. She looked west, the Houses of Parliament. Big Ben.

That rings a bell.

Lilith gave a bark of a laugh at her own weak joke.

Oh, that's why I'm awake. The little bastard is in trouble.

Without much thought, Lilith pulled a broomstick out of the air and, with it between her thighs, sprinted across the apartment and leapt straight through the enormous picture window.

Iris and Alfie were standing in the cage; the Divine's headless body lay on one side and Blake's was on the other. Iris was standing back a little, letting Alfie examine him. She let her gaze flicker over to Sabrina who was standing on the other side of the room, near to where Vikram was still encased in a bubbling field of energy. Keeping Vikram prisoner seemed to be quite demanding, as Sabrina sounded weary when she said, 'Are they both dead?'

Alfie straightened up and turned. 'His neck's broken. And that's without all the power of the Divine dissipating through his body. He didn't stand a chance.'

What a guy.

When Iris heard that familiar echoey voice in her head, she turned, excepting to see the ghost of her dead brother Matt. In fact, she had chastisement ready for him on her lips – something about where he had been all this time. But, when she turned, the dead man walking she saw standing just outside the cage wasn't Matt.

'Blake? Oh, God, no.'

Seems like a girl like you is kind of greedy when it comes to personal demons, huh?

Iris turned back to the body on the floor. Alfie was crouched back over it, ignoring her. She turned back to Blake – the Blake who had to be a figment of her imagination. 'You are *not* haunting me, Blake.'

Nah, course not. It's just your overactive imagination again. What's the root of it this time? Just can't let me go? Racked with guilt over me biting the bullet?

Iris frowned. 'Maybe it's my need for some kind of damn explanation. You're his son? You're Dr Tobias's son? I met your parents. They came to the wedding.'

Yeah. You just met them the once, didn't you?

'Yes.'

And you didn't think that was odd?

'Maybe, a little, with you there was a lot of odd.'

Iris realised that Alfie had come over to her and was stroking her arm saying, 'Iris, are you OK?'

She brushed him away. 'Just a minute.'

I never knew he wasn't my father. That guy. The one you met. My mother's husband. Maybe he didn't know. When I was eighteen, just before I went to university – I was going to go to University College in London, really excited – he turned up. Dr Tobias. I got home from my last day of school and there he was. Said he had stuff to tell me.

'And what did he tell you?'

Everything. The big reveal. Lycs and vamps. Witches and magic. How he was an Ancient Beast. The warrior wolf. His plans to find the wolf that would kill the Ancient Beasts and protect the Silver Crown. He knew he'd be the first to go. He'd read that somewhere. He thought if he could protect himself the rest of the Silver Crown would be safe. Safe from you, Iris, as it turns out.

Iris inhaled, realising something that felt like a shattering inside her. 'He wanted to protect the Silver Crown because they controlled the Divine Wolf, didn't he? He knew that when I came along and destroyed them it would all fall apart.'

Blake shrugged. *Well, he never said that to me. I don't know.*

'I do,' Iris whispered. 'It's all my fault. I caused this.'

Blake was staring at Iris. He shook his head slightly. Iris felt a thick tightness at the back of her throat. 'Oh, God.'

And then a loud haughty voice shouted, 'OK. I'm here! Where is he?'

Iris looked up to see Lilith marching through the door, but, before she got anywhere near them, before Iris could even say anything, Sabrina shouted quickly, 'I got the prince for you so you can't do anything bad to me.'

Lilith stopped and turned. 'Sabrina! Oh fuck, when I passed out, did my . . . ?'

Sabrina shrugged. 'Yeah. Kind of. A bit.'

Lilith sighed heavily then looked up at Vikram trapped in the magical bubble. 'Oh, God, and he got out too.

OK, OK, hang on, darling.' She shouted the last part of her statement in the general direction of Iris, Blake and Alfie.

What? What? Hang on. Are you here to help me, or what? Lilith!

Lilith, who had been stalking over to Sabrina, turned and looked right at Blake's ghost. 'I said, in a minute.'

Blake rolled his eyes as Lilith walked over to Sabrina. Just before she reached her, Sabrina suddenly yelled out in pain. 'I can't – I can't hold him.'

The bubble containing Vikram suddenly looked a lot thinner. Lilith whirled around and shot her arms up, flanking Sabrina in exactly the same position. Another wave of energy shot from her palms and wrapped itself around Vikram.

'Damn,' Lilith shouted as if she had been burnt. 'He's so strong.'

Iris looked at Blake. 'So, what ... ?'

What's Vikram?

'Yeah.'

Well, he looks like a vamp and he smells like a vamp and he keeps out of daylight like a vamp ...

'But he isn't a vamp?'

Blake screwed up his face. *No he is, but ... Right, before the vamps cut themselves off from humans, all kinds of weird stuff went on. Mostly stuff done by vamps and humans to lycs and witches, but it cut all kinds of ways. Loads of humans tried to control lycs and vamps to make weapons. Didn't try that so much with witches. Humans don't get to control witches very often.*

Iris thought she saw Blake preening as he said this.

But there was a lot of stuff about getting lycs bitten by vamps to see if they could then be a sort of bestial vamp. Vamps have psychic abilities. Some stronger, some weaker. Some uber, uber – like Darius Cole. The idea was that if the lyc had a vamp handle on brain control they could be conscious when they changed. Mongrels.

'Fuck. An army of rational Beasts. Like what the Divine wanted.'

That's always the dream isn't it? Werewolves you can control. Command.

'It didn't work though?'

Nah. I got books and books on it. The poor puppy dogs just died. As if the vamp teeth were silver. Now weirdly your little nursey and her blood cleaning – that might've done it. But I digress . . . It didn't work, and then, one day, somehow, some vamps got their hands on him up there.

Blake pointed at Vikram, now being held by a straining Sabrina and Lilith. He seemed to be fighting inside his bubble, shouting and kicking out.

'And what's he?' said Iris.

'He's an Ancient Beast. Number twelve. The one who was missing.'

'I thought the Divine was number twelve.'

She is. She is now. She had to take his place after he was bitten. It has to be twelve, you see, for the Silver Crown's power to work. That's why the Doc, why Dad had to keep attending the meetings. And that's why when they lost the prince – Vikram – they had to use the Divine. Before that, I think they kept her permanently in some kind of suspended animation on account of her being such a dangerous insane mega-bitch.

'But when they lost the prince, how come they didn't just get his eldest living cub to ascend, like they did with Alfie?'

The story is he never had any cubs. Never bit. Ancient Beasts are conscious when they change, remember. Soppy old thing didn't want to do it. He's always portrayed as the runt of the Ancient Beasts. The prince is a kind of sarcastic nickname. 'Course, once he'd taken the vamp bite, it was a different story. He was ferocious and scary. Some people say he went to Transylvania and inspired Dracula stories, but that's probably bollocks. But he certainly is strong. Look at him fighting two fucking witches.

'So what happened to him? Back then I mean?'

Oh, they caught him in the end. Lycs and vamps together. Lycs took custody. Locked him up in a witch prison. Seems like Lilith was the one holding his key.

'So how'd he get out?'

How the fuck should I know?

Iris was about to say something back to Blake, something about him seeming to know everything else about what was going on, but Lilith, who was sweating with the work of containing Vikram, turned and shouted, 'Iris. When did you last see Matthew?'

Iris frowned. 'Matthew?'

'Your dead brother's ghost,' shouted another voice. It was Cate, who had just come barrelling, skidding down the stairs. Without stopping or looking around, she lifted her hands and started shooting energy into the bubble holding Vikram.

'Yes. I know. I know who he is.'

'When did you last see him?' shouted Lilith.

The power from the three witches was getting noisier, a fizzing roar now.

'Um, at Cobalt.'

'Before I opened the morphial connector?'

'Um, yes.'

'And you haven't seen him since?'

'No.'

'Fuck!' Lilith shouted. 'He got through her gateway.'

'He got through my what?'

Lilith turned a little towards Iris. 'Vikram has been sealed in a witch prison for over two hundred years. Not in the temporary holding zone like Sabrina – locked up tight deep within it, never getting free. But I let him out, briefly, to help prime you for the morphial connector. I had total control over him. You were never in danger . . .'

'When he took me out the night before full moon.'

You needed a vamp to make Iris psychy enough for the

connector and you decided to use The Prince! Blake looked incredulous.

'Yes,' said Lilith. 'Why not? He was the easiest vamp for me to find. I knew just where he was. No reason to think I couldn't shut him right back up again after. Well ... Except, OK, somehow, he must have realised you had a psychic opening. The fact you see your brother's ghost. He used that. Sucked Matthew out of your mind and sent him back instead.'

'But he works for Cobalt?'

Oh, God, Iris. No he doesn't. Just 'cause he wanders around there. He's a vamp. He can go where he likes. He can even control who can see him.

Iris looked at Vikram, twisting in the bubble. It didn't seem real. First he had been a normal bloke. Well, a normal vampire-hunting bloke. Then a vamp. Then a vamp and a lyc. Then a vamp and an Ancient Beast. And now ... Now he was 'Matthew?'

'He's not Matthew. Not exactly. He's using your connection to Matthew to exist outside the prison dimension. Matthew must be trapped there in his place. But, if you call Matthew to you, and if, at the same time, we force him back, we might be able to reverse their places again.'

'But I don't call Matthew. He's just a hallucination.'

Lilith gave Iris a look so terrifying she felt sorrier for Blake than she ever had. 'Call. Him.'

Iris closed her eyes. Strangely, though Alfie was right by her, she felt the threads of the morphial connector. 'Matt?'

She saw him, like a flash, a rush of images and knowledge. He was in a small gold cage, suspended in darkness. He looked cold and confused.

Iris? Iris, is that you? Oh, God, Iris. I think I made it to hell.

'You need to come back.'

I don't know how.

Iris felt him. Felt the connection between them. It wasn't like the morphial connector. It was something deeper, stronger. Twins, together in the womb, two tiny bodies wrapped around each other for nine long months. She knew Matt was real. The Matt she saw. The Matt she'd always seen. He wasn't a hallucination. Wasn't guilt. He was real. Death couldn't divide them.

Iris reached out. She felt her hand pass through something and then she saw it in front of her as she looked at Matt, tight and scared in his cage.

She opened the door of the gold cage. The black void was suddenly like a cold sucking rush. Somewhere she saw Vikram's face, huge and ghostly all around them, like smoke in the dark. She grabbed Matt and pulled.

56

When Iris opened her eyes she was lying on the floor of the Silver Cage, still next to Blake's body. She rolled over slightly and saw Lilith, Cate and Alfie standing over it.

'He knew,' Lilith was saying. 'He knew he was the heir all along. He could have seen that prophecy at any time.'

'Who knows how much he knew, or how long he knew it,' said Cate.

Iris lifted her head. 'He knew he was going to die? To pay the price?'

'I'll tell you what he did know,' said Lilith's tight haughty voice. 'He knew that there aren't many surefire ways to cheat a magical prophesied death except . . .'

'A witch's binding,' said Iris.

Lilith reached out and touched Blake's cheek. 'Come on, baby, you don't get away from me that easily.'

Blake's eyelids fluttered and opened. He looked at Lilith and then over at Iris. 'Oh, it's my better half. So witch-binding really is that strong, huh?'

'No,' Alfie said, sounding almost angry, as he straightened and pulled away from the huddle around Blake. 'You're joking. He *cannot* be alive. He took all the Divine's power and dissipated it.'

'Iris took the power of eleven Ancient Beasts through her body.'

'Yes well,' said Alfie, 'that doesn't make any sense either. There's no way she could be able to live with that sort of power without protection.'

'Iris doesn't have any protection. Except *you*. Except

loving you. Otherwise the power of eleven Ancient Beasts would have killed her. You're a werewolf and a very strong one at that. You gave her the support. Even when you were under the thrall of the Divine. You kept her alive. I know you don't believe in werewolf life mates. And, frankly, I've always thought it a bit of a strange trope for a species so prone to sluttishness. But you two have a bond. Now more than ever. She's bound to you. All that power is still inside her. It'll take a century for it to all leak out of her through you and dissipate. She needs you to keep it stable. If you die, she dies.'

Iris nodded, shocked.

'Woah,' said Alfie softly.

'Yeah.' Lilith grinned. 'How's that for some life mating?'

Alfie grinned and walked over to Iris. He reached out to her with one big beefy arm and pulled her to her feet. As he took her into his familiar embrace, he said, 'Thank you for rescuing me.'

'Oh, that was nothing,' Iris whispered into his mouth as he pressed a kiss on to her. Then several more.

Alfie took his time, nuzzling her, grating his very prickly stubbled chin over her cheeks and neck. She sighed and gasped, jelly-putty in his arms. He slipped his teeth over her jawline and bit down. Her legs were water.

'And I'm sorry,' he said, finding her ear again and licking it once before continuing, 'that I, well, you know, chained you up in that cavern.'

'Well,' said Iris, stiffening a little at the sore spot of the memory, 'like I said, I understand. Thrall.'

'That's always what fucks it up for us,' he murmured. 'Thrall. I don't know how you can go on trusting me. Not when you know how werewolf loyalty can be. If I get caught thralled to some other Beast . . .'

'Well, you won't,' said a voice behind Alfie.

Alfie turned and moved a little and Iris saw Blake standing behind them.

'Look, Blake, I know you know a lot about lycans and prophecies and shit, but . . .'

Blake shrugged, as Alfie trailed off. 'Not that. You won't get thralled again because there are no other lycs who can thrall you. You're top of the tree, Alfie. The most powerful lyc in the world.'

'I am?'

'Sure, you're an Ancient Beast, aren't you? Heir to Tobias. Which kind of makes you my brother or something, but that's just gross considering we had sex that time.'

'What?' said Alfie.

'I'll let Iris explain all that later. But you are the only Ancient Beast left alive since Vixy did her thing. And with no Divine either, well, you're it. Top dog.' Blake paused and pulled out his tobacco. 'Well, apart from Prince Vik. But he's been sealed forever in a witch-prison dimension. They were meant to stick Sabrina back in there too, but she appears to have done a runner.'

'But he escaped from there once,' Iris said, pushing Alfie's fingers away from the teasing spot on her jawline. 'Why can't they just kill him? I'll kill him. I'm meant to. The prophecy . . .'

Blake made a face. 'Well, witches don't go in for so much just killing. Anyway, what did he ever do to you, Iris? He was on your side.'

'What do you mean? I *have* to kill him. He's an Ancient Beast.'

'Yes and the last time you killed a batch of Ancient Beasts you let the Divine Wolf loose on the world. I mean, Iris, just 'cause something's in a prophecy doesn't necessarily mean it's such a great thing to do. How would you even kill him? He's lyc and vamp.'

'Why are you talking me out of this? I thought you were all about killing lycs?'

Blake had rolled his cigarette now. He placed it in his mouth and lit a match by pinching the head tight and dragging his fingernails over it. It flared and he sucked his roll-up to life. 'I thought I was all about interrogating them, but it's shades of grey, Iris. That's all I'm saying. Shades of grey. There's no real reason to kill Vikram, but there's no way he can safely be allowed on earth. You're just pissed off at him because he bit you.'

'What?' Iris pushed her way past Alfie and took a step round him towards Blake. 'What did you say?'

Alfie snaked his arms around Iris's waist and held her as Blake said, 'He bit you. Lilith freed him and sent him to you. It was part of her plan. Just get him to give you a little bite to make you slightly vampy so the conduit would work.'

Iris tipped her head back to look up at Alfie. 'Would that even work?'

Alfie shrugged.

'You could ask Lilith, but she's gone with Cate to make some magic thing for Sabrina.'

'Oh, she left you behind. Honeymoon over?'

'Yeah, yeah. Shut up. Look, Vikram is nothing even to do with Cobalt. He's a vamp. He bit you.'

'So. It doesn't work like that with vamps. It'd take more than a nip to make me . . .'

Blake interrupted her. 'Hey, Alfie, does Vixy smell different to you?'

Alfie sniffed. 'Maybe a little. Hard to really tell.'

'Alfie,' Iris squeaked, hitting his left arm.

'Yeah, well, nothing we can really do about it one way or the other. I'm going to sleep with my windows shut for a while though.'

'Blake, if I am "a bit vampy", I'm not going to bite you.'

Iris stopped talking, as Alfie suddenly went rigid behind her, then bellowed in pain.

'Oh my God!' Iris shouted. 'The moon.'

'Oh fuck,' said Blake, 'get him the cage.'

'No, no, no!' Iris turned on Blake, pushing him into the wall behind him as Alfie fell convulsing to the floor. 'The cage holds his form. It'll work like the collar. The two opposing magics will kill him.'

Iris looked at Alfie on the floor, more animal than human. Blake had forgotten. She knew how easy it was to forget what Alfie was. She could barely believe it herself.

As the animal – the wolf that was Alfie – got slowly to its feet, Iris whispered, 'He's an Ancient Beast now. It's still Alfie in there.'

Alfie snarled.

'You sure about that?' Blake whispered.

Iris raised her crossbow as Blake drew into the gap between Iris and the wall.

Iris looked into the creature's eyes. Gold. She thought of that moment. That moment months ago that had started it all. When Alfie, wolfed and dangerous, had sprung back into her life.

She was lying on her back on the damp grass. Night. The rough ground of that wild part of the university parks, twigs and stones in her back, wolf breath on her face. When she had finally opened her eyes, she had seen nothing but wolf – silent, slavering wolf.

Her first thought had been *teeth*.

My, my, what big teeth you have.

Above those teeth, golden eyes. The air was cold, the damp grass even colder. *Yes, much better, focus on the eyes. Not the teeth, the eyes.*

My, my, what big eyes you have.

In her memory, and there, in the cellar of the Silver Crown, Iris looked deeper into the wolf's eyes . . .

It was like a flash of an image. Subliminal. She saw – or *thought* she saw – just for a fraction of a second, not a wolf, but a man. A man she knew, recognised.

'Alfie?'

The wolf just stared at her.

'Alfie,' she said again. 'Is that you?'

You really think he can hear you?

Iris turned her head, slightly. In the corner of the cellar was Matthew.

Iris smiled at Alfie. 'Yes,' she said. 'Yes, I do.'

57

Friday, 14 March 2008

Lilith stretched out on the bed in her fanciest underwear. 'Oh nice,' she said, when Blake, who was straddling her waist, held up the four sparkling cuffs, each with a neat length of chain attached.

'You recognise them, then, baby?'

'How could I not? One of the Sacred Silvers. How did you get hold of them?'

Blake shrugged. 'Well, the rest got taken to Cobalt, but people tend to forget about these. Everyone always thinks Collar, Crowns, Cage. They forget about the fourth corner: the Silver Chains. And I thought, you know, do I trust Cobalt? Who does? Better if all those powerful objects aren't in the same place.'

As he spoke, Blake leant down and let the tail ends of the chains from two of the cuffs snake their way around the bedposts. He slotted Lilith's wrists into place as she said, 'Well, they are pretty. But you do realise they won't hold me any more than a bunch of stuff you bought in the hardware store.'

Blake shrugged. The second manacle was fixed and he ducked down to kiss her nose. 'I know. But the fact it, it's all artifice, isn't it? I mean, when I chained up Iris, I always knew that if she really asked me properly I'd let her free. It's just about suspension of disbelief.'

Lilith nodded.

Blake moved down the bed to fix her ankles.

'And how about you?' said Lilith. 'Are you going to *believe* I'm not going to kill you?'

Blake was on all fours facing away from Lilith. He straightened his knees, still doubled over so he could look at her through his legs, her face framed by the split at the back of his white coat. 'You know, I'm not sure if you can.' He dropped back down again and went back to his work, fixing her second ankle into its cuff.

'You think?'

'I'm pretty sure, if you take a witch's binding, that witch can't kill you. I'm sure that's part of the "even beyond death" clause.'

'Which you did a bit of research on, I take it.'

Blake spun around and came to rest with his face just above Lilith's, his body caging hers on the bed. 'A little. Just to be safe.'

'Right, well, you know, these things aren't always so clear-cut,' Lilith said, a little breathless in her bondage. 'I mean, it's not like there has been any proper research. No case studies.'

'Well,' said Blake, dropping into a kiss before pushing back up as her lips chased his hopelessly, 'I happen to like research.'

'Hmm, and I don't suppose your stealing these chains has got anything to do with the fact that these are the same ones that Alfie the werewolf used to chain up the ex-wife who you are still in love with.'

Blake grinned at Lilith. He sat back and pulled off his tie, the only other item he was wearing with the white coat. He winked. 'Oh, I really think it's time for you to shut that witch mouth,' he said.

After Blake had gagged Lilith with his tie wrapped twice around her head, he shifted quickly and drove into her. She was so wet and ready. She loved this. He ploughed her hard, snapping his slim hips back and forth, rotating them to make her dance as she writhed and wailed into her gag underneath him.

'You're a bad witch,' he whispered, when he slipped

his fingers down and on to her clit. 'I can feel how wet you are. Bad, bad witch.'

Lilith moaned into the tie twisted into her mouth.

'What would they think if they could see you now? Mistress of more than seventeen covens. If they could see how I chain you up like an animal, like a *werewolf*, and make you scream like this. Is that what witches are meant to do?'

Lilith panted a response into her gag.

'I can't hear you, witch! Is it?'

Lilith shook her head frantically, making a muffled sound like 'No, no.'

'Thought not. Now fucking come for me, bad witch. Bad, bad witch. Bitch. Killer bitch. Killer fucking bitch.' And Blake came too, as Lilith did. Screaming up to meet her. His mind with Iris. With Iris forever.

Alfie and Iris stood on the drawbridge of the medieval castle they had found, incongruously sitting squat in a side street just round the corner from Waterloo station.

'Well,' said Iris, looking up at the heavily baroque frontage, 'that's a lot of gargoyles. This has to be the place, right?'

'Kind of says Witch Towers to me,' Alfie said. He was trailing a hand on her waist. Ever since he'd woken up human after the full moon he hadn't stopped touching Iris.

'I can't believe this is really here. I mean, right here.' Iris gestured around them. 'It's a bit of a giveaway, isn't it?'

'Oh,' said Alfie, reaching for the bell pull, 'I'm sure you can't find it unless she wants you to.'

The boom of the bell echoed somewhere inside the castle.

'Unless *they* want you to,' Iris said. 'Blake lives here too now.'

'Yeah, I'm just enjoying a last few moments pretending he actually died like he was meant to.'

The whole castle was over the top. As she led them through the entrance hall, Lilith claimed that Blake had asked to have the castle back, insisting she didn't always choose such opulent style.

In the huge baronial dining room, Iris and Alfie were sitting opposite each other about halfway down a long table. It was all reds and golds and dark wood. Super-gothic red candles dribbled wax all over the white linen tablecloth. Everything that ought to sparkle sparkled. Everything else was drab and dark.

Lilith was at one end of the table, Blake at the other. The table wasn't so large that Iris couldn't make out the cuff marks on Lilith's wrists. They were a very familiar shape. She glanced at Blake, who winked. Clearly, he had seen her looking.

Damn but Blake looked sexy tonight. What had he done? He seemed to be fizzing with sexual energy. Iris looked back at Alfie and, as with every time she looked at Alfie, her heart turned over at how beautiful he was. She let her gaze drift from one man to the other, over and over. She remembered that night locked in the cellar of the pack house, all thinking they were going to die. Both their cocks and both their tongues inside her.

Lilith said something and Iris shook herself. 'Sorry. What?'

'I just asked how it was going at Cobalt.'

'Oh, right,' said Iris. 'Well, fine. I'm managing the lycan division, which is looking good, great resources. We're still a bit light on the research side.'

Iris paused and Blake coughed into his soup, muttering something like, 'Not that place. No way.'

'Oh, and they still haven't fully reclassified lycans as non-mythical. That'll have to wait until they appoint a new director for Cobalt. There's talk of Merle Cobalt, you know, the daughter of Erin and Charles, but she's still thinking about it.'

'Merle Cobalt! She's married to a vamp.'

'She's married,' said Alfie darkly, 'to Darius Cole.'

'Well, exactly. She's also about twelve years old.'

'I think she's twenty-six or something, twenty-seven, maybe,' said Iris. 'Anyway, I don't know. That's what they're saying.'

'Fucking nepotism,' said Blake.

Iris laughed out loud. 'You're talking nepotism! Son of wolf!'

'Never mind that now,' said Lilith, in a voice that calmly silenced everyone else's. 'How about you, Alfie? Are you at Cobalt too?'

Alfie shook his head before answering, 'God, no. I've pretty much decided that isn't the answer. Besides, now I'm, well, whatever I am...'

'King of the Dog-faced People has a nice ring to it,' said Blake.

'Well, whatever. Anyway, I'm trying to put that role to use. I'm going back out to visit the Carci Gate next month, find out what they're doing there. I'm going to travel. Try and work with all the werewolves in the world to figure out what we are going to do about this thing. One possibility is to re-form the Silver Crown. Find the heirs to every Beast Iris killed and help them to ascend like I did.'

'Alfie,' Iris said.

'But we haven't agreed if that's the best thing to do yet. It's complex. There's lots of grey.'

'I'll bet,' murmured Blake, sounding almost sensitive.

'I'm back living in the pack house in Oxford. Got the rest of my pack there too. I'm working with Leon on the mythological stuff. And I'm working with Pearl on the science. Iris told me about what she did to save Zac's life. Well, almost. It's pretty interesting. But the main idea is total lock down. To get every werewolf locking himself up at full moon. To prevent reinfection.'

'You'll never do that,' said Blake.

'Well, I just don't know,' said Alfie, 'but that's the only goal that makes sense.'

'And, if you do do it, that'll be the end of lycans forever, eventually. No more bites, no more beasts. You'll die out. Well, except you, I guess you live forever.'

'Well, said Alfie, slightly shyly, 'that's another thing we just don't know.'

'He's working with me, anyway,' said Iris, changing the subject. 'On no, not for Cobalt, as he said. But he's liaising with me. We're out catching lycs and tranqing them. Then he comes and talks to them about lock down. Binds them to it with thrall.'

'Wow,' said Blake, 'sounds like a kind of liberal lycan utopian vision. I give it six months before you're back to killing them, Iris.'

Iris sighed, realising the best move was to change the subject yet again. She turned to Lilith. 'So how about Vikram? Is he contained?'

'He's back in the prison that had him contained for hundreds of years until I decided to let him out. Should be OK so long as I don't fuck up again.'

'Did, um –' Iris paused, looking down at the dark wooden table top. 'When he bit me, er ... Do you know what that did?'

Lilith pouted. 'I'm not sure. I asked him to make sure you were psychically open. Some people are already, but vamps are good at suggestion and psychic manipulation. I don't actually know what he did.'

'Face it, Iris,' said Blake, 'he vampirised you, one way or another.'

'Did he do anything to me that might have changed things with me and Matt. I mean with Matt's ghost. I know he replaced Matt somehow in order to be free of his prison. But, well, something's ...' Iris let her gaze slide over to where Matt was standing in the corner of the hall. He shrugged at Iris. 'It's just ever since he came back, he's, well, he's still here. He used to come and go, even in the beginning when it was bad. He's never been around all the time.'

'Oh that,' said Lilith. 'Well, you called him to you.'

'So, do I, what . . . ? Tell him to leave again?'

'No. I doubt that'll work. You need to free him. There's something keeping him here on earth. You need to do what he left undone.'

'But I've done that. I killed the Beast. And then when that wasn't enough I killed all the rest of the Silver Crown. Oh, God, Vikram! Is it because I haven't killed Vikram?' Iris turned to Matt. 'Is it because I haven't killed Vikram?'

Matt shrugged again. *I don't know.*

Lilith laughed, her now familiar loud bark echoey in the vast room. 'How could killing the Silver Crown be something Matt left undone? What did he leave undone when he died?'

'What?' said Iris. 'I don't understand.'

'You're too blinded by vengeance to see it, Iris,' said Lilith. 'What was Matt doing when he died?'

And then Alfie said softly, 'Oh, God. I don't believe it.'

'What?' said Iris.

'The photographs. The photos he was taking of me when the Beast attacked us. He left the photo shoot unfinished. You said he had plans. Certain pictures of me he wanted to take. He never finished it.'

Iris shook her head, 'There is no way . . .'

'Well,' said Lilith brightly, 'I'm a witch. In fact, some might even say I'm a bad witch.' Her gaze flickered over to Blake and back again. 'I notoriously don't like to give straight answers. But, look, after everything else you've done to lay your demons to rest, would it hurt to give it a try?'

58

'Are you sure he wanted me like this?' Alfie said as Iris tightened the ropes that held him to the tree.

'Absolutely. He showed me a picture. Is this right, Matt?' she said, turning.

Behind her, Matt nodded his approval.

The moon was full. Alfie was still in his human form. Something magical holding him there. Iris had taken the silver ring – the one she had worn on a leather thong around her neck since Alfie had come back into her life and returned it to her – and placed it on his little finger. It hadn't burnt him. Lilith had taken care of it all.

Alfie was topless, in his jeans, the same ones he had on that night. Iris couldn't believe he still had them. Hadn't the hospital removed them? The police taken them?

But, Alfie insisted, these were the very same ones.

He was tied to the tree with thick white rope. Iris had found it in a box at her flat. The same stuff the police had retrieved from the site. She couldn't believe she still had that.

And the picture was there too. The cute little bondage cartoon Matt had shown her that night of the half-naked guy tied to the tree. The image he wanted to capture in Alfie's flesh.

Alfie's chest was forced out by the way his arms were drawn tight behind him. Blake had helped with the roping up, but he'd gone off into the trees to talk to

Lilith. It was just the two of them. Matt's ghost was still floating around somewhere – but Iris couldn't see him just this minute.

She crept closer to Alfie and kissed him.

Alfie gasped. Iris increased the pressure, pressing her way hard into his helpless mouth. Alfie writhed a little, his moans wet and sharply aroused.

Iris drew back, ignoring his blatant frustration, and whispered, 'It's been a long journey to get back here.'

Alfie made a low laughing sound. 'I've certainly been around the block a few times to do it.'

'Is that some kind of, "I've been an enormous man-slut" confession?' Iris snaked her hand down Alfie's body and stroked his hard cock through his jeans.

'You know what I did. What I was like when you pushed me away. I tried a million women in my bed. But none of them could stop me thinking about you.'

Iris kissed him again. 'Except the Divine.'

Alfie shook his head. 'Even with her, even in the depths of that thrall, you were with me. Even before the connector opened, you were there. The witches are right. There are too many bonds lacing us together, Iris.'

Iris darted her head close and flicked her tongue over his top lip. Beautiful wolf. She stole another glance at the full moon. Lilith had taken care of that too. Right now, it was like Alfie wasn't a werewolf. Like it had never happened, like they had turned back time. 'I want you to fuck me,' Iris whispered. 'I want to climb on to your magnificent cock. Right now. But will it ruin the pictures? You'll have your jeans on, but you'll need to have a bulge there. I shouldn't let you come yet. You ought to be hard.'

You can fake the bulge with something if need be.

Iris turned, irritated. 'Oh, leave us be, Matthew, please.'

Sorry, sis, you know I can't seem to do that.

'God, Matt, is this going to work? Will this make you

leave forever?' Iris felt a lump in her throat as she said that.

I have absolutely no idea, Matt said wryly and wandered a little way off into the trees. But he didn't vanish the way he used to.

'You won't need to fake the, uh, bulge,' said Alfie. 'Even though Lilith has held my form, the moon's still affecting me. You could fuck me all night tonight and I wouldn't go soft.'

'Really?' said Iris, arousal hitching her breath. 'That's very good to know.'

Iris got Alfie's jeans down, tugging them hard to force them through the tight gap between his bare arse and the bark of the tree. He was already so hard, precome wet on the tip. Sap sticky.

Iris kicked off her trousers and underwear. She kept her rough-soled combat boots on. She put her hands on his shoulders and then her arms around his neck, bracing her legs and getting some purchase on the bark as she climbed him and the tree until she perched above Alfie's cock.

'Fuck,' he said softly, 'you're so fucking strong.'

'Yeah, killer bitch me.' Iris laughed and then gasped as she sheathed her already wet cunt on to Alfie's cock.

Alfie gasped too, his face twisting in quick ecstasy.

It was so strenuous to fuck this way, Iris loved it instantly. She loved it when she had to work for it. Years of training had taught her to race, to fight, to capture. She worked herself on Alfie's cock. Faster. Her leg muscles screaming as she fought to keep herself tensed against the tree with the grip of her thick soles.

She slammed herself over and over on Alfie's cock. Feeling the trees all around her. Feeling the weight of this place, where the Beast had torn them apart, killed Matt, bitten Alfie, changed her forever.

And something coursed through Iris. Maybe it was the absolution she had always wanted. Maybe not. But it was something raw and powerful. Alfie moved his head and bit her neck and she almost but not quite fell. She screamed and bucked, twisted on his cock, threw her head back and looked right at the moon.

What was she? Warrior wolf. Vampire? Witch? Killer bitch? She felt like a little bit of everything rolled into one.

Only human.

Author's Note

My first and forever thanks to Ewan who did everything he could to make the survival horror of creating these books easier, short of actually writing them for me. And, believe me, if I could have talked him into that, I would've. Thank you. I love you. Thanks also for buying a white coat from the army surplus just so I could check a few facts.

To Adam, who went down on his knees in production to give me workable deadlines and, according to legend, once right on to his belly. I'm still waiting for photographs.

To Madelynne Ellis who made all three books better by giving it to me scarily straight and told me to tie Alfie and Leon together – just for you, M! To Kristina Lloyd who taught me so much about sex and writing and writing sex. And who likes white coats too.

To everyone at Lust Bites. Everyone in Oxford. My family. My kids. My cat. And Rob – I don't know if you did anything much to help with this book, but I like you. And I'm going to call you as soon as I have written this.

Also, because I can, I would like to thank Iris Instasi-Fox, Alfie Friday, Blake Tabernacle, Lilith, Cate Ray, Leon Whitesnake, Zac Booth, Misty Sun, Aurelia Toto, Pearl White, William 'Pure' White, Ella Pepper, Erin Cobalt, Charles Cobalt, Darius Cole, Merle Cobalt, Vikram Rose, Malcolm Tobias, Hera, Sabrina and Matthew Instasi-Fox for spending a really strange year with me.

Silver werewolves, my God, I can't believe I wrote all that.

Visit the Black Lace website at
www.black-lace-books.com

LOOK OUT FOR THE ALL-NEW BLACK LACE BOOKS – AVAILABLE NOW!

All books priced £7.99 in the UK. Please note publication dates apply to the UK only. For other territories, please contact your retailer.

A GENTLEMAN'S WAGER
Madelynne Ellis
ISBN 978 0 352 33800 6

When eighteenth-century young lady Bella Rushdale finds herself fiercely attracted to handsome landowner Lucerne Marlinscar, she does not expect the rival for her affections to be another man. However, the handsome and decadent Marquis of Pennerley has desired Lucerne for years and, when they are brought together at the remote Lauwine Hall for a country party on the Yorkshire Moors, he intends to claim him. This leads to a passionate struggle for dominance – at the risk of scandal – between the highly sexed Bella and the debauched aristocrat. Ultimately it will be Lucerne who will choose the outcome – and his decision is bound to upset somebody's plans.

POSSESSION
Mathilde Madden, Madelynne Ellis, Anne Tourney
ISBN 978 0 352 34164 8

Three otherworldly short novels of shape-shifters and possession:

Falling Dancer: Kelda has two jobs: full-time bartender, part-time exorcist. She meets vengeful spirits and misguided demons wherever she goes. She wishes the spirit world would leave her alone so she could have a relationship that lasted longer than twenty-four hours, but when she's contacted by a sexy musician who wants her to solve the mystery of his girlfriend's disappearance, she can't help getting involved . . .

The Silver Chains: Alfie Friday is a werewolf. For 7 years he has controlled his curse carefully by locking himself in a cage every full moon. But now he's changing when it isn't full moon. His girlfriend Misty travels to South America to try and find a way of controlling Alfie's changes, but discovers the key to the problem lies in Oxford. The place it all began for Alfie and the place he has vowed never to return to.

Broken Angel: After stealing a copy of an ancient manuscript, Blaze Makaresh finds himself being hunted down by a gang of youkai – demons who infiltrate human society in order to satisfy their hunger for sex and flesh. When the Talon, an elitist society of demon-hunters, come to his aid, he's soon enmeshed with the beautiful Asha, and the dawning of an age-old prophecy.

To be published in March 2008

CASSANDRA'S CONFLICT
Fredrica Alleyn
ISBN 978 0 352 34186 0

A house in Hampstead. Present-day. Behind a façade of cultured respectability lies a world of decadent indulgence and dark eroticism. Cassandra's sheltered life is transformed when she gets employed as governess to the Baron's children. He draws her into games where lust can feed on the erotic charge of submission. Games where only he knows the rules and where unusual pleasures can flourish.

PHANTASMAGORIA
Madelynne Ellis
ISBN 978 0 352 34168 6

1800 – Three years after escaping to London with her bisexual lovers, Bella Rushdale wakes one morning to find their delicate ménage-a-trois on the verge of shattering. Vaughan, Marquis of Pennerley has left abruptly and without any explanation. Determined to reclaim him and preserve their relationship, Bella pursues the errant Marquis to his family seat on the Welsh Borders where she finds herself embroiled in his preparations for a diabolical gothic celebration on All Hallows Eve – a phantasmagoria! Among the shadows and phantoms Bella and her lovers will peel away the deceits and desires of the past and future.

To be published in April 2008

GOTHIC HEAT
Portia Da Costa
ISBN 978 0 352 34170 9

Paula Beckett has a problem. The spirit of the wicked and voluptuous sorceress Isidora Katori is trying to possess her body and Paula finds herself driven by dark desires and a delicious wanton recklessness. Rafe Hathaway is irresistibly drawn to both women. But who will he finally choose – feisty and sexy Paula, who is fighting impossible odds to hang on to her very existence, or sultry and ruthless Isidora, who offers him the key to immortality?

GEMINI HEAT
Portia Da Costa
ISBN 978 0 352 34187 7

As the metropolis sizzles in the freak early summer temperatures, identical twin sisters Deana and Delia Ferraro are cooking up a heat wave of their own. Surrounded by an atmosphere of relentless humidity, Deanna and Delia find themselves rivals for the attentions of Jackson de Guile, an exotic, wealthy entrepreneur and master of power dynamics who draws them both into a web of luxurious debauchery. The erotic encounters become increasingly bizarre as the twins vie for the rewards that pleasuring him brings them – tainted rewards which only serve to confuse their perceptions of the limits of sexual experience.

THE NEW BLACK LACE BOOK OF WOMEN'S SEXUAL FANTASIES
Edited and compiled by Mitzi Szereto
ISBN 978 0 352 34172 3

The second anthology of detailed sexual fantasies contributed by women from all over the world. The book is a result of a year's research by an expert on erotic writing and gives a fascinating insight into the rich diversity of the female sexual imagination.

Black Lace Booklist

Information is correct at time of printing. To avoid disappointment, check availability before ordering. Go to www.black-lace-books.com. All books are priced £7.99 unless another price is given.

BLACK LACE BOOKS WITH A CONTEMPORARY SETTING

To find out the latest information about Black Lace titles, check out the
website: www.black-lace-books.com or send for a booklist with
complete synopses by writing to:

Black Lace Booklist, Virgin Books Ltd
Thames Wharf Studios
Rainville Road
London W6 9HA

Please include an SAE of decent size. Please note only British stamps
are valid.

Please send me the books I have ticked above.

Name ....

Address ....

....

....

....

Post Code ....

Send to: Virgin Books Cash Sales, Thames Wharf Studios, Rainville Road, London W6 9HA.

US customers: for prices and details of how to order books for delivery by mail, call 888-330-8477.

Please enclose a cheque or postal order, made payable to Virgin Books Ltd, to the value of the books you have ordered plus postage and packing costs as follows:

UK and BFPO – £1.00 for the first book, 50p for each subsequent book.

Overseas (including Republic of Ireland) – £2.00 for the first book, £1.00 for each subsequent book.

If you would prefer to pay by VISA, ACCESS/MASTERCARD, DINERS CLUB, AMEX or SWITCH, please write your card number and expiry date here:

....

Signature ....

Please allow up to 28 days for delivery.